THE LIVEABOARDS

❁

Lynne Baumgardt

iUniverse, Inc.
New York Lincoln Shanghai

THE LIVEABOARDS

iUniverse books may be ordered through booksellers or by contacting:

iUniverse
2021 Pine Lake Road, Suite 100
Lincoln, NE 68512
www.iuniverse.com
1-800-Authors (1-800-288-4677)

This book is a work of fiction. Names, characters, and incidents either are products of the author's imagination or are used fictitiously. Any resemblance to actual events or persons, living or dead, is entirely coincidental.

ISBN-13: 978-0-595-36167-0 (pbk)
ISBN-13: 978-0-595-80612-6 (ebk)
ISBN-10: 0-595-36167-6 (pbk)
ISBN-10: 0-595-80612-0 (ebk)

Printed in the United States of America

I would like to thank my wonderful husband Al for his computer expertise and patience; and my daughter Heather, my dearest friends Judy and Lane, and fellow liveaboards Sheila and Clair for their encouragement.

CHAPTER 1

❀

Genuine liveaboards are people who do not have a regular land-based dwelling, and they tend to be unusual in that they float endlessly, attached to any fixed spot on earth by relatively flimsy lines which can be untied in minutes. Liveaboards usually do have a slip or port or well in a marina that they currently use as their "home base" for several reasons. This spot they rent by the month. The clientele at any marina changes a good bit each month.

Many people at Sunset Marina on Lake Guntersville in Alabama call themselves liveaboards. They spend every minute in good weather on their boats and love "simply messing about" in boats. They even have a second mailbox at their marina so that in the summer they have to check their mailboxes at "the house" maybe only once a week. Some say they use their houses mostly for storage so that makes them liveaboards.

But visiting your boat often isn't at all like living aboard. When they get sick, or when the marina water has broken again and their on-board water tanks are empty, or when the head springs a leak and the stink of their own waste is strong in their noses, the wannabees "go home" until the crisis passes. For genuine liveaboards, "home" is the boat.

—A Genuine Liveaboard

"If we sold the house quickly, Dorie, we could move onto *Sun Spot* this summer and fix her up good enough so we'd be comfortable next winter. We'd have to put this place on the market now, though." Fred motioned to one of the piles on the dining room table. "Average time to sell a house in this part of Huntsville here is about five months. Course, I reckon we could get rid of it faster if we'd be willing to go below the assessed price."

"But surely we won't do that." Dorie tried to keep the panic from her voice, a blend of the crisp Wisconsin where she grew up and the softer northern Alabama where she had lived with Fred for thirty-five years. "Why can't we just spend the summer on *Sun Spot*? Plan to not come home at all the whole summer. Janie and her boyfriend, assuming he's still around by then, would be happy to sleep aboard when they come in August, and the others could always go to the Holiday Inn or the new Hampton Inn in Guntersville if they want to. We could decide then if we really want to winterize her and..." her voice tapered off uncertainly at his scowl.

"Now, sugar." Fred drew the word out until it was anything but sweet. He waved at the table covered with neat piles of paper, proof of his diligent research. "We're not getting any younger, sweetheart. I can't see spending all our retirement money keeping up two homes. You know this place is at the point where it needs things, big budget things that I can't do. Like a new roof, for instance. Like the Andersons."

Dorie moved toward the picture window to escape that tone of voice. When had he started talking down to her as if she were one of their kids, a voice overly patient and a little too loud? It was insulting.

The Andersons' lovely home was across from theirs and slightly down the steep hill; its new brick-red roof and crank-out windows with blinds between the glass almost glowed in the cold January sunshine of northern Alabama. It did make their place look kind of battle worn. Four kids and thirty-five years could certainly wear out a house. Not that they hadn't made improvements over the years. Well, not so much improvements as upkeep. Fred had always been meticulous about that.

"And what the hell do we need five bedrooms for anymore?" he said to her back. He came across the room and thrust his latest budget printout into her face, jabbing at it with his index finger. "We can fix up this big old house and rattle around in it waiting for the kids to visit, or we can fix up the boat and be real liveaboards. Have an adventure. Put in a water maker and take her down to the Gulf even like Bobby Ray and what's her name, that pretty girl, at Sunset Marina. Key West. The Bahamas. Do something just for us for a change."

His blue eyes had faded a little but had lost none of their intensity, and his passion startled her. She hadn't seen him this excited about anything in years. Not even the Greek Islands cruise they had taken for their silver anniversary. Hadn't that been just for them?

"Let me just stir the pasta sauce." She patted the arm that held the budget. "And go to the bathroom," she added as she escaped around the high counter and into the kitchen.

"You're going to use the aft head," she heard him mutter and knew he was practicing nautical lingo.

Since he had fallen in love with and closed the deal on a 45-foot 1975 Chris Craft Commander three months before, their surfeit of bedrooms had all become staterooms, the family room the main salon, the kitchen the galley. Fred's enthusiasm for the old boat had been charming at first and Dorie had breathed a sigh of relief that he wouldn't be like so many men who worked their entire adult lives and then didn't have a clue about what to do with themselves in retirement. Taking *Sun Spot* as far as physical labor and TLC could take her would be a wonderful hobby for a pattern maker good with his hands, a handy man that designed parts for engines similar to boat engines and so understood them. Before he had gotten so busy the last few years before retirement, Fred had helped a neighbor restore a houseboat at Ditto Landing Marina and had loved it, she knew, even though she resented the time it took him away from the family. With four kids, he was needed at home, and she had told him so. Of course, all the kids were up and out now.

But still, to sell the house, their comfortable home here in Huntsville, and actually live there? She hadn't thought he was serious when he talked about it before. He would come to his senses when he figured out the tremendous amount of money and dedication it would take to make *Sun Spot* even remotely seaworthy or comfortable for more than a weekend. This wasn't like the runabouts they had always dragged the kids behind on a Big Bertha—this wasn't even a houseboat—and the Gulf of Mexico wasn't the tame Tennessee River.

Dorie turned down the heat under the sauce and stirred it with a wooden spoon. She liked to make a triple batch in her biggest stockpot and then freeze it in containers for lasagna, ravioli, ricotta-stuffed shells, or she added sausages or meatballs for spaghetti. But this pot probably wouldn't even fit under the hood of the Chris Craft's three-burner Princess, circa 1975, stovetop. How in heaven's name could she be expected to really cook on that dinky thing in that dinky little kitchen!

She turned to survey her spacious kitchen with its gleaming appliances surrounding her like old family friends. Why, their casual dining island with built-in turntable was bigger than the entire galley on that boat, so a bigger stove wasn't even an option! And if you had something in the small oven, you couldn't use the burners on top at the same time because there was a switch you moved up for the burners or down for the oven. She stirred the thick tomato sauce angrily. The pasta would get cold while you were heating up the garlic bread!

She huffed into the small bathroom off the utility room. "Aft head, my eye," Dorie whispered into the familiar mirror above the sink. "Aye, aye, my eye," she mock saluted herself and snorted. At fifty-seven she was still taller than average but no longer thin or even blond, and although her boobs had expanded to a D cup, they were also headed south in tandem with a roll of fat around her middle and pouches hanging loosely from under her arms. Four children and gravity had taken their toll, and she felt very much like the grandmother she was. She had given up bleaching her fine hair to let it grow out to chin length, as her hairdresser had assured her was most becoming to her heart-shaped, albeit now pudgy, heart-shaped face. The trouble was that her mousy, ash-blond hair had no oomph even though she dutifully slathered it with mousse and set it in rollers every other day. She ran her fingers under to fluff it at the temples. Yeah, right. Maybe it was time she changed hairdressers.

She tucked the lifeless stuff behind her ears and leaned into the mirror. Her eyes were still her best feature, though, an interesting grayish green and large for her face even pudgy as it was. On impulse, she rummaged in the drawer for her favorite green eyeliner and leaned in again to apply it to her eyelids before standing back and squinting at her handiwork. Thank God for her eyes.

She tinkled and flushed the toilet. And that was another thing. The water swished around the white porcelain, disappeared magically into a distant reservoir somewhere out there, and was replaced with sweet, clear water. The Chris Craft had a one hundred gallon holding tank. Swell. "Like I want to sit on a hundred gallons of my own pee and poop." Dorie almost caressed the terrycloth commode cover. "And then have it all pumped out, have everybody stand around and watch it go through a big, snaky tube until somebody yells, 'Hold it, Mel, we're out of room. We got to pump this shit into the big tank first. Man, you got some holding tank on this Chris. I'm having trouble getting up enough vacuum on this thing to get to the bottom!'"

"Dorie?" Fred knocked on the bathroom door again. "Who the hell you talking to in there? Dorie?"

She flushed again for the sheer pleasure of it. "I was talking to the toilet, Fred, and I don't want to discuss it." Embarrassed, she tried to brush past him in the hallway but he put his arms around her, pinning her to his chest.

"Honey, honey, hold on now, sugar pie."

Fred had grown up in Wisconsin too; in fact, they had met during their senior year at the University of Wisconsin, but he sounded so much more Southern than Dorie did. Said insurance with the accent on the "in" and vehicle with a "hic" and bedroom suite as "suit." Dorie just couldn't do that although she did lapse into a "y'all" now and then even when she wasn't trying to be funny.

"I'm sorry." The condescending tone was gone and he kissed her cheek and waited until she looked up into those pretty blue eyes of his. "I really am, Dorie. I know we haven't talked about this enough, and I guess I'm pushing you because I want it so bad." Even ten years ago he would have said "badly." "I just get so gosh damned excited thinking about the two of us, just me and my first mate, taking off on our own yacht any ole time we want to, going up to Chattanooga or Knoxville or down to Green Turtle Bay for a month or two. Just us two old salts."

"We can do that right now, Fred. There's nothing to stop us from hopping in the car and…"

"But it's not the same at all, honey. You'll see." He rubbed her back and she arched more closely over his belly, which had expanded just a little since he had retired, she noticed, and against his warm, wide chest. She used to be able to feel his ribs, but he still felt good and looked good too, his brown hair going silver at the temples, his six-feet-two-inch frame still straight and athletic. She was proud of her handsome man.

"I think Captain Larry did a number on you," she murmured into his shirt-front and he laughed and hugged her tighter. Fred and Captain Larry, who had brokered the Chris Craft for Riverfront Yachts in Louisville, had brought *Sun Spot* over seven hundred miles on the Ohio River to the Tennessee River and Sunset Marina. Dorie had promised to take care of their married daughter's boys while they were on business in Beijing for two weeks. So instead of learning to enjoy their old "new" boat with a hired professional captain to guide them, Grandma Dorie had driven to Nashville and toted two wiggly elementary aged grandkids back and forth to school, church, soccer practice, the PTA craft and bake sale, an overnight at a neighbor's, roller skating, the movies, out for pizza. Lord love them but they wore her out.

"Captain Larry and I had a ball, my honey, but nothing to like what you and I are going to have floating at the end of a hook in an isolated cove, nobody else around." He nudged at her breasts. "Nobody to have to wear clothes for." Fred hadn't talked sexy like this in ages and she pulled back, feeling the burn of a blush creep up toward her ears.

"Oh sure," she frowned, "and scare the coots half to death." She pictured herself running around topless, those lovely rolls of fat bouncing along with her D-cup boobs. Since she had turned fifty, she had gained two or three pounds every year and had gradually grown to a size extra-large. She couldn't seem to get rid of those extra pounds no matter what she did. Well, it was true that she hadn't exactly mounted a full-scale attack on the problem. Something else always seemed more important.

Their love life had been non-existent for months, but they were grandparents, for heavens sake, and Fred had been so preoccupied with retirement plans and then with that stupid boat. Oh, they kissed good morning and good night, but when he put his arms around her as he was doing now, she was sure that her flabby body repulsed him as much as it repulsed her, and she was ashamed and pulled away. At night, she hurried into her nightgown while he was still in the bathroom. Nope. At fifty-seven, her topless days were definitely over.

"You don't scare this ole coot, sugar." He slapped her lightly on the fanny. "How about if we dress nice and warm and go down to the boat, check on how the engine room heater is keeping up?"

"I thought you did that yesterday."

"Well, we can't be too careful." He headed for the front closet. "Don't forget to turn off that sauce, Dorie," he called as he shrugged into his heavy suede jacket.

"What about the Packer game?" Dorie demanded as she almost twisted the knob right off the stove. "I told Marla we'd be there at 3:00." The Andersons were from Illinois originally and it was their turn to host the Sunday football party for the other "damn Yankees" (the ones who wouldn't go home) and the few Southerners in the neighborhood who enjoyed pro ball. "They're playing at Green Bay," she called and he turned in the doorway.

"Why don't you call them and explain. You haven't been to the boat for a month or more. Anyhow, they probably won't even miss us." The garage door gizmo began its hum as it broke the seal.

But she would miss them, she thought, as she dialed up Marla. Even though Fred didn't think much of her husband. George wasn't good with his hands, had to hire someone to change the washer on a leaky faucet, Fred had scoffed. But George never complained about paying a plumber and so what if he wasn't handy. She yanked her jacket over her heavy sweater, hanging on to the bulky sleeve ends as she jammed her arms through the jacket arms. And what about her garden, her lovely garden! She stood there like a scarecrow in a cornfield, her mouth drooping in dismay with the realization. "Liveaboards don't have gardens," she said to nobody before she heard the impatient honk of the car horn and let her lumpy arms thump down in disgust. "I'm coming! Hold your horses, Fred!" she hollered but he was already in the breezeway door.

"What's the problem?" he asked, his mouth thin with irritation.

"Liveaboards don't have gardens."

"Oh, for Pete's sake, Dorie." He grabbed her arm and propelled her, not very gently either, through to his van in the garage. "You can have big pots or something."

CHAPTER 2

Sunset Marina is one of several on Lake Guntersville in northern Alabama, a lake created in 1939 when the Tennessee Valley Authority built the Guntersville Lock and Dam to help control the Tennessee River and generate electricity for the area. The resulting lake is huge, covering over 800 acres, and offers boaters and fishermen a lovely recreational paradise in the foothills of the Appalachian Mountains.

Although in the Sunbelt, Northern Alabama is about as far north as you want to go to liveaboard all year round. Of course there are folks who will live in Massachusetts chipping ice from around their boats for drinking water, but you know those people are crazy. Many Southerners think spending winter on a boat at Sunset Marina is crazy too. Lake Guntersville did freeze over completely in 1940, the first winter the lake existed, and once in a while you wake up to a skim of ice in the shallower areas. You have to get those space heaters going in the boat and bundle up pretty good against those cold north winds coming straight down the Tennessee River.

But winter here is short and can be a special time on the water. With no noise of motors or sounds of voices, you hear that quivery call of the loons and the assorted clucks, honks and shrieks of all the other birds and ducks that winter here. You hear the sound of the little waves slapping against the hull of your boat and the snap of halyards on the sailboat masts when the wind comes around. This being the Sunbelt, every two or three days you get a few glorious hours in the winter sun and a magnificent sunset going down over purple mountains all to yourself. The Tennessee River seems to take this opportunity to renew itself and you can see bottom in places you couldn't at the end of a busy summer. In the wintertime, the peace and beauty of the place just seem to seep into your soul.

—A Genuine Liveaboard

"There's hardly anybody here." Fred looked pleased as the minivan crunched over the nearly empty gravel parking lot, dodging potholes filled with water. "Nobody here yesterday either," he remarked cheerfully as he pulled his sweat suit hood up around his face and came around to get her as he always did. "Put your earmuffs on, sweetheart," he ordered as he helped her out and clicked the lock button. "Don't want another ear infection."

"Okay, daddy," she said in a sarcastic, little-girl voice and snapped the fake fur muffs hard over her ears, but he was already halfway down the half-sunken walkway and turned impatiently to wait for her to catch up before starting out onto their pier.

"Careful of ice in those shady spots, Dorie. You really should have worn your rubber-soled boots."

"I'll certainly consult you more carefully on the proper way to dress…" but her sarcastic retort died as a flock of herring gulls wheeled down from the metal roof above them, screaming annoyance at being disturbed. They draped into two graceful arcs on either side of them, sending curls of white feathers afloat, first in the air and then on the water. Dorie stopped to watch them resettle fitfully on the metal roof of the long pier parallel to theirs. "Oh my," she breathed. Herring gulls, much prettier than their name implies, have snowy white breasts, dove-gray heads and gray wings tipped with black. "Were they here last time? Last time I was here?"

"I don't think so. At least not so many." Fred gestured behind him toward the fuel dock. "I think they came for the winter soon after the coots arrived."

"Oh my," she said again. In the shallows bobbed hundreds of small black exclamation points, pigeon-like birds nervously huddled together, their black heads and white beaks disappearing under the cold water from time to time. They made a strangled honking sound, discernible now that the gulls had quieted. Dorie had noticed them on Lake Guntersville before but only a few, not this huge number.

"I don't know how old those coots are, but they do look as if they scare easy."

"If we don't get to where it's warm pretty soon," she laughed, and jiggled around on the pier, "whatever I have to scare them with will be frozen solid and probably fall off." It was much colder under the metal roof, which was designed primarily as protection from the harsh Alabama summer sun. She puffed at him so he could see her breath.

"Now that would be a crying shame, sweet pea." He draped his arm over her shoulders and drew her along quickly past houseboats, fishing boats, pontoons and cruisers of all sizes and in all conditions bobbing side by side. They heard noise coming from one houseboat, canned laughter, but the drapes were tightly drawn, only a pencil of light visible in the gloom under the roof. There were no signs of life on any of the other boats. "Feels kind of spooky, doesn't it?" The delight in his voice was so obvious that she just grunted noncommittally rather than complain again. She really couldn't feel her toes.

Sun Spot was one boat from the end, her port bow now partially lit by the afternoon sun, and even through all those clothes she could feel his heart beat more quickly as he stopped for a moment to just look.

Dorie followed his adoring gaze past the bow pulpit, (which cradled a surprisingly small anchor for all that boat, she thought) up to the teak gunnels around the front, and aft to the enclosed back deck.

"She's really something, isn't she? Weighed out at 66,000 pounds, 33 tons, when they launched her!" Dorie had heard all this before. In 1975, Chris Craft didn't yet trust such a thin material as fiberglass and had applied many more layers than newer boats now had, all adding to the stability and weight of an already heavy 45 long by 15-foot wide, flush deck, flying bridge model. He shook his head in amazement and guided her to the metal folding ladder he had tied to a roof support in an effort to steady it. She held it for him as he unsnapped the blue canvas, very dirty blue canvas, lifted the wooden bar, which squeaked as he folded it back, and motioned for her to wobble her way up. Their combined weight made *Sun Spot* dip a little and they rocked pleasantly from side to side until she steadied. Thank heavens Dorie didn't get seasick easily, but even on the enclosed back deck she could see her breath.

"Wait just a minute, hon, just let me check that ceramic engine room heater and we'll get some heat going up here. This baby warms up faster than you might think." He winked at her before he unlocked the little door, hooked it back, and folded up the companionway hatch to access the curving staircase. The whoosh of sickly sweet diesel fuel smell nearly knocked her over. "You get used to it," he grinned before disappearing below.

Get used to it, my fat butt, she thought. She hadn't realized before that it was so strong, but the weather had been much warmer then and they had been able to open up, diffuse that cloying odor.

The furniture on the back deck was wicker but sturdy; a couch, two deep armchairs with wide armrests, and two straight-backed chairs, probably meant to be used with a table which was no longer there. The cushions were a mottled blue vinyl with piping that had been white originally but now was dingy yellow. In fact, the wicker, now uncertain beige, might have been white once too, she decided. The indoor-outdoor carpeting looked newer but was curled up and ragged around the edges and shredded around the round hatch where it had been inexpertly cut out. The hatch could be propped up to provide more air flow to the aft cabin below it and also provided an escape route from the cabin, so she knew it was important, but it was inconveniently situated smack dab in the middle of the deck's sitting area and looked God awful. Behind one of the seats facing the helm station, which looked so complicated she refused to really look at it, there was a wet bar with liquor storage below and a fold-down counter. The ladder to the fly bridge also folded, this time up onto the roof of the deck.

She sat down in one of the damp, lumpy armchairs. Well, she could make new cushions. She had replaced their patio furniture cushions and they'd turned out okay. Then decide about the wicker. But if she made the cushions and then found out that the wicker was shot, all that work, not to mention money, would be wasted.

"Engine room heater seems to be fine, Dorie," Fred called from somewhere under the floorboards but whatever he said next was drowned out by a mighty squeal which vibrated her chair before it dropped to a deep, pulsating hum. The diesel fuel was joined by an acrid, burning smell that made her eyes water. "Now we'll get warm in a hurry," he peered up from the bottom of the stairs, rubbing his hands together in satisfaction. "Got the reverse cycle pump for the heat going. Don't worry. That smell will burn off when she gets going."

"Uh huh." Or maybe she would just get used to that too. No, wait. Everyone man, woman, and child living in nearby Anniston, Alabama, had been issued a gas mask by the government in case of a chemical leak as caustic material was being removed from storage tanks underneath the town. Maybe *Sun Spot* could qualify too.

"Why don't you come down into the main salon, honey, so we can close that door. I have a surprise down here, something I know you'll like."

"Is it a government-approved gas mask?" she asked hopefully before stepping over the high threshold and down the four-step, curving staircase. Very elegant if she didn't break her neck on it first.

"What?" he asked from inside the refrigerator door.

"Nothing," she shouted over the drone of the "furnace" and jammed her earmuffs into her jacket pocket.

"Well, how about this?" He triumphantly waved two plastic flutes and a bottle of Korbel Brut, her favorite champagne. "I thought that we might celebrate, just the two of us together on *Sun Spot*. We have never really been alone on this boat, Dorie. Did you realize that?" Fred wrapped a paper towel around the bottle and got the cork out without spilling a drop. "To us," he tapped and they both sipped the delicious effervescence. "To our grand adventure together, my honey and me," he toasted again and kissed her softly, beautifully, on the lips.

She had to love the joy she saw in his face as the bubbly warmed her at last. Or maybe it was the sun now moving down low enough to fill the entire living room, main salon, with its cheerful glow and she finally felt warm enough to take off her jacket.

"I chose this slip because I figured we'd get some of that sun in the winter-time," he said, gallantly taking her jacket from her and draping it over a hook with a flourish that said 'See? Coat hooks and everything!' "Course we'll get it in the summer too, but not so bad as if we were right on the end. I think that boat next door will block it in the summer." He gestured toward the Luhrs Sportfish rigged for deep-sea fishing docked in the outermost slip.

"That boat looks like it belongs in the Gulf," Dorie said as she craned to see the top of the tuna tower which barely made it under the metal roof. In fact, part of it probably had to be dismantled to get under at all. "I'll bet it's just stored here temporarily for the winter. Not much need for a fishing tower to catch crappy and catfish on Lake Guntersville."

He shrugged. "Cross that bridge when we come to it. Anyhow, the air conditioners work. At least the surveyor said they did. It was really too cool to test them properly though, so we may have to have the Freon checked when it warms up."

"Are they as quiet as the furnace?" She couldn't keep the sarcasm from her voice. True, it was beginning to throw a lot of heat from the grate above the hide abed and the burny smell seemed to be less sharp but the constant thrumming was getting to her.

"I know it's loud, honey, and it's not really a furnace but you can call it that if you want to. It's a reverse cycle pump. The air conditioning will be about the same but more efficient. There's a vent in the forward ceiling and another control like this one in our cabin above the foot of your bunk. I've been looking on the Internet for quiet, wall-mounted heaters that work on a thermostat. And I want variable wattage options so we can use our fifty-amp service to best advantage. Well, actually, we have two thirty-amps on a splitter cord. There's only so much electricity we can pull at once, you know. Then we'd use this beast for emergencies."

As he rattled on, he roamed the salon walls from behind the hide abed sofa and two barrel chairs, to behind the table that doubled in size when you opened it and spun the top around, to behind the end table onto which a rather nice nautical lamp was bolted. The little galley was in a corner and that was out of the question. "But you have to help me decide where the heater in here should go. We can't put anything right in front of it, a course."

"Hold on!" She gripped the counter and Fred braced his feet as *Sun Spot* suddenly heaved, her lines creaking with the strain. "What on earth...?" Nobody in his right mind was boating out there today!

"Tow boat," Fred smiled, "and she's got a right heavy load, I reckon."

"And do you 'reckon' we have to live aboard to place space heaters, Bubba?"

At her sour tone, Fred stopped his prowling and set his glass on the counter. "No, we don't have to do that, I guess." He smoothed his palms along the wooden counter rail and looked at her with wounded eyes. "I'm just getting frustrated, I guess, coming here every day and..."

"Every day? You've been here every day?" She had assumed he was puttering around in his workshop at one end of the garage while she was playing bridge at her monthly luncheon, meeting with the education committee at church, getting in her Master Gardener volunteer hours, T'ai Chi classes. Since the last child, Teddy, had finally gotten squared away as a bonafide dentist and moved out two years before, these things had mushroomed to fill the time. And after Fred had retired, she had kind of stayed out of his way, figuring he needed some breathing room. As an independent pattern maker, Fred had always worked so hard, even on weekends when there was a rush job for his shop.

But why hadn't she known that he had visited *Sun Spot* every day? Long before retiring last April, ever since the houseboat episode, in fact, Fred had talked constantly about boats. He expounded on the virtues of trawlers versus cruisers, diesel versus gas, Detroit diesels versus Caterpillars. The new golf clubs the kids had gotten him as a retirement gift had been used only once and then on a couples' outing, which she had pushed him into and it was clear he had only tolerated. Then he had taken off for days at a time, calling her from this or that marina, disappointment clear in his voice, until he had found this old Chris Craft. He was using his entire severance money to buy it, he had told her. Didn't ask her. Told her. And that wasn't chicken feed even with the kids up and out, the house paid off, a decent portfolio of stocks and bonds, and a nice pension coming in every month. That money could have bought a lot of cruises to a lot of places.

"We really have to discuss this, Fred." She put her glass down beside his and shook her head when he offered more.

"What do you think I dragged you down here for, Dorie? I know you enjoy the Packers and that hunk Brett Favre."

"I enjoy doing a lot of things, Fred. You seem to enjoy doing only one thing."

"Sometimes I stay only a little while, take a few measurements." He looked sheepish, refusing to look at her, and she pulled him over to sit on the couch beside him.

Dorie put her hands on his. "When you bought this boat, Fred honey, I thought we could some fun with it, maybe for a few summers. You'd have fun fixing it up without spending a fortune. Maybe I could make some new cushions for the deck furniture, like I made for our patio, you know? Use it for a summer home. Invite our friends for cocktails and a cruise around the lake. When we got tired of that, we'd sell it. Now what's wrong with that picture?"

He sighed and squeezed her hands. "I'm not sure I bought the right boat for that, Dorie." She sat up straighter. "I wanted a good quality craft, one worth working on, and you know Grandpa Langford had a Chris Craft on Lake Michigan, a wooden one. Real beauty but constant work. I thought being fiberglass might make it easier. But not a houseboat because you're so limited to the river with that." He was looking straight into her eyes, worry creeping around the edges of his mouth. "I realized when Captain Larry showed me all the bells and whistles on this thing, all the work to just keep her running and all…" He hesitated before plunging through the rest of his confession. "I realized when we brought her down from Louisville that maybe this was more than I'd bargained for, Dorie. The engine room alone half scares me to death."

"But why, Fred? You love engines. You design parts for engines."

He stood up in agitation, puffing out his cheeks and blowing hard. "Just to change the oil, these old Detroit diesels require twenty-four quarts of heavy-weight. Twenty-four quarts! Before we fired them up each morning, we climbed into our crap clothes and crawled underneath to check things out. Had to add some oil every single time. Had to add some to the generator too and check the transmission fluid."

"Are they defective, the engines? Wasn't the surveyor supposed to catch that?"

"No, no, Detroits always use a lot of oil, I know that, especially these old 8V71's. No, everything works as advertised, but…" he looked sheepish again, "what I hadn't realized was how tight it is down in that engine room." He pointed at the floorboards. "And how much time I was going to have to spend down there and, well, c'mon, let me show you." He pulled her up from the couch and guided her down two steps into the forward cabin in which there were built-in bunk beds on the port side, the bottom three-quarter size and the top a single. To the right were built-in drawers, a mirror and a full-length, if shallow, closet. A head with a big v-shaped shower completed the forward area. She had thought it would be fine for guests, non-claustrophobic guests.

She backed up against the bunks so he could pull out the steps they had just used and open the engine room. The smell of diesel fuel and oil assaulted her again, but Fred seemed unaffected as he turned on a light and motioned for her to crawl in after him down the narrow center aisle. "Be careful you don't brush up against anything, Dorie," he looked around back at her anxiously.

"I'll be careful," she said, hesitating only a second before allowing her old but clean jeans and old but clean hands make contact with the oil-stained vinyl that covered the crawl space running the length of the engine room.

She had looked down here before, had made appropriately impressed noises when the huge and filthy machines were first pointed out to her. She might as well have been in a mockup of space capsule at NASA for all the meaning they had for her, these grimy behemoths with tubes and wires and hoses going everywhere and countless knobs and gauges, very neat but very, very dirty. "What's that?" she stopped, startled by a high-pitched, quivery cry, followed by another coming from somewhere right outside the hull.

"Just loons."

"Inside and out."

He was a few feet ahead and had turned around to face her, and she realized that his shoulders filled the workspace completely. Forward the path narrowed for a few feet and he would have to edge through that sideways. "There's a step down from the holding tank. That's it."

"The fresh water tank?" She climbed over the little ledge.

"Nope," he said cheerfully and laughed at the face she made. "I didn't realize you were so squeamish about stuff like that."

"I changed enough diapers and cleaned up after enough sick kids to know what I would rather not get 'up close and personal with,' thanks anyway."

"Well, I could put in a Y valve. Maybe I should do that for emergencies anyway, even though they're finally illegal here in Alabama as of last October."

"What will that do?"

"Make it possible for us to pump overboard, into the lake."

"Are you kidding?" They were face-to-face, knee-to-knee, in the bilge discussing human waste, and she found that she was interested in spite of herself.

"Honey, you spend some time at most any marina on the river, and you'll find that there is never a line at the pump-out." He shrugged. "That's what Larry said. I haven't been here long enough to know. Maybe it's different here."

"But that's awful!"

He shrugged again. "Maybe, maybe not. Compared to what industry dumps, and what even one dairy or hog farm or chicken ranch dumps, or what runs off from fertilized lawns, I don't know. I thought about installing a waste treatment system, like a Raritan Lectra San or a Purisan, but they're pretty expensive and you still have to dump the treated stuff. Some states like Florida have banned the dumping of even gray water." He stopped at her look of confusion. "You know, dishwater or laundry water."

"I need to read more," she said sincerely. God knew there were piles of magazines in the garage workshop, *Liveaboard, Heartland Boating, Power and Motor Yacht, Passagemaker, Boat U.S. and West Marine Catalogs*, piles of them. This was another world, like snorkeling when you lifted your head from the amazing beauty under the water to gaze at the amazing but totally different beauty above. Not that this ugly, cramped, smelly engine room qualified as beauty, of course not, but Fred and she had been living in different worlds. That much was obvious.

Fred leaned forward, bumping his head on a cross bar before ducking under it, and managed to put his arms around her for the second time in one day. "I think I bit a hog in the ass, Dorie," he said into her neck, "and it makes me scared and happy at the same time. I can fix up this old girl sweet as pie, but I can't do it by myself. There are too many things and it's going to cost the world even if I do most of the work. And it's not worth it, and it's not fair to spend all that, unless you want to think about living aboard, making this our new home."

"Hold on just a second, Fred." She pulled away to look straight into his eyes. "We're down here so you can show me how miserable the engine room is and how you don't fit down here. You don't fit, I can see that. I don't even fit down here, and…" she held up a finger to stop him from responding while she took a breath. "And why in heaven's name would you want a boat that's so hard to service and needs so much work? We'd probably lose some money, but why not sell this old thing, buy a newer boat, maybe not so big, that isn't such a dinosaur and that we could enjoy right away. Why this boat, Fred?"

"I know everything you're saying, Dorie. I go around and around with myself every night, but then I come down here to the marina and I see the possibilities and, well, remember that old 1937 Ford Victoria? It was a six passenger coupe that Motown Motors had on their lot?"

"Yes," she said guardedly. Was he losing it? She prayed for simple dementia.

"I wanted to restore that thing so bad."

"You did? I didn't realize. My knees are hurting."

"I know, I know, but just hear me out. I wanted that Ford because I knew I could learn how to fix it up, have a ball. But we were putting Teddy through dental school and you had already given me such hell about working on Tom's houseboat, so it was out of the question at the time."

"Fred…"

"No wait now." He was struggling, his face contorted with the effort to express himself. "I want to restore this old boat because, in spite of how this engine room scares me to death, I think I can do a good job at it. I have to learn a lot, I know, but I don't want a toy boat, Dorie. This old girl is special. We're only the third owners in twenty-nine years. I have a record of her since she was launched in April of 1975. And I know how happy you are doing your social things, but I can't spend my retirement just golfing or playing cards."

"I also keep up a big house, Fred, and cook and do your laundry!"

"No, now I didn't mean it that way." He held her resentment off with his palms. "I know how hard you work. I can see that. And that's my point. I don't want to do this alone, and I don't see how you could keep up that house and this boat too. See, I wanted you to understand how hard it will be to work down here so you'd know we have to do this now, while we can, while I can still crawl around down here. I'm almost fifty-eight…"

"Little late for a mid-life crisis," she said tartly. Her knees were really throbbing now. "Let's finish this discussion upstairs."

"No." He grabbed her shoulders and shook her a little. It didn't hurt but this wasn't her Fred and suddenly her knees didn't seem so important. "I'm sorry but we finish it right here."

"Okay," she said in a small voice.

"You know how happy I was to get that early retirement package?" She nodded yes. "But you don't know how long I hated being chained to that computer, do you?"

"You never complained."

"What good would it have done, to complain? I wanted that '37 Ford so bad I could taste it. Instead I got a new John Deere so I could mow that fucking lawn, keep it as nice as the Andersons'." The bitterness in his voice shocked her as much as the shaking had. "And when I saw *Sun Spot,* I fell in love, just like with that Ford, only much more. That would have been a nice hobby; this is a way of life. It's now or never, and not doing it would just about break my heart, but I can't do it without you, Dorie."

She knew he could see the love in her eyes as she acquiesced. Isn't that what she loved most about him, his passion, his drive?

"And I'm not thinking we'd do this liveaboard thing forever, Dorie. I have no idea how long, but you know those A-frame drawings I had made up years ago? When we get too old or we're tired of the boat, maybe we could find a spot in the mountains and build that, just two bedrooms up in the loft, remember?"

"Okay."

He looked at her carefully and gently took both of her cold hands in his bigger warm ones. "I didn't hurt you, did I?" She shook her head no. "I just feel that this a chance to do something different, have that adventure, just the two of us."

"Okay."

He gave a small laugh and kissed her on the cheek. "C'mon, let's finish that champagne before it goes flat on us."

"I can't," she said solemnly.

"Why not? You had only one glass." He had his hands on her big hips, urging her to turn around and crawl back out over the holding tank.

"I can't get out. My knees won't work anymore."

"Move it!" He swatted her lightly on the rear for the second time that day.

"First mate abuse. It's not a good thing."

"I'll show you some real abuse when we live aboard," he grinned. "We'll make this old tub rock and roll, just you wait."

CHAPTER 3

Sunset Marina has seventy-six slips ranging in length from 30 to 60 feet and is not the smallest or grandest marina on Lake Guntersville. Regulars pay monthly rent according to slip size, as apposed to transients who usually pay daily by the foot. Sixty slips are undercover and are more expensive than open slips, which are on a separate dock occupied mainly by sailboats. Yearly slip rental is cheaper than month-to-month, but most are willing to pay that extra fee for the freedom that goes with it.

Even though there are twenty-six mailboxes with names on them, at present there are eight boats occupied by genuine liveaboards. This is the breakdown:

Married couples---------------------------------3 boats
Unmarried couples------------------------------1 boat
Single man, women visiting---------------------3 boats
Single man, women never visiting---------------1 boat

These numbers could change by the time you read this, of course. People come, people go.

—A Genuine Liveaboard

"Lady?" Vernon called as he unzipped the winter Isinglass and bent to squeeze his belly through the smallest opening he could make and still get onto the forward deck of the houseboat. The television was blaring so she had to be home from her sister's. "Lady, where you?" he called again as he rezipped the plastic carefully. It was several years old, and he noticed some new tears, and one section of the zipper base had begun to unravel again. He pursed thick lips around his cigar stub and grumbled. "Can't get nothing good, nothing to last these days. Just keep shelling out for the same damn things over and over."

"What' s the matter, Vernon?" His wife rocked the sliding door that opened onto the deck just enough to get her head through. "What you doing out there, fool?"

"Now, don't you be calling me that. You know I don't like that, Lady." Vernon's full head of gray hair had been cut just yesterday but shaved up too high in back and on the sides, the pale bottom strip making his ears seem to stick out above his black glasses and give him a vaguely retarded look. His niece charged him only half price so he couldn't say too much, but Lady said, get her to stop doing that or go somewhere else. He just couldn't though. After all, she was family and those barbershops just charged too damn much.

He struggled to close the sliding door, adjusted the curtains, and moved a pile of newspaper fliers and catalogs from his recliner to the couch, which already had a pile of its own in addition to several plastic bags filled with merchandise to be returned. If Lady saw something she liked, she held it up, and if it looked right, took it home irregardless of what size it said on the ticket. After all, what could a size 26W mean to those itty-bitty Taiwanese or Koreans? Too bad her eye wasn't all that good.

"Damn it," he said softly and moved his cigar over to the left side of his mouth. That bottom tooth on the right hurt like the dickens whenever he forgot and bit down on it. Probably cost him more Goddamned money for a dentist just to pull it. Two or three fliers printed on shiny paper slid off the couch onto the floor, and Vernon checked to see that Lady had turned back to "Law & Order" before he nudged them under the couch with his foot. He could tie a string around that rotten tooth and the other end to a doorknob and slam the damn door real hard. If he had a door to slam, that is. All these here sliding doors got jammed up with crap all the time so you had to shove till you was blue to get them open all the way.

He rocked restlessly while he waited for the program to be over, one foot jiggling up on his toes. He had promised Lady that he wouldn't say hey to Jack Daniels before 3 o'clock, and by God, he intended to keep his word no matter how bad his mouth hurt. He chewed on his cigar and spat into a paper towel.

"Jimmy talked to me today," he announced loudly when he saw her edging over toward the computer in her rolling barrel chair. Lady was hooked on computer solitaire.

"Which Jimmy?"

"Jimmy Lassiter." Jimmy and his wife Georgie owned the marina. Well, the bank probably owned most of it, but they ran the place, collected the rent. "Jimmy says that slip at the end will be open sometime next month. That

Henderson guy finally sold. A couple in Knoxville, he said. They be taking the boat out of here soon as the weather gets good."

"That so?" Lady was definitely interested.

"That's a 60 footer, that slip. We'd have room for the Bayliner and the Bombardier; we put the Bayliner in kinda cattycorner. Only stick out a little. Nice view too."

"Yahuh," she agreed. Now he had to haul the boats from where they were stored on trailers in Cousin Elizabeth's back yard and get them into the water at the public boat launch. On a real nice day there might even be a wait at the launch. Then reverse the process at the end of the day. He had tried leaving the 25-foot Bayliner overnight in an empty slip, but that money-hungry Jimmy had seen it and added transient dockage to their monthly bill. He had also tried leaving the boats on their trailers in the parking lot, but Jimmy said there was a storage fee for that too. Georgie was all right but that Jimmy Lassiter was no favorite of theirs. "More money," Lady said. That woman could almost read his mind!

"Not only that, but Jimmy says he won't rent that slip on a month-to-month. Now, why does he say that?" Vernon had never, in all his years as a live-aboard, taken a yearly lease. That defeated the purpose of living on a boat, being mobile. "Why does he tell me about that slip and he knows how I feel? I done explained it to him and to Georgie so many times."

By God, it was after 3! He reached into the cupboard for the Jack Daniels bottle with one hand and his favorite glass with the other, then added three ice cubes, just the way he liked it. He rolled the Jack around on his tongue savoring that first smoky bite. Made him forget that sore tooth altogether. Lord but he pitied folks, like Lady, who didn't drink nothing, not even sweet wine.

"Jimmy knows how I feel," he said again, much aggrieved. Vernon pushed his black glasses up higher on his nose. Had to get those damn things fixed too one of these days.

"Yahuh," Lady again agreed. Except for the Lake Guntersville Yacht Club where you had to put down several thousand dollars and then pay a monthly fee, they had lived at just about every marina that provided water and electricity on the Tennessee River from Florence to Shell Mound, just south of Chattanooga. And, by God, they had made a lot of good friends along the way.

"We going to invite those new ones, them Yankees, to the party, you think? I may a seen that boat before somewhere." The Jack had lost its bite now but nothing smoothed you over like good whisky. Good whiskey and good music. He relaxed in his recliner, put up the footrest. "She looks kind of pretty in a prissy way. You can always tell those Yankees, how they carry theyself and talk and all. Him, I don't know. Didn't get a real close look." He caught her eye as she rolled over to the computer table, and she nodded. "Okay. I'll invite em first chance I get." Then he put in the "Country Favorites" CD and turned it up loud. Lady wouldn't care now that she was into the solitaire game.

Dorie was struggling to cut through a section of carpeting with heavy scissors when, out of the corner of her eye; she caught him ambling toward her. "Hey, how you?" The fat man with an unlit stump of a cigar in his mouth bent over the side of the dock to spit brown juice into the water and took a sip of his drink from a paper cup before smiling up at Dorie again. His nose was a heavy drinker's nose, she thought, red and purplish veins standing out in the afternoon sunlight, but maybe his nose just looked redder because of those heavy black glasses. And what a goofy haircut! "Ain't I see your boat over to Alred Marina before? I used to be at Alred's and I thought maybe you come just for I left outta there for over here?"

She blinked, needing a moment to understand the sense of it. "No, no, this is a new boat for us. We brought it down from Louisville. This is the only place we've docked the boat on Lake Guntersville."

"Well, welcome to Sunset!" He held up a chubby hand and when she leaned down over the stainless steel rail, he gave her fingers a little shake and she saw that one of bows on his ugly glasses was ringed with duct tape. "I'm Vernon Johnson. Everybody cept Lady call me VJ, so you just call me VJ too." His voice was too loud and reminded her of the flight of a finch, kind of hiccupping. "That's our little ole boat over yonder." He motioned several slips behind him to the houseboat that had the curtains tightly drawn.

"Nice to meet you. I'm Doris Langford. Everybody calls me Dorie. So you're the mysterious person who lives there! We've been wondering."

"Oh, ain't no mystery about us," he laughed and bent to spit again. "Lady, she don't like the cold, so we got to button up right tight. Me, I ain't so bothered by it irregardless, but it don't seem so bad this afternoon now the wind has died. So you and your man just bought this boat, huh? That's a nice, solid boat, yessir." He stepped back to admire it, his small eyes squinting. Another sip. "Yessir."

"Well, thank you, VJ. We have so much to do we don't quite know where to start, and we've been working like idiots." She gestured at the carpet remnant she had spread out over the top of the hull so she could cut it to fit the engine room floor and resisted swiping at the grease on her jeans. They went home filthy and exhausted every night.

"Y'all ain't liveaboards, are you? I see you going back and forth some-wheres."

"Right now we're wannabees, I guess. We've got to see about selling our house in Huntsville. I have no earthly idea about what to do with all the stuff we've spent thirty-five years accumulating. What did you do when you moved aboard?" VJ's houseboat seemed impossibly small for even one person, let alone two, but then she had been reading stories about couples who got along just fine on 22-foot sailboats, so what did she know?

"Oh, you'd have to talk to Lady bout that. In fact, I want y'all to come to a party we're having on Sunday afternoon. Hey, how you?" He extended a hand up to Fred who had heard their voices and emerged wiping his hands on a paper towel. He admired the boat a while for Fred's benefit before returning to his invitation. "We gone pretend it's summer and have us a fish fry. Give you a chance to meet some other folks around here. We got a lot of good folks here, real party people!" VJ saluted them with his nearly empty paper cup.

"Well, that sounds just fine to me," Fred said and put his arm around her. "Honey, you up for a party? What time on Sunday?"

"Bout 3 o'clock. We generally start bout 3 in the winter cause we still got us some sunlight unless it be raining or some damn thing. Don't matter ever which way." He waved good-bye. "Now, you need anything, you just got to knock on the boat. No, y'all ain't got to bring nothing," he called, as he weaved his way back down the pier.

"Boy Howdy, I reckon he be having a party all by hisself," Dorie said when he was out of earshot.

"Now, not everybody speaks the king's English like you, school teacher." School teacher. That seemed like about five hundred years ago. She had taught English 101 at Huntsville University when they were first married and Fred was doing his pattern maker apprenticeship. Before Freddie came along. "How you coming with that carpeting? I thought you might need a board to put under-neath so you could bear down with this cutter instead of using scissors. What do you think?"

"I think that's a good idea."

"You know, at first I thought carpeting the engine room was silly. It's just going to get dirty right away. But then I realized, so what? What a relief it's going to be for these poor old knees and elbows."

"Good. Chop, chop," she pushed him away. "I don't want to lose the light and have to haul this out again tomorrow."

Back at his boat, Vernon put the paper cup on the crowded counter, pursed his lips at the mess left over from lunch still sitting there, and filled his real glass. "They coming, Lady, and they both Yankees as I spected."

Lady looked over at him from her chair in front of the computer and pointed to a scrap of paper next to the telephone. "They fix your glasses for you free if call and make an appointment when they not too busy," she said and returned to the screen. Since her sister give her that game disc, that's all Lady wanted to do was play solitaire.

Vernon didn't like games or TV much and he wasn't much of a fisherman, but he did enjoy one particular chat room, and if she ever finished playing, he'd like to talk awhile. Some real nice folks. He had already made his daily e-mail report on the air and water temperature and precipitation to *Lakeside News*, the twice-weekly newspaper that covered several communities around them—Lakeside, of course, Guntersville, Arab, Grant, Good Hope, Albertville and Boaz—but he still had to do his weekly bird count for the Audubon Society. They all got together in January to take an official count around the entire area, when the results were published in the *News*, but he kept his own records year round. He specialized in waterfowl, but he enjoyed an occasional bird watching foray on land.

Vernon was pretty proud of the fact that he was the first one to recognize the trouble with cormorants. Now, the great blue herons stayed all year, but the cormorants were supposed to migrate north in the summer with the loons, coots, grebes, ducks, seagulls, and geese. They all started leaving about March 1, give or take for the weather, when the purple martins started coming into the nests made of gourds that Vernon took down every fall, cleaned, and hung back up on poles around the marina in late February, if it was warm enough. Not too soon or the damned brown-headed cowbirds would get in there first and the martin scouts would look elsewhere for the summer. That had happened only one year, he was proud to report.

But for the last three winters, double-crested cormorants started staying year round, for some damned reason—Vernon had been the first to realize that—and they had just about killed all the trees on a couple of small islands in the lake. Just pooped them to death so only the dead trunks, swarming with cormorants, remained, their colonies getting larger every year. Vernon rocked nervously in his lounger. What to do, what to do? So far the catch at the many bass tournaments held on Lake Guntersville seemed unaffected, but that had to change if the cormorants were allowed to go unchecked.

Lady was still at that damned game. He shook his head in dismay. Her backside filled up the barrel chair and the fat of her upper arms draped down in folds over her elbows, and there was even an extra fold now creeping over the neckline of her sweatshirt. Poor Lady. She had been heavy before the accident, a big woman, but nothing like this. As though she could read his thoughts, she turned her head to look at him, and he tried to smile at her around his cigar, but she turned back to her game without returning the smile. Well, that new Yankee lady was even prettier up close, had real warm, kind of green speckled eyes and a nice full bosom.

Vernon decided on Patsy Cline and returned to his chair. Over the years, he hadn't been as faithful to Lady as a Christian man ought to be and he felt bad about that. Lady was a good woman, a good mother, had stood with him through some tough times. "Stand By Your Man." That's what Lady had done. Even after the accident that was all his fault. Him and Jack Daniels.

The tears welled up and he looked at the back of Lady's head with affection. He would try not to let that Dorie charm him into anything because you never knew with Yankees how they might react to something. Try as he might to control it, especially since the accident, once in a while Vernon might have a little too much Jack and get frisky with the ladies at a party, might say something or put his hands where they didn't belong. By God, his true friends would call him on it. Put him back on the right path in a nice way, not mean or nothin. And he would apologize and try even harder the next time. But with these here Yankees you never knew how they would take it. That Fred was skinny but he looked strong, and he was taller than Vernon. Could probably pull a pretty fair punch. She was a right pretty thing though. She had just enough girth to her to give a man something to hang on to, but she wasn't so big you'd wallow around.

"That's enough," Lady said as she turned off the game, and Vernon was so startled he almost spilled his drink.

"Huh?" He felt the telltale warmth creeping up his neck, the beet-red guilt, but Lady only heaved herself out of the chair and lumbered down the narrow hallway to the head.

CHAPTER 4

❀

You've heard the joke that boats are defined as holes in the water into which money is thrown. And maybe you've seen a cartoon where a little man wearing a captain's hat, always whistling and smiling, climbs into his car, drives to the marina, fills a dock cart with money from his trunk, throws the money at his boat, and drives back home, still whistling and smiling.

Some of the same people who tell these jokes persist in believing that living aboard is economical, a waterfront view without the exorbitant price per square foot of shoreline property. They envision themselves at anchor in a lovely cove catching fish for supper, their only expense a six pack and a bar of soap for a bath in the warm, crystal clear lake. They tell themselves that on a boat they will be content to live simply, get back to the basics, that they don't need "much" to make them happy.

Well, liveaboards are not all created equal.

—A Genuine Liveaboard

Concerning the house, they hadn't signed with any one realtor yet but had met with three different companies in the past month. Each one had been willing to take the listing but had suggested that they first do just about all the things that Fred was not willing to do and why he was selling the house in the first place. They put that problem aside for now.

None of this bothered Dorie as much as she thought it would. Now that she had committed herself to the boat, she found herself looking more at her home as a house, as real estate. Her biggest problems were the garden and some of her possessions. What about her own mother's china and her adorable corner hutch? What about the cobalt blue pitcher and matching glasses and the gorgeous antique cedar chest that her grandmother had left them in her will? The Tiffany lamp that the kids had pitched in to buy for their thirtieth? The sterling serving platters? My God, the Christmas ornaments they ritually exchanged each year. Some of them were delicate works of art!

These things bothered Dorie quite a bit and no one at the Johnson party had offered any real suggestions. Just a lot of shoulder shrugging and not much sympathy. Not even from Sylvia, the one called Lady. Maybe they thought she was bragging, like complaining about how much it costs to run your personal airplane, but she wasn't. And she didn't think their attitude was fair because everybody had things that were precious to them even if they weren't especially valuable to anybody else, didn't they? And not a soul at the party seemed to miss gardening; they equated it with pulling weeds and mowing the lawn. No one seemed to get pleasure out of watching things grow, and Dorie couldn't understand that at all.

Concerning where to best begin work on *Sun Spot*, they attempted a rational approach. They would each list, in descending order with most important things first, what should be done on *Spot*, and then they would compare their lists.

FRED'S LIST

Two 30 amp, 50' power cords plus y splitter cord	$300
Power cord repair kit	$75
New automatic bilge pump, 12V, Rule 2000	$200
New switch for forward 110V bilge pump	$35
Second-hand (half price per Jimmy Lassiter)	
Xantrax inverter 45 amp. battery charger	$2200
Spare diaphragm water pump, 12V, 4 gal. Per min.	$350
Direct line crossover valve to shore water/drinking hose	$25
Racor water filter w/shut-off valve/3 disposable filters	$70
Stainless steel thru-hull cable/telephone inlet	$90
New lines, assorted:	
2 60' 5/8	$150
2 40' (5/8 and 3/4)	$70

FRED'S LIST (Continued)

2	25' (5/8 and 3/4)	$45
	New stainless steel thru-hull power cord inlets	$160
	Sanigard holding tank vent filter/replacement element	$140
	Three in-wall thermostat heaters, variable watt settings	$750
	Cordage for 250' emergency 5/8 anchor line	$200
	Amp meter	$50
	Y-valve and pump for emergency pump over	$175
	Remodel aft cabin, Queen bed partly over stbd muffler	$2800
	2500 watt inverter/panel/2 gel cell batteries	$4000

DORIE'S LIST

Get rid of diesel/oil smell

Build more galley storage for pots, pans

Make hanging closet into pantry

Replace boarding ladder with stairs

Buy microwave

Replace salon fold-out couch with den fold-out couch

Check condition of wicker deck furniture for new cushions

Buy/Build back deck table

Buy washer/dryer and design/build cabinet for it

Remodel master bedroom—king bed

"We didn't say you had to put down the prices of things," she protested until the great disparity in the two lists hit her and she started to laugh. Were they both thinking about the same boat? Had they been married for 35 years and knew each other inside and out? Were they both on the same planet? She held them up side by side. "Not too close a match," she said.

"You think?" Fred pretended to scrutinize the lists before laughing too. "I thought of one thing more but it won't cost much. I want to cut a hatch right here," he outlined a rectangle in the middle of the main salon floor, "that I can lift out when I'm working down there. Give me more air movement. And maybe I'll mount a wall fan below too. Just a cheap one."

"Cheap, huh?" She retracted his list and studied it more carefully. "Are your estimates for real, Fred? Twenty-two hundred dollars for a battery charger? Don't we only have two batteries? Didn't I crawl over them in the engine room?"

"Yes, you certainly did." He seemed pleased that she had remembered. "But those are 8D batteries and they weigh 150 pounds each and cost almost $500 apiece. We have a lot of DC power on this boat. For instance, the bathroom lights are strictly DC. I don't know why. That charger," he pointed to the list, "was put into a 55-foot Ocean Alexander over at Aqua Yacht Harbor in Mississippi, a brand new Oceans, and it couldn't handle all the DC power called for, according to Jimmy Lassiter. You know, the marina owner," he said in response to her uplifted eyebrows. "He's a buddy with the manager there, so it's really new, but we can get it for half price. I think it's a good deal. We'll probably never have to replace those 8D batteries."

"You can buy four batteries for that money, and don't we have a battery charger already?"

"Yes, it works but it's not a good one."

"Let's move that down on your list, Fred."

"Someone else will snap it up if we don't, Dorie. This really is a good deal."

She sighed. "I'm beginning to understand why we can't do the house and this boat. I suspect if I bought 'nautical' potholders, the price would triple."

"But if the boat sank, y'all could fish those potholders right out of the drink, just snatch 'em up floating on by. Think of the joy in that!"

"I gets de-lirious just thanking about it, Bubba. But really…" the numbers were just beginning to sink in. She had had no idea. "Do all the people at Sunset spend this kind of money on their boats?"

"A few might. That Bobby Ray Reynolds and the pretty girl with the brown hair…"

"Sarah," she supplied. "Her name is Sarah and she's not such a girl anymore." She had met them at the party.

"Anyhow, Bobby Ray and Sarah have that gorgeous Jefferson on the other pier, and they keep it immaculate."

"Sarah's just a girlfriend," she interrupted. "She doesn't own that boat. They're not married because Sarah said she doesn't want to be his fifth wife."

"Well, anyway, I'm going to get you over there to look at it some weekend when they're here. It's a beauty. Course it's a $400K beauty, too. But look at the majority of the boats here. Look at VJ's piece of shit, excuse my French. And that's why they sink to the bottom or burn up first and everybody cries and says, "Oh dear, what a disaster!' It's not a disaster; it's just poor, make that non-existent, upkeep. When's the last time you think VJ's boat was hauled out and the bottom checked?" She shrugged. "Not since he bought it, that's when. Probably got blisters so deep they should be sleeping in life jackets!"

"Blisters in life jackets! I'd like to see that," she teased.

"English teacher."

"Sticks and stones." She stuck her tongue out at him.

"Listen, Miss Smartypants, I hate to tell you this, but we can't just replace this couch with the one in the den."

"Don't you think it would look better? All these shades of beige are so…beige."

"Honey, think about it. How would we get it down here?"

"Well, how did they get this one down here?" She plumped down on it and felt the wooden frame press into the backs of her thighs.

"It's made to come apart. See, the back comes off here," he demonstrated, "and the arms here, and then there's just the fold-out spring structure. See, it's upholstered for that."

"How do you know that, Fred?"

"Well, I looked. I'm a pattern maker, sweetheart, and we're just born curious about how things are made, I guess, and it wasn't built-in like the bunks, for instance, so I figured it had to come apart on purpose."

Pretty ingenious, she had to agree, and scratched that off her list. Beige it was, for now. "So all of the couch comes apart in pieces that you could uphol-ster and then put back together?"

"That's just what I said, Dorie."

"I know, I know. I'm just thinking that maybe I could recover it myself. I've always wanted to try that." She put "Recover couch" on her list. In the mean-while, she would replace the cushion foam so at least they didn't hit bottom when they sat down.

"Come down here a minute, sweetheart," Fred called from the aft state-room. "I think those Sleep Number mattresses with the inflation pumps would be good, don't you? I'll order them UPS Next-Day Delivery, if they'll do that, so we'll have them by the weekend."

"What did you and Captain Larry do for beds, if these are so bad?" Dorie asked. They had slept for three nights in a row in their built-in twin bunks, very dated but adequate, she thought. Fred, however, had done nothing but complain about his hips, his back, his neck. Like spending hours in that engine room had nothing to do with his aches and pains.

"I honestly didn't even think about the comfort of the beds then, Dorie. I think I passed out every night. We might have overdone the martoonies a little too," he smiled. "And we slept in sleeping bags on top, so that maybe gave me some more cushion. Sometimes I slept on the couch. I don't know, but that mattress," he pointed at the offending bunk, "is killing me. I don't know why you aren't hurting more. Yours is even shorter than mine." He lay down on top of her coverlet, his head jammed against the quilted headboard, to demonstrate how his feet would have to climb up the wall of the closet if he wanted to stretch out. At least on his side, he could close the door to the cabin and let his feet hang over. With the door closed, however, he complained that it was too stuffy in the cabin, so he had attached an eye bolt and hook to the end of his bunk and to the back of the door to let in air but still allow for foot room. Much better, but the contraption rattled annoyingly whenever the boat rocked. He said he was working on that.

"I didn't say I wasn't hurting, Fred, but mine is big enough." Well, as long as they were complaining. "I can't seem to get really warm, though, no matter how many covers I pile on."

"Well, no wonder!" Fred had lifted her mattress and pulled up the hinged door underneath it by its ring handle. Four drawers took up the space under each bunk in the front, but behind the drawers were assorted gizmos and wires and more storage space. Under her bunk, the space was open all the way to the hull. In fact, that's where the official Coast Guard documentation numbers had been ground into the hull so that it would be traceable if the boat were ever stolen. The original owner had done this and the numbers stayed with the boat forever. That was great, but the draft coming up from the cold hull was almost palpable with diesel fuel smell and cold enough to make her shiver. Here she had been piling blankets on top and the problem came from underneath.

"We can fix this, Dorie. You get some of that dense foam that campers use for under their sleeping bags and I'll just staple that to the underside of the lift-up door and along the sides here. Hey, look at this mildew." Sure enough, black crud coated the wood along the aft wall and had begun to permeate her mattress along the back edge. No wonder the mattresses had been piled up on the inside bunk when Fred bought the boat. "Mine's okay," Fred announced. "Just that much closer to the engine heat, I guess, but mildew is going to be a winter problem with yours no matter what kind of mattress we buy. He propped it up on edge. Let me think about this. Go ahead and get the foam though, honey."

"I'll put that on the top of my shopping list," she said wearily. There just wasn't enough time in one day. They would definitely go home to their king-sized Sealy Posturpedic tonight. "But those self inflating beds are expensive, Fred. If we're going to remodel back here anyway, put in a queen bed, redo the closet, isn't that awfully pricey for a short-term solution? Neither one of us had temporary new mattresses on our list."

"Neither one of us knew then what it was like sleeping down here long term, and any kind of remodeling back here won't happen for at least a year, honey. Not if you want that washer/dryer combo when we do it." He pointed to the old-fashioned make-up table that was in a corner next to the closet, its corroded mirror surrounded by small round lights. Tearing this out and putting in a small machine that washed and dried ten pounds maximum per load in the same tumbler would cost about $3,000, they figured, if Fred designed the cabinet and if they saved shipping charges by picking up the machine at a Boat U.S. store in Atlanta. For bigger things like quilts and throw rugs she would still have to go to a laundromat.

"Are you sure a twin-sized would fit on my bunk?" A twin contour sheet fit Fred's mattress but she had to use double-ended, elasticized garters underneath to keep her sheet taut.

"Well, that's a good question." He whipped out his tape measure. "A very good question. Hmmm. Going to be tight but I think so. Worse comes to worse, we could remove the headboard on your side."

"I think we'd better check on those mattresses in the forward cabin too, Fred." He grunted assent while she donned her blue rubber gloves and went yet again for the bleach bottle and bucket.

"Same problem up here," he called cheerfully. "Say, I know what, Dorie." She could hear thumps as he struggled to set the bigger bottom mattress on its side. We can use one of the new inflatable mattresses for the top bunk here when we remodel back there. And the second one will come in handy when the kids visit, you'll see. Then it won't seem so wasteful."

"Okay," she said, trying not spill any of the solution on the bedding and keep her head away from the bleach fumes." Thank God for bleach.

But bleach didn't seem to do much for that diesel smell. Nor did Spic and Span, several kinds of carpet cleaner or Fabreeze. When they got home that night, Dorie wearily dumped their duffle bag with accumulated work clothes on the laundry room floor and gasped at the sickly sweet stench. You did kind of get used to it while you were cooped up and preoccupied with projects inside the boat, but the diesel reek from these clothes after just three days was horrible. Think what the curtains, the carpeting, bedding, towels, eventually everything on that boat would be like. It couldn't be good for them to breathe that either.

"We've got to do something, Fred." She had insisted he join her in the laundry room." She shook her stinky jeans at him in disgust. "This just isn't normal."

"Is it really that bad?" He was so tired, his blue eyes bloodshot with fatigue, his face still smudged even though he had washed it before leaving the boat.

"Oh, honey, it's terrible. I don't think I can live with this smell. I really don't." She was so tired herself she was almost dizzy, but whenever she had brought it up over the last three days, he had pushed it aside as being unimportant, fussy. "At that party I talked with several people who have diesel engines, Fred, and they said that all boats, especially old ones, are bound to have certain problem odors, but not like ours, Fred. Their clothes and hair weren't permeated like this!" She shook the jeans at him again, getting more and more angry as he just stood there, propped up against the washer, looking at her as if she were demented. "You have to face up to it and do something, whatever it takes, to get rid of this, and I mean it!" Her voice was rising hysterically but she didn't care. His stupid list of pumps and bazillion dollar battery chargers and she had to get something she wanted too if she was to be expected to live there, for Pete's sake. "This was at the top of my list, you know!"

Fred held up his arms wearily. "Okay, okay, Dorie. Just back off a minute and let me explain." He sank down onto the floor, stretched out his long legs in front of him and leaned against the washer. "C'mon down here, honey. I can't stand up anymore." He looked so sad and defeated that all the mad went out of her and she followed him down and propped herself against the companion dryer.

He didn't look at her. "I didn't want to tell you, but I know there's a fuel tank leak because I started noticing fuel in the port engine sump just before we made it here from Louisville, maybe the last two days. Not too bad and I was hoping it was just the hard running we were doing, but I don't know. Captain Larry said to just watch it when we took her out again but, of course, we haven't had that chance. That may be part of the problem, though I suspect it's not all of it."

He pursed his lips and gave her a sideways glance before plunging ahead. "I think we've also got a hole in the riser on the outboard side of the port engine. This is allowing fumes to come back into the aft cabin. I could smell it real strong while we were pushing it, running at about 2200 rpms to make good time. I think we might have blown a hole in her then." He gave out a short laugh. "When you buy a boat that's nearly thirty years old, I guess that's what you get." He studied his hands. "I'm sorry, Dorie. I should have told you. I was just hoping it would be tolerable until we got some other stuff out of the way, but I guess this has to go right to the top of my list too. This old girl hasn't been used much the last few years, and some things just won't stand up to the strain of hard running. I'm sorry."

"So how do you get these leaks fixed?" She felt hurt that he hadn't told her. She had thought they were in this "adventure" together now, but maybe she was just expected to tidy up behind while he had one. "I'm sure you've thought about that," she said coolly.

That sideways look from him again. "For the riser leak, I located a guy on the internet who lives in Florida and who specializes in tracking down these old parts. I'll e-mail him tomorrow and see if he can find a new one. It's going to be expensive, I'm certain of that. We'll have to have *Spot* hauled out at Aqua Yacht Harbor. That's the closest place that can handle our weight. Alred's Marina could drag us out on a sleigh but I don't trust that. For the fuel tank leak, I don't know what to do. Have to get somebody in to look at it first. A guy named Diesel Don is supposed to be real good and probably not so busy this time of year. I'll call him tomorrow too." He reached over to squeeze her thigh. "Don't you worry, honey. We'll figure it out."

"Oh, I'm sure you will, Fred." She was careful not to slip on the greasy clothes as she pulled herself up. "You're very capable. Well, I'm off for a hot shower and bed. These clothes can wait until tomorrow too."

"Dorie, I'm really sorry about the leaks," he called to her retreating back, but she pretended not to hear then or later when he slid into bed.

She had dropped everything to participate in this whole-heartedly with her husband, and she was starting to really enjoy it too. There was something very satisfying about solving problems together, being inventive, creative, whatever you wanted to call it. Setting up the little galley was like playing house, a challenge trying to use every available square inch to advantage. She had cleaned the three-burner stove and had just begun to cull her recipe books for more one-pot, casserole-type meals that didn't require too much last minute preparation and had decided to buy a six-quart slow cooker with a Corning ware center for cleaning. She could use the lift out center in the oven for other dishes too. Her stainless steel electric wok was perfect but she had to figure out where to store it. She was having fun.

But he didn't think she was strong enough, or maybe intelligent enough, to understand serious "boat" trouble. She may not understand all the mechanical workings or the terminology, but she sure understood trouble. Who the hell did he think got Dentist Teddy into therapy before he overdosed on laughing gas? Ha ha. While good old Fred was lusting after a 1930-something Ford Victoria, she was desperately trying to keep Teddy in medical school, and she had done it too. Teddy was doing fine now, was happy. And Janie, the third one, she was a pistol. Had to take her to the Birmingham Planned Parenthood where they had counselors her own age. That kid wouldn't listen to anybody else. Fred had been working at Cape Canaveral when Junior almost shot his eye out with his new pellet gun. She had told him Junior was too young for that but would he listen?

"So much for lists," she said angrily to his back, sat up, and turned on her reading lamp. He didn't roll over but his head shifted on the pillow and she saw his neck muscles tighten. "Don't you patronize me with your lists and your fancy schmancy internet connections. What else should I know about *Sun Spot*?" He mumbled something. "What? Fred, don't make me…"

"Okay, okay." He rolled to face her. "Don't use the cattle prod again, warden, I'll talk."

"That's not one bit funny, you asshole!" She was up on her knees now, fists clenched and eyes blazing mad. She punched her pillow in frustration.

"Take it easy now, Dorie. I know it's not funny." He sat up and ran his fingers through his messy hair. "I'm sorry. I'm making jokes to keep my own spirits up, Dorie, and I really am sorry about not discussing it with you. I wasn't trying to insult you. Honest. I was trying to ignore what I suspect is big trouble." He sighed. "In addition to those leaks, I think there's something wrong with the port transmission. It just doesn't shift right since I had the engines realigned in Louisville."

She punched the pillow again. "What good did it do to have the boat surveyed if none of this was detected?"

"A survey can't predict how long old parts will hold up, Dorie. I don't think I got taken or anything. I think…well, I don't know what to think, really. The shaft logs were my idea after I bought the boat. Maybe I should have left them alone." He had that sheepish look again. "Maybe we should cut our losses and sell *Spot*. You sure haven't had much fun so far."

"How do you know?"

"All you've done is work."

"We've been at it together for all of two weeks. I have always worked hard, Fred. And I'm not a teenager who requires instant gratification. You're not the only one who's sat on the John Deere when they'd rather be doing something else, you know. I raised four kids pretty much on my own through the important stuff. What do you think you've lived with all these years, a marshmallow? A powder puff? Cotton candy?"

He held up his palms in surrender. "Do you want to sell this boat?" he asked very seriously.

"No."

"Do you want to sell this boat and buy a newer one, as you suggested before?"

"No."

He propped up on one elbow." You're sure, because…"

"I'm sure, Fred. A commitment is a commitment. When I said I'd live aboard *Sun Spot*, I meant it. I'll do whatever it takes to make that happen, starting with getting rid of the damned diesel smell. But I'm also sure that I won't be a second-class citizen on this 'adventure' we're having. I won't be talked down to and I won't be protected. You've never done that before."

"I should have asked you before I bought it, Dorie. I should have. I thought maybe when you got to know the old girl you'd fall in love with her too and…"

"Well, that may happen yet but if you don't lose that hang-dog face pretty soon, I'm going to have to hurt you, Freddy." He threw an arm around her and bit her ear gently before blowing into it. She kissed his forehead. "Let's sell this place as is, take what we can get, and run with the money. No," she amended that, "let's see *Spot* run!

CHAPTER 5

✽

The village of Lakeside had been a pleasant but sleepy little Southern town of about 4,000 landlocked by water and mountains before Redstone Arsenal and then NASA located in Huntsville, only forty-five miles to the northwest. Lakeside is still landlocked but will never be quite as sleepy. These sophisticated Huntsvillians, who come from all parts of the globe, have recognized Lakeside for the ideal recreational and retirement community that it is. Prime waterfront property has grown more and more expensive, as it has everywhere, and summer shacks are being replaced with huge homes and refurbished boathouses along the shoreline.

Some of the newer people aren't too thrilled to be in close proximity to Sunset Marina, even though the marina was here long before they came. They complain about the higher levels of fecal matter found around the marina, which is especially true in summer. Enough complaints like these around the state has led to the implementation of the Marine Sewage Act in October of 2003, making it illegal to discharge untreated sewage into any lake. Other states have had similar laws for years, but other states have had better pumpout facilities for years too.

In 1982 Lakeside became the second town, soon after its neighbor Guntersville, to go wet in a dry county in Alabama. You've heard that joke that the only place Baptists don't recognize one another is in the liquor store. There's a fair amount of that around here in the Bible Belt.

—A Genuine Liveaboard

"What are you going to wear?" she had asked him the day before the boat party so she could bring good clothes from the house. The clothes they had been working in were destined for the garbage, several sets of them. They were planning to sleep on the boat together for the first time after the party and she was excited.

"The baby blue cashmere sweater, pleated navy gabardines, and..." he was wedged in the narrow deck space between the hull and the outside rail trying to secure the weather-beaten power cord more neatly along the guard rail, "crocodile loafers with the tassels but no socks. How does that sound?"

"Smashing if you owned any of those items. And what's with the no socks? Isn't it a little chilly for no socks?" She was handing him the cord holders from the dock below, dancing around now and then to keep warm.

He grunted as he struggled to kneel sideways and still use both hands. "I just thought wearing no socks was supposed to be yachty looking." His sweat suit hood kept slipping down over his eyes. "You know, Dorie, I think we're doing this backwards. I should be down there and you up here." They switched and it went much better.

"I think I'll wear the lime green sweater that Mindy sent me for my birthday," she said. It was tunic length and would cover her sins.

"Honey, I don't think it matters at all. Clean would be nice. Pick anything for me."

"Speaking of clean, it's going to be kind of fun to try the shower for the first time. How is it? You never said."

They finished with the cord but it still looked tacky, coated with a gray, greasy film. "I used a cleaner made just for these things but it sure didn't work. Used it on the fenders but it's no good. Expensive too. Oh well. The aft shower is okay, but it needs a new showerhead. Let's try the big one forward, together."

She had looked up at him in alarm. "Would we have enough hot water to do that? The hot water heater isn't very big."

"Twelve gallons. We'll have plenty."

But before the party, Dorie used the aft shower while he was still putting stuff away from the day's work. "To test the showerhead for myself," she had told Fred.

By 3 o'clock the music coming from VJ's outside speakers was so loud the seagulls disappeared and the coots huddled at the far edge of the harbor, calling back and forth in agitation. A dog somewhere on the other pier barked for a long time before someone managed to quiet it. Yessir, it was going to be some party.

"How you? How you?" Vernon beamed at his guests, shaking hands with the males and throwing his meaty arms around the females in what started as a fatherly bear hug but ended with Vernon's free arm, the one without the paper cup and cigar, pressing the side of a breast before he let go. "This ain't no Valentine's party, but you my Valentine" he whispered to his favorites. But not to that pretty new Yankee woman. He'd have to get to know her better first. Her and her husband. "How you like that CD? 'Party Favorites of the 80's.' You like it? And a nice day too, ain't it? The Lord smiling on us today!"

It was a gorgeous mid-February day in Alabama the Beautiful; afternoon temperatures had reached 60 degrees, winds out of the south but light. Winter wasn't over but was on its way out. Vernon would have to get his gourds up soon for the martin scouts. Coots and gulls were starting to gather and geese were doing practice runs for their northbound migration, criss-crossing the lake in V formation.

The group on the little front deck, Isinglass doorway tied back, was a mixture of men and women who squeezed companionably onto two loveseats, two chairs, and the forward ledge of the floor, sending outer coats through the open patio doors and on back and stashing carry-along drinks in baskets and coolers in the corners. Women joined Lady in the main salon, loading their Saran-wrapped trays of food on the table until Lady said to eat. A couple of men were milling around on the dock in front of the houseboat, smoking unfiltered Camels that they put out in a coffee can filled with sand. Vernon had set up plastic chairs and a card table on which large paper cups, an electric deep fryer, a bag of cornmeal, assorted spices, and a large can of peanut oil waited. Under the table was a cooler filled with bags of ice.

Vernon was quick to realize that Fred and Dorie had arrived empty handed. Well, they didn't know, and he ushered them through to the galley, introducing them as he went, especially to Lady, and fixed them up from his bar. Fred had gin and she had vodka and diet coke. He pointed them to the ice chest and said to just get more whenever they were ready.

"Me, I'm ready too, VJ," a tall man with a set of tin eating utensils hanging by a cord around his neck held out an empty paper cup and Vernon laughed.

"Don't pay him no mind, folks. This here Ronald the Mooch." He introduced them. "You get to know him soon enough, he smell your cooking."

Ronald didn't seem one bit offended. He shook his utensils at them and had a nice smile. "Always prepared, just like the Boy Scouts. I really like your Chris Craft. What year is she?"

"You come back later, Ronald, when you really out of luck." Vernon left them to get acquainted as Ronald pulled a pint from his jacket pocket and grinned as he filled his cup.

"We always love your music, VJ, you old sweetie," said a doll-like blond woman with very big eyes and a teeny waist cinched in tight. She had an arm around Vernon, well, almost around, and sounded as if she had started her own party some time before. "You save me a dance, now, VJ." She gave him a squeeze and tottered back inside. Vernon followed her but she scrunched in next to her boyfriend. Then he thought he might turn the music up a little, but Lady gave him the evil eye and he decided it was probably loud enough and worked his way out again to the dock where he jigged in time to Tennessee Ernie Ford. The Jack was doing its thing and he felt fine. Life can be beautiful.

"Turn that damn music down, VJ," Bobby Ray Reynolds stuck his head out the flap. "We can't hear ourselves talk in here!" The volume lessened considerably and he got irritated for a second until he saw it was Lady had done it.

"That was a tad loud," said one of the smokers named Robert Marvel who reached inside his jacket for a Chihuahua hardly bigger than his hand. "I could feel Gracie shivering in there and it ain't the cold, it's that loud music hurts her ears." He gently placed the little dog on the pier where she shook herself and disappeared under the table.

"Whyn't you bring your own music for Gracie, she so fussy. Big rat," he muttered.

"Now you got no call to talk about her that way, VJ. You know what that sweet little dog means to me."

"I know, Robert Marvel." He patted the shorter man on the shoulder. "You and Gracie both a Marvel," and they laughed together at the old joke.

"Hear that, Gracie?" Robert bent to scoop her up from under the table where she had deposited a little puddle. "VJ says you're marvelous. And he's so right." He gave her a kiss and she sent out a tiny pink tongue to lick his lips.

"Yuck," said the other smoker who was named John. "I don't allow Sandy to do that. You never know where that tongue been last. Or maybe you do and that's worse," he laughed.

"Why didn't you bring Sandy today? Gracie likes Sandy," Robert said, tucking her into his shirt pocket. Her big popping eyes and pointed ears stuck out of the vee of his jacket zipper.

"Sure, and when it gets too cold out here, I can just stick that seventy pound moose right here in my jacket." He held out his arms as if he were pregnant with Sandy and staggered around the pier.

VJ laughed so hard he like to fell over. "You bring your Sandy to the next party, John. When we be outside, we got plenty room for dogs."

Dorie and Fred stood in the patio doorway and listened to the conversation on the porch. Bobby Ray Reynolds and Sarah occupied one loveseat across from Jimmy Lassiter and Georgie. Sailboat Dave sat on the ledge beside his girlfriend, an attractive woman with a beautiful long brown ponytail she could just about sit on, and a big man named Matt who kept trying, futilely, to scrunch up to give them more room. He kept apologizing to Sailboat's girl-friend who kept telling him it was all right. Perched on a cooler in the corner was a slight man with a pitted complexion, his arm draped awkwardly around the shoulders of the petite blond with the big pale-blue eyes whose name was Yolanda. Ronald the Mooch had reclaimed one chair and in the other was an old man with a tremendous white beard. His name was JV.

"Ain't that something?" the old man twinkled at Dorie. "I'm John Vernon and he's…" he thumbed over his shoulder at their host who was spitting into the lake, "Vernon John. You believe we was Siamese twins separated at birth? Only thing is, when they split us up, I got all the brains and good looks. Only thing VJ got was rhythm. Boy can dance, but…" he shrugged and laughed. Nobody contradicted him.

"So, anybody shop in Huntsville of a Sunday yet?" Bobby Ray asked nobody in particular. He was close to Fred's age but looked older, not fat but worn out, his face deeply lined. He turned to Fred. "I'm referring to the new law where they can sell liquor over there on Sunday."

"I figured that," Fred said. "We live in Huntsville so we've been following it."

"That so?" Bobby Ray said. He wore expensive jewelry, a fouled anchor hanging on a thick gold chain and a Colonel Sanders ring with big diamonds, but he was dressed in jeans just like the rest of them, jeans or sweats and tennis shoes. "Really aren't too many people here from Huntsville." Heads bobbed in agreement. "Most Huntsville boaters, they go to Ditto Landing or Bay Hill. Like I'm from Grant and Sarah, here, is from Guntersville." Yolanda lived in Albertville with the scrawny boyfriend, who had piped up in a high, reedy voice. The old man with the white beard said he lived on a mountain near Arab and Ronald was a liveaboard now but had lived in Boaz before.

"Well, we're hoping to move here and live aboard too." Fred smiled at Ronald the Mooch and winked at Dorie.

"I wish we could get more folks from Huntsville to come here," Jimmy Las-siter said. "I don't know why more of them don't. We got plenty of empty slips."

Vernon stuck his head in. Seems he had been listening after all. "Maybe you charge less and don't insist people take year leases when they prefer month-to-month, you wouldn't have so many empty slips."

"Now VJ, no business at a party," Jimmy Lassiter admonished.

"That's right, VJ, even if it is your party," Sailboat Dave chipped in. "Them are the rules."

"He started it," Vernon, protested, "talking about empty slips!"

"No, now I was only observing, VJ, just making an observation. Here, you have some of mine." He turned to his wife. "Georgie, where's our stuff?" Georgie reached into the basket behind the loveseat and poured some Jack Daniels into VJ's cup. She was a good-looking woman but quite a bit older than Jimmy.

"I'll talk to him about that," she whispered in VJ's ear and he beamed, mollified, and gave her a quick hug.

"You a sweet thang, Georgie," he mouthed.

"So what about that Sunday law?" Bobby Ray persisted.

"I thinks it's right up there with gay marriages," Sailboat's girlfriend said loudly and everybody made some kind of noise at that. The two smokers gathered with VJ around the open flap.

"Ain't that something?"

"How do you figure those two things are alike?" Bobby Ray asked when he could be heard.

"I think they're alike because they both mean that morality is going down the drain," the girlfriend said with conviction. "You people just don't seem to know right from wrong no more even when it hits you over the head. Everything is right there in the Bible."

"Victoria doesn't drink or smoke anymore," Sailboat apologized to the group. "She's born again."

"I'll drink to that," Ronald the Mooch said, "and I'll do it on a Sunday too!" He made a big show of taking a sip.

"Yah, what about drinking on a Sunday?" Victoria asked, flinging her long ponytail around her shoulder so she could play with the ribbon on the end. Sailboat had a ponytail too but it wasn't as long." If you drink on Sunday, why shouldn't you be able to buy booze on Sunday? What's the difference?"

"If you still drank, honey, you'd understand," the old man said and patted her knee.

"You're full of beer," she said unkindly and JV pulled back as though she had slapped him. "Jesus doesn't want you drinking or buying booze any day of the week. It's sinful any time. Sunday don't make any difference. That's my point." There were a few polite "Amen's" from around the group but nobody would meet her eyes as they studied their paper cups. They would have moved away from her if there had been any place to go.

"Well, I don't care about selling alcohol of a Sunday," Bobby Ray said loudly into the uncomfortable silence, "cause I think Victoria's right. If y'all are going to sell the 'Demon Rum,' y'all might as well do it of a Sunday too. It's hypocritical not to." There were a few sideways looks at Bobby Ray's clever sidestepping. Victoria looked as if she had bitten into a lemon but she stayed quiet, obviously confused. "But that gay marriage thing," he went on loudly, "is something else. I just don't get it."

"Or maybe, after messing up four of them, you just don't get marriage, period," Sarah said quietly and looked, wide-eyed around the group.

"Me neither," Robert the Mooch laughed. "I don't get marriage neither," and everybody was so relieved they got silly.

"Do you get it?" they turned to each other in mock seriousness and then laughed hilariously when it seemed nobody did.

"Time to get your fish and hush puppies on, Vernon," Lady decided. Inside, Lady and her helpers had loaded down her table with plates of veggies and dip, homemade and store-bought potato salad, two kinds of hot bean dishes, spicy chopped tomato and avocado, deviled eggs, chili dip in a crock pot, Doritos and chips, coleslaw with pineapple, cornbread in a skillet, lemon pound cake, brownies, paper plates, napkins, and plastic utensils.

"Y'all come on in and get you started now," Lady ordered.

"It all looks wonderful," Dorie said as Lady handed her a plate.

"Summertime, I make fried okra and creamed corn, maybe some Crowder peas with those hot peppers for flavor, but you got to have fresh for that." She sounded apologetic. "Even them tomatoes don't taste like much this time of year but the avocadoes are all right and they go good together so I made em anyhow."

"I think it's wonderful," Dorie said again and began to take a little of everything to be polite. Lady looked pleased and pointed out who had contributed what so Dorie could give the proper compliments later. "Do you think if I made something Italian, like stuffed manicotti, people here would eat it?" Dorie had moved to stand beside Lady at the back of the small room to let others at the table.

"I believe they would," she said, thumping her huge body down into her chair with the rollers. Next to her, Dorie felt absolutely svelte. "Got to take a load off. Some of em probably won't be able to say it, but they usually can eat it. I see you working hard on that boat, girl. That boat your idea?"

"No, it wasn't."

"Yahuh," Lady grunted.

"But now that I'm into it, I'm really enjoying it. I think I'm going to like living aboard. I just can't figure out how you do all this great food in such a tiny kitchen." She moved to let someone through to the head. "Galley," she amended. "I think there's a knack to it."

"Yahuh," the big woman agreed, "but don't forget that most dock parties women bring dishes so you don't have to do it all. I've been doing it so long, I don't rightly think about it no more, but you'll catch on. You should talk to Shirley about that." She nodded toward a woman who wore her thick salt and pepper hair in a topknot and was fussing with the dip. "Shirley and her husband Matt, they live aboard over to C Dock. As far as cooking, you've got to do things in stages, little by little, I guess."

"I'm sorry, but I feel funny calling you 'Lady,'" Dorie blurted out.

The big woman seemed to really look up at her for the first time, and Dorie looked back. Lady had the warmest brown eyes fringed with long lashes, and her hair was a pretty silvery gray, which curled beautifully around her round cheeks. "That's what I'm most used to, but my Christian name is Sylvia and some folks do call me that. Sylvia Angelina. Now ain't that pretty?" When she smiled, her eyes disappeared altogether.

"It's lovely, Sylvia Angelina, and so is your hair. If my natural hair had turned out like yours, or like Shirley's, I would be happy to be gray."

"Oh, mine ain't natural, honey, but thank you." She raised her hands to gently pat her hair and Dorie noticed that her nails were manicured and painted a pearly pink. "My friend Catherine does it for a bunch of us. She's a cosmetologist over to the 'Scissor Works.' I'll give you her number before you leave."

Sylvia scooted the chair back a little and looked her up and down with pursed lips, and Dorie felt her cheeks flush and mentally searched for a place to set her heaping plate down, but there wasn't any. "You're a real pretty woman just like you are," Sylvia said kindly, "but I believe you'd be even prettier with your hair blond again. It was blond, wasn't it?" Dorie nodded yes. It had been so long since anyone had told her she was pretty, she didn't know how to respond. "Thought so from your fair coloring. You can be proud you look so good at your age. I looked pretty good too up until that auto wreck. I'll tell you about it sometime. But you," she shook a fat finger at Dorie, "you better be sure you know what you're getting into, girl. You think you going to make that old boat a palace if you just work hard enough."

"Can't it be?"

"Sure, if you want to work that hard all the time and be too tired to have any fun in life. It's always going to be just a old boat! Plain and simple. Now, go out and get you some fish while they hot."

Outside, Vernon deftly dredged fillets in his seasoned cornmeal, and after a few minutes, he lifted them out of the oil with a slotted spoon and onto a paper-lined tray. He alternated frying hush puppy batter and fish. "Sailboat caught them crappies last couple days," Vernon said, not wanting to take all the credit. "They good, huh?" Dorie and Fred ate the hot fragrant curls right from the tray with their fingers, as the others who had gone outside were doing, and told him they were delicious. "I use this here stuff called 'Limon' in the corn-meal," he beamed. "It's a Mezican seasoning."

"Your name is Dorie, right?" The big man who had sat on the ledge of the front deck towered above her. She stepped closer to him to let others at the tray and found herself mesmerized by the gold flecks dancing in his eyes as the winter sun sent its last shimmering light over the water.

"Yes, I am," she said, "and you're Matt, I believe." She wiped her greasy hands on a napkin and held one out in greeting.

"That's right." He grasped her extended hand in his much larger one and Dorie found herself not at all unhappy when he hung on to it for a moment. He was gorgeous when he smiled and his soft Southern accent was deep and old fashioned, courtly. "I'm surprised you remembered with all these strange folks, Miss Dorie." He smelled wonderful too, an old-fashioned scent like Old Spice but not that. She couldn't put her finger on it and she couldn't stop gazing into those eyes.

The spell was broken when Yolanda stumbled getting off the boat. Her boyfriend caught her from behind by her tiny waist and held her up until she pushed his hands away. "Leave me be, Phillip." The last part came out a hiccup. "I'm fine." She teetered down the walkway and grabbed at the table, but Matt steadied her this time and she gave him a wobbly smile and patted for his big hand to release her." I just need some of VJ's fish, is all, right VJ?" She suddenly lurched at Vernon, draped her arms around him and yelled, "Ow, dammit!" when a few drops of hot oil from the slotted spoon hit her hand, and this time she would have reeled right off the pier into the water if Ronald the Mooch hadn't intercepted her.

"Leave me be, Ronald," Phillip said in a very good imitation of Yolanda's voice complete with hiccup. "I'm just fine," he added, pirouetting and fluttering his eyelashes. Phillip was not attractive to begin with, his narrow shoulders rounded and complexion lumpy with acne scars. And that high voice didn't do a thing for him either. "Maybe a jump in the lake would do her good," he said to Ronald.

Vernon had dived under the table for the cooler. "Now, Phillip, this little lady just had a little too much happy juice. Put this ice on it, honey. We all done that some time or nother. I member carrying you to your car, Phillip, that one time you had too much rum and Coke."

Sailboat Dave and Victoria emerged from the boat, Victoria charging ahead and looking determined. "We got to get going, VJ. Victoria has to get up early," he said apologetically.

"But you ain't even had no fish yet," VJ protested. "Your own fish!" But Sailboat just waved and trailed after his born-again girlfriend, pulling his cooler of beer.

Yolanda had grown very still, leaning with her back against Ronald, one arm outthrust with a paper towel around the ice. Her big blue eyes were closed.

"I know, VJ," Phillip whined, "but she's been getting too sloppy, passing out at every party, for God sake." Phillip's high voice got higher. "It ain't no fun toting home a drunk every night and then sobering her up for work the next day."

"Maybe they work her too hard at that diner. That ain't no easy government job, being a waitress, you know," Vernon argued as he finished the fish, a big pile mounding up on the tray while everyone who was outside contemplated Yolanda. "On your feet all the day long."

"Hey," Ronald laughed, "am I supposed to hold her like this all the night long?" The sun was setting and the temperature dropping with it.

"Shit if I care," Phillip said. "You can take her home too. See what she put out for you, all I care," he sniffed.

"We don't talk that way around the ladies, boy." Vernon had had enough of him.

"You bring that girl inside," Lady ordered from the porch." And get that fish in here if you done. It's too cold for cavorting around out there." She turned on the bright outside spotlights and everybody squinted in the glare. Gracie gave a little squeal and pulled her head inside Robert Marvel's jacket.

They all took something inside while Fred helped Ronald with Yolanda. She weighed all of ninety pounds so they could almost carry her. Vernon grumbled and decided to leave the hot oil until tomorrow, but he moved it off into a corner. Man came with a lady, he was responsible to get her home, no matter what. He would tell Lady he didn't want that faggoty Phillip on his boat no more. Yolanda, poor sweet thing, she could come anytime. She needed somebody better than that Phillip. He would think about this. He grumbled some more. He never even got to dance once.

Inside, the party was at full tilt—too crowded, loud and silly now that Victoria had left. "Glad that girl took her Jesus with her," someone said and there was nervous laughter at that. "My Jesus turned water into wine at a party like this."

"Bet you Jesus don't let her have no fun in the sack no more neither," someone said and there were appreciative snorts until VJ said that was enough. People were entitled to their own opinion. No need for blasphemy. They put the flap down against the cold but most weren't feeling any chill. Yolanda wasn't the only one drinking too much though she was the only one to pass out, and they laid her on the bed with the coats while Phillip found a seat in a corner away from VJ. The fish disappeared and then folks went after the lemon pound cake and the brownies. Whenever one person moved, another had to adjust, and there was some good-natured pushing and grab-ass but nobody minded.

Every once in a while, Vernon would turn the old-time country music up, and a little while later, someone would turn it down. "You can hear 'Your Cheatin' Heart' only so many times," Ronald told Robert Marvel.

"Gracie don't like it even once when it's so loud," he replied and gently patted the tiny dog sleeping in the crook of his arm.

"Now how they gonna enforce that new law about waste disposal?" John asked. "And how is that annual inspection of every shitter in every marina going to take place when I hear we got two Marine Police from here to Chattanooga. Two!" He caught Vernon's eye. "Sorry, VJ, I'll watch my language, but my Sandy poops more than I do and it all ends up in the lake and nobody cares about that. It don't make no sense."

"You shouldn't be charging your regular people to use your pumpout," Vernon said to Jimmy Lassiter. "That sailboat marina don't charge at all if you slip there."

"You're supposed to clean up after that dog," Jimmy said, ignoring Vernon. Vernon got up to turn the volume up again. "I put a shovel right there by the telephone pole for you to clean up."

"And what am I supposed to do with it after I pick it up with that shovel?" John asked.

"Oh, yeah," Jimmy grinned. "I see your point. Maybe you've got to use baggies."

"Okay," John pointed a finger at him. "I will load up your garbage cans with baggies full of shit. No problem. Be specially nice about August."

"In one of these gay marriages like they're doing in San Francisco," Bobby Ray Reynolds said, "what I don't get is how do they know which one is the wife and which one the husband?"

"They don't say 'man and wife,' Bobby Ray," Sarah said. Sarah was one of those people who looked kind of plain at first; in fact, she wore no makeup, but then you saw the beautiful structure of her face, high cheekbones and firm chin. She had a flawless peachy complexion and her shining brown curls complemented shining brown eyes. "They just say 'married persons,' or something like that." Sarah wore only one piece of jewelry—a marquis-cut emerald ring that had to be three carats—which she waved at them now.

"Well, that's good," Bobby Ray said, "because I'd sure as hell hate to be the wife if my husband was another man."

"That's only cause you ain't gay, Bobby Ray," John Vernon said, stroking his long white beard. "I don't believe we got any gay folks at this marina, do we, Jimmy?"

"What you asking me for? What am I, the sex Gestapo?" Jimmy laughed. "Hell, I don't know and I don't care long as they pay the rent on time. Don't ask, don't tell."

"Well, I think we would know if they was," VJ said and gave Phillip a long, hard look. "They got these here little mannerisms." He stuck his pinkie into the air and wiggled his hips in his chair.

"You mean like waving a stinking cold cigar around all the time?" Phillip shot back and wiggled his own hips so everybody laughed, but it wasn't the comfortable laughter like before.

"Watch yourself, boy," Vernon growled.

"You watch yourself," Phillip growled back. He was really pretty good at imitation.

"You watch yourself do what?" Yolanda asked blearily from the hallway and all heads turned her way. "Do what?" she demanded. "I think I had too much vodka," she told Lady and Lady agreed with her.

"You take her home now, Phillip, and tuck her in," Lady said.

"Yes Ma'am, I sure will," Phillip had the good grace to respond nicely. As if given a signal, they all rose to go too, laughing as they elbowed each other for coats and jackets, gathered up platters and coolers, told each other again how good their food had been, and said their thank you's.

"Let me help you, Dorie." Matt held her hooded jacket for her, waited for her to zip up, and gently snapped the tab under her chin. "Don't want you to catch cold now," he smiled and patted her shoulders before turning to find his own jacket in the pile.

"Where's Shirley?" Sarah asked from the other side of the bed as she shrugged into a huge sheared beaver swing coat.

"How pretty that is and practical too," Dorie said, edging around the bed to admire the coat, but Sarah brushed past her and into the hallway without a word.

"Now, ya'll don't need to go," Vernon protested, trying to hug the women goodbye and stop them from going at the same time. "The evening young. Ronald, I got some Jack left just for you!" But even Ronald the Mooch was partied out.

Sometime during all of that, Dorie had asked Sylvia what she liked about being a liveaboard. "I've never had the chance to talk with a woman about it before," she explained.

Sylvia thought for a while. "I love the colors. How the light on the water changes things as the day goes by. I like the city lights on the water at night too. I like the color of water and the smell of water. And when the boat moves, I'm moving directly from a powerful force of nature. Jesus is rocking me in his hands and I sleep real good when my back isn't bothering me too much. I like knowing that Vernon and me could move any time we want to, but wherever we go up or down the river, we would know people. Mighty interesting folks, too, from down and out river rats to millionaires. Some got PhD's; some ain't graduated grade school. And they're always ready to talk and to party, specially party. Sometimes a little too much, but they're sort of on vacation and pretty happy when they come here. I have to say I like it, yahuh." She pursed her lips in thought. "But you should talk to Shirley sometime, and there's another one here lives aboard with her husband, but I don't know them too well. Over on D dock. She's standoffish. You'll know her though cause she's got one brown eye and one blue." Sylvia twinkled her eyes at Dorie and they both began to laugh. "I'm not kidding you, honey. God plays some strange tricks on us!"

CHAPTER 6

❀

For as many boats as there are registered in the United States (The state of Michi-gan has the most, you might be surprised to know), there are few liveaboards, and while everybody knows their names at Sunset, some wish to live quietly or just don't socialize much on the docks. Others make it their business to set the social standards and define manners, just as the oldest residents in small land-based communities did long ago before everybody moved every ten minutes. They see themselves as repositories of marina information, matchmakers, role models.

Oh, about the Marine Sanitation Law that Alabama finally put into effect in October of 2003, those two marine police that John thought couldn't or wouldn't be able to do the inspections have set a date in March, 2004, to do just that at Sun-set. There will be some scrambling now.

—A Genuine Liveaboard

"I think you've lost some weight, honey. Look how those pants bag around your backside."

"Really, Fred? You think so?" They were building her "pantry" in what had been a deep, narrow hanging locker next to the curving staircase. Dorie had measured the sizes of the cans and jars she used most often so she wouldn't have to readjust the shelves all the time. "I haven't had the nerve to step on the scale at home." She hadn't had the nerve for a very long time, but working on the boat, she sure hadn't much chance to snack, her biggest downfall. "That next one should be tall enough for the twenty ounce cans, at least eight inches."

Fred grunted and concentrated on the saw, which he wielded at the edge of the table protected by a thick plastic cloth. Not exactly an ideal workshop. The pre-finished shelves they had found at Lowe's were the right width but not the right length, so he had to saw only the short way but was still making a mess.

Dorie knelt to figure out the next setting but decided to take off her sweatshirt first. Spring had arrived full time on a Saturday, and it was warm inside even with the windows open. They would have to buy fans soon. Getting to the cans and jars in the back would always be difficult, she realized. The closet was too narrow to put in runners for pullout shelves, which would have been ideal. Well, she would keep a running list on the laptop. Other people did that all the time, but she had never had to be so organized before. When she ran out of mushroom soup, they bought a case at Sam's Club and had enough for a year. "Those were the days, my friend," went through her mind and she started to hum an out-of-tune version of the catchy melody.

"Don't tell me," Fred said around the pencil between his teeth, "you're wishing you were playing bridge with those cronies of yours."

"Actually, I was lusting after a year's supply of mushroom soup," she said and bobbed her fanny at him.

"The diesel fumes are getting to you, Miss Dorie, but you sure do look fetching in that tee shirt."

"Yah?" She blushed and looked down. "You sure it's not my new blond hairdo?" She patted her head to draw his attention away from her body. She had gone to Sylvia's hairdresser who had highlighted her hair with fine blond streaks and given her a variation of the old Pixie from years ago. It was wash and wear and she knew it looked better.

"I like the blond again, but, no, I was admiring your tits, baby." He wiggled his eyebrows Groucho Marx style and flicked his pencil like that famous cigar. She straightened her torso and sucked in her stomach. Well, tried to. "How about we try out my bunk for two tonight. I've got this wonderful air mattress and your sleep number is my sleep number, my little chickadee," he leered.

"Aren't you mixing up Groucho with W.C. Fields, and does this have anything to do with the fact that I spiked your Pepsi with Viagra?"

"Can you do that?" His eyebrows went up on their own this time and she laughed.

"Come on, boy. Use that hacksaw to get this pantry done and then worry about sleep numbers."

"It's not a hacksaw, Dorie. It's a handsaw." He put it down on the table. "How would you feel about my trying Viagra?" he blurted out.

"I don't know," she started to say when they both heard the tapping on the hull.

"Hello the boat, y'all? Anybody home?" Fred made a face asking whether whoever it was had heard his question, but Dorie shrugged that she didn't know.

It was the beautiful Sarah bearing a paper plate covered with plastic wrap. "Permission to come aboard?" she asked before crossing onto the back deck and gracefully stepping over a toolbox and various cans arranged by size. She wasn't as tall as Dorie but her legs in very short shorts looked a mile long and shapely, her arms thin and firm in a khaki sleeveless blouse, that peachy skin glowing. She wore the usual sneakers but with lace-trimmed anklets, the kind Dorie bought for the girls when they were little. "I made some macaroons to sweeten your afternoon," she said brightly and offered Fred the plate. "Didn't you say coconut macaroons were your favorites?" she asked him and he said they were and made appreciative noises over the plate before handing it to Dorie.

"Look Dorie, macaroons!" he said as though she had just appeared.

"Your favorites!" she said, matching his tone. This was news to her. She thought her pecan dreams were his "favorites," but what did she know, the dumpy wife of thirty-five years. But that wasn't fair to Sarah who couldn't help it that she was gorgeous, had curly brown hair, and was twenty years younger than she. "Thank you," she said sincerely, "that was very thoughtful of you."

"Sit down, Sarah." Fred patted an armchair and Sarah glided into it while Dorie plopped down on the couch and Fred took the matching chair.

"Y'all have been working so hard," Sarah smiled at Fred and tossed her hair back, her teeth impossibly white. "Bobby Ray says to come over later for a drink. We're here for a couple three days while he has some work done on the generator, I guess." She rolled her big brown eyes at him and recrossed her lovely legs. "I don't pay much attention to those things. Bobby Ray always has to hire someone to do his boat work for him." She gestured gracefully. "He's not handy like you are, Freddy."

"Oh I can't do all of my own work either," Mr. Modest replied, but his chest swelled in his tee shirt and he had a silly smile. Probably from the strain of starring at those sexy naked legs stretched out under his nose.

"In fact," Dorie said, "we're waiting for a call from Aqua Yacht Harbor to let us know when they can haul us out and fix some things Fred can't fix." She hadn't meant to sound snappish, but it didn't seem to matter because she might not even have been there. Sarah's eyes never veered from her handsome husband who seemed to be basking in her adoring gaze. He was unconsciously making small adjustments that called attention to his manly physique.

"Well, I just wanted to thank you again, Freddy," Sarah gushed, "for fixing that disposal. I just never clog up the one at Bobby Ray's house but there's something about the one on the boat…" She threw up her hands and the emerald ring the size of New York City flashed. "Bobby Ray says I do it on purpose because I don't really like the boat, but that just isn't true." Fred nodded sympathetically. "I just can't seem to find enough to do down here, is all, so I get into trouble." Up with the hands again. "So we'll see y'all later for drinks?" she asked him.

"Thank Bobby Ray for us." Dorie said too loudly and stood up. "Ask if we can have a rain check until after we get back from Aqua, will you?"

Sarah seemed to notice Dorie for the first time. "Y'all are so lucky to be married to such a talented man, darlin, and so good lookin' too!" Dorie bridled. At the marina, "darlin" was what you called any woman whose name you couldn't remember. Ronald had told her that it was sort of a running joke at Sunset. "I do hope you appreciate him." Extra big smile at Fred. "But can't y'all take a little time out just for fun? We'd really, really love to see y'all."

"I'm afraid we're on kind of a tight schedule because of that lift out. Watch your step on that ladder, now," Dorie said unnecessarily as she edged her through the doorway, "and thanks again for my husband's favorite cookies, darlin. I'm sure he'll enjoy them."

They were silent as they watched Sarah undulate down the stepladder and up the pier, as slick as hot oil until she slid unto Vernon's front deck and disappeared. "Well, that was interesting," Fred said and grinned at Dorie. "You didn't ask me if I wanted to join them for cocktails." He turned back the plastic wrap on the cookie plate and bit into a macaroon. "Not bad," he decided and offered her one. She waved him away and he looked at her sideways. "I went over there to borrow Bobby Ray's bollard loop so I could make one for us to use through the locks." He reached behind the couch and pulled out a contraption that looked like a big lasso, the loop part covered with clear, thick plastic. "See, you throw the loop around the bollard," he demonstrated, "and then you attach this end to a cleat. Bobby Ray says it makes going through the locks a breeze if you have your fenders placed right." Fred cleared his throat. "Well, let's finish that pantry so you can get her stocked," he said as he bounded down the stairs. "Aren't you going to help measure?" he called up after a minute.

"Hey, Dorie, you coming up for air?" It was Sailboat Dave beside the boat rummaging through his yellow fishing wagon. "You are working entirely too hard, girl. Making us all look bad." He offered up a small, thin box. "Give this caliper back to Freddy, will you? Hey, Freddy!" he called when he spotted him through the open window. "Thanks a lot. I think I got her fixed, thanks to you, buddy. You were right. It wasn't metric." She took the box. "See you, Dorie. Oh, hey, I thought you should know. Victoria and I broke up." He shrugged elaborately, his black ponytail flopping down his back, his broad smile sweet. He was a young-old hippie born too late for Woodstock and when he wasn't working as a welder, he was fishing or out on his sailboat or both, getting so sunburned he looked more like a full blooded Cherokee than the quarter he was.

"So you and Victoria broke up, huh?" Dorie said, leaning over the rail."

"Oh, yeah, she was nice, but once she found Jesus, she just couldn't abide me drinking or smoking pot," he shrugged again and rubbed the beginnings of a beer belly, "and I can't for the life of me see any harm in either of em. I don't have anything against religion but I mean, pot isn't like crystal meth or ecstasy or cocaine or any of them, you know? Pot doesn't do brain damage. It's even legalized as a pain medication in several states. Well, the crappies are hitting good. See you later."

Sailboat nearly collided with Vernon as he turned the yellow fishing wagon around on the pier. "Hey, watch out, boy," Vernon hollered. "You like to poke my eye out all them rods! No, I don't want no beer. How you, Miss Dorie?" he called up. Vernon carried his paper cup a little earlier than usual and his cheek was swollen on the right side. "Freddy, you in there?" he cupped his hands, careful of his cheek, and peered into the side window. "I come to get back some of that gin you got off me few days ago. Lady won't let me have none til 3 o'clock but my tooth hurting so bad I don't know what to do."

"Hang on, VJ," Fred called. "Come on up and sit down."

Vernon climbed the ladder with surprising agility but huffed and puffed when he sat down. His cheek really did look terrible, so swollen his eye was half closed. His bony white knees stuck out of black shorts. "When you getting those stairs? You order them over to Alred's?" They had. "Well, I hope they come quick. That ladder too hard on my poor old knees. Bless you," he said and took a good swig. "Oh, me. I hurt so bad. The dentist give me antibiotics but he can't do nothing until this swelling goes down. Says I can't chew them cigars no more or I lose all my teeth!" Vernon got a refill in less than a minute. "Sarah tell me you ain't got time to party over to their boat this afternoon. She real upset about it." He looked hard at Dorie. "She think you don't like her."

"We like her fine, VJ, her and Bobby Ray," Fred assured him. "I think Dorie's just worried that we won't have the boat ready to go to Aqua when they call, you know. Wants everything just so." He smiled at her and shook his head. How silly she was.

"Well, how bout you come over there for just a little while then. That be a good thang to do now. Sarah's a real nice person you get to know her." Vernon got one more refill and left.

"Let's get that pantry done and then get cleaned up," Fred suggested.

"No, I think I'm done working for the day."

"You are? It's only a little after two. I thought you wanted that pantry done." He sounded confused.

She had worked every day on *Sun Spot* for the past two months, every day all day except Sunday mornings when they had driven into Huntsville for church. And the boat had shaped up a lot but was far from what they wanted. She had agreed to ignore the diesel smell because they couldn't do anything about it yet except to put all their clean clothes, towels, sheets, etc., in plastic bags. Diesel Don, the local expert, had been too busy to take on new customers for a while so they had to wait for any prognosis on the leaks until they took their trip to Mississippi. Her hair might look spiffy at the moment but her hands and nails were a mess in spite of rubber gloves, and she hurt all over from bending in odd spaces. But she had felt good before that visit from Sarah and the others. Alive and vibrant and proud to be working with Fred to make even small improvements. And he was regaining interest in sex, thinking about Viagra. But something wasn't right here. She couldn't put her finger on it exactly.

They had tried to fulfill the top of their lists. Fred had set up his new power cords, the automatic bilge pump, and the crossover valve for the new water hose so they could use dock water without first filling their own holding tanks and then pumping it up. He had cut a lift-out door in the floor of the main salon, which Dorie covered with a multicolored oval rug that she found at Home Depot. He had torn out the old storage cabinet beside the refrigerator and built a new one for pots, pans and assorted rubber-sealed, clear plastic containers for crackers, cookies, and cereals—anything they wanted to stay crisp. Dorie had searched everywhere and found a microwave that would fit exactly on top of the cabinet and then he built a frame for the microwave so it wouldn't jump off the cabinet when *Spot* got frisky. She found a cute pattern in thin, sturdy Corelle dishes for the small cupboard above the sink and lined everything with rubber. The camping pad stapled to the underside of her bunk worked fine for the cold, just as he had said it would, and with a layer of inter-locking rubber tiles to allow ventilation under the new mattresses, their beds were mildew free and very comfortable. But they had always slept together and, even though they hadn't made love in forever, she missed talking quietly before sleep, touching him in the night. He said he slept like a rock.

They had listed the house with a realtor who seemed competent, and Dorie had come up with a plan concerning their possessions. The cedar chest from her grandmother and the Tiffany lamp from the kids they would keep. The chest would take the place of the end table, which they would give away to anyone on the dock or throw out. It would support the nautical lamp and a small TV as well as provide storage for seasonal clothes. The Tiffany would be bolted down in the forward cabin. In fact, it would be just right after Fred added support to the base.

By Easter weekend in mid-April, Dorie and Fred would have disposed of the trash and taken whatever else they wanted. The kids would come to the house for one last time and decide what they wished to have, with the understanding that they had to get the stuff out within two weeks, no exceptions. Everybody but Janie, their wild child, thought they were crazy and said so, but they had their own lives to lead. End of discussion. Then Movers and Shakers would hold a weekend tag sale, of which Dorie and Fred would get a percentage, and cart off the rest. Voila! A lifetime of accumulation disposed of within just a few weeks. She had even lined up a cleaning service to vacuum and polish after their home was empty because she wouldn't have her big Hoover anymore and, anyway, it would be too sad. The photo albums and framed family pictures they would take aboard to scan into the computer when they had more time.

The only thing she couldn't figure out was what to do with clothes. None of the kids would want them even if they did fit. They planned to rent a storage space but it wasn't suitable for clothes. She had three formal gowns with bags, shoes, and wraps to match. She had worn them on the cruise and the dusty rose at Fred's retirement party. And she counted 34 pairs of shoes. She didn't even particularly like shoes; it's just that she had to have the right ones for different outfits and they lasted forever if you seldom wore them. She'd find out if Goodwill took in slightly used shoes. She seemed to have a lot of coats and there were also outfits that she had worn once or twice and then gotten too fat to fit. If she were losing weight, halleluiah praise the Lord, should she keep some of the smaller ones?

Fred didn't have so many clothes except that he had an inordinate number of button-down shirts that he had worn for work everyday. Goodwill would appreciate them. He had his own tuxedo and a lovely camelhair coat. If they went on another cruise, they would need her gowns and the tux. They had agreed that they wouldn't store anything with any of the kids, but these clothes might be the exception.

So when, in all this sorting, measuring, consulting, ordering, shopping and planning, not to mention flat-out working, had Fred had time to fix the lovely Sarah's disposal, counsel Sailboat on repairs, and drink Vernon's liquor in the daytime? While she was shopping? Meeting with the realtor? Ah, yes. Viagra. Was it possible the lovely Sarah, who got into trouble because she didn't have enough to do, had something to do with that? And if Fred was interested in Sarah, had there been others in the past? Never in 35 years had she thought this way. She felt as if she didn't know this man.

"You finish the pantry, Freddy old thing." He looked at her as if she were nuts. "I'm going to do my nails and take a nap. Oh, and I'm adding a garbage disposal to my list. Don't know why I didn't think of it before."

They found Bobby Ray's 52' Jefferson to be as new, spacious and luxurious as VJ's houseboat was old, cramped and run-down. This time, Dorie brought a basket with their own liquor and a two-pound can of mixed nuts to pass, and this time, she was going to party. She even had a vodka and diet Coke while waiting for Fred to shower.

"Whoa," he said as he emerged from the aft cabin, "you got all gussied up."

"I'll take that as a compliment, however old fashioned," she said, sipping her drink. She had taken special care with her makeup and, in her sorting clothes at the house, had found a linen-blend pantsuit that had been too small last spring. She was thrilled that it fit her now. It was a color called celadon, sort of celery green but softer, and it went especially well with her blond hair. It felt good too. She stuffed a shawl in the basket for when it got cold later. It was still only early March and, although it was an unseasonable 66 degrees now, that wouldn't last.

On the way they met tiny Yolanda meandering along to the party on the arm of Phillip. "I got canned today," she said cheerfully, her eyes not quite focused. "I don't care," she assured them. "I can always get a job."

"Sure," Phillip said sourly.

"You're so mean to me," she whined and punched him on the arm before tripping on a metal connecting plate on the dock and grabbing him to keep from falling.

Most of the party was outside on the extra-wide end pier that ran parallel to Bobby's boat and inside the main salon and enclosed back deck. They arrived to a chorus of greetings and Bobby Ray gave Dorie a hug and shook Fred's hand before inviting them aboard. Sarah welcomed them with a shriek as they climbed the high wooden stairs and threw her arms around Dorie and then Fred. "I am so glad y'all changed your mind! Dorie, you look so pretty! What have you done to yourself? I love that suit!" Sarah was dressed as she had been earlier except for pants instead of shorts. Her white teeth sparkled. "Now, c'mon and make yourselves at home. I'll just put your little old goody basket in the corner over here! What lovely nuts. I love nigger toes! Have you had the tour? Well, of course you saw it, Freddy," she nudged his chest with her shoulder, "but Dorie, I'll be glad to show you around while Freddy fixes you a big ole drink. It doesn't take long." She led the way.

The new Jefferson was impeccable, done in mauves, sea foam green, and old rose. It had a separate and very inviting galley two steps down with a convection/microwave oven, small dishwasher, full refrigerator, coffee maker, built-in blender, garbage disposal, the works. It also had a built-in booth big enough for six. Sarah had covered the table with what she called "heavy hors d'oeuvres"—hot wings, sausage balls, egg rolls, cheese, hard salami, taco dip with Fritos, small Reuben sandwiches, hot dogs wrapped in crescents, Pizza Bites, and some things she couldn't identify.

The master stateroom was forward and had a walk-around king-sized bed, something Dorie would now think about every morning while she struggled to make up their twin beds against the wall. Two guest staterooms were aft, one with twins and a smaller one with bunk beds. Most of the furniture was custom built and Dorie thought it was beautiful and said so.

"Oh, thank you, but my only real contribution is the silk flower arrangements," Sarah said. Dorie dutifully admired the vases, pots, and urns that she now realized were everywhere and loaded down with mauve, sea foam green and pink flowers, spiral twists and sparkly doodads. "I took an artificial flower arranging course in Huntsville." Sarah looked at her so expectantly that she found one arrangement she really did like, a graceful concoction in shades of green, and effused over it at length. "I like that one too!" Sarah said.

"That's Bobby Ray's second son," she pointed to a picture beside the vase of a young man at attention in an army uniform, his Adam's apple looking prominent and vulnerable. "He's in Iraq," Sarah said simply, and Dorie was grateful all over again that her Teddy hadn't enlisted as a way out of his trouble with drugs. She murmured her understanding of the fear that must be in their hearts. The younger woman was trying, she had to give her that. Vernon had probably talked with her too.

When they got back to the main salon and aft, Dorie could see that just about everyone from Vernon's party and some who were new to her had arrived and were milling around outside, their voices loud and excited. She couldn't remember all the names and was glad to find that Sylvia had claimed most of one couch and looked set for the duration, a can of diet soda in her chunky hand. "Come sit," she invited and patted the seat next to her.

"Here you go, Dorie." Fred handed her a paper cup and disappeared down the wooden staircase after Sarah, leaving them alone in the salon.

"Have you heard about the inspection?" Sylvia asked. "That's what everybody's all excited about. They're going to check that everybody's got a current registration tag and to see that everybody's using their holding tanks instead of pumping overboard. You got your tags?" Dorie nodded. Fred had done that first thing. "You use your holding tank?" They did. "Well, you're in good shape then."

In fact, they had pumped out just last week. If they were careful and didn't use too much water to flush and used the john at the marina once in a while, they could go for three weeks. Dorie had hoped for a ride on the lake after the pump out, her first real ride, but the wind had come up from the north and they were just glad to get back into the slip afterwards. Fred had promised that they would anchor overnight in Honeycomb Creek the first nice weather window.

"Yah, I used to like to anchor out too," Sylvia said. "Now, I don't know. I worry that something might happen and there we'd be, stuck out there, and I just don't enjoy it no more. Hell to get old and worry about your health all the time." Dorie hugged the big woman in sympathy. She knew that Sylvia went to various doctors and took pain pills constantly for her back and hips. "I do still enjoy a boat ride though," Sylvia assured her.

"Hey, Dorie, how you? We all glad you come." Vernon rooted in his cooler and refilled his drink. "You want more Cocola, Lady?" She didn't. "C'mon down, Lady," Vernon sipped, his cheek so swollen that his right eye was closed entirely now. "Jimmy telling us about that inspection. Hey Matt, Shirley!" he greeted the newcomers. "You met Dorie in that Chris Craft? Matt and Shirley here got a real nice Monticello."

"I'm glad to see you again," Dorie rose and smiled at the woman with the distinctive gray topknot. She hadn't realized before how thin Shirley was. A bulky sweater had camouflaged her stick figure then. Beside her, Matt was the picture of robust health and no wonder he had towered over Dorie at the fish fry. He had to be six foot five and looked like an ex-football player, thick but still well built. Light brown hair graying at the temples set off those distinctive gold flecks in his light brown eyes.

"Always glad to see a pretty lady again," he kissed her cheek sweetly and gave her a squeeze before letting her go and she found herself blushing. Sandalwood was what he smelled like, an aftershave her father had often used and that she loved. Men didn't seem to wear aftershave anymore.

"C'mon now, Dorie." Vernon startled her by taking her now empty cup from her hand and expertly refilling it. Shirley had taken her place next to Sylvia on the couch and they were already engrossed in conversation. "We get you some ice on the dock and hear what Jimmy have to say about this mess. She mine," he said to Matt over his shoulder as he ushered her out the door. On the pier she made a beeline for the ice chest and out of Vernon's grasp. She raised her cup in a salute to Fred across the crowd, but he just winked and made no move toward her.

"Yes, they're going to do this annually, they say." Jimmy Lassiter was holding forth to the group. "You get a sticker every year, just like the registration sticker."

"I don't never even take my boat out of the slip," Robert Marvel grumbled, petting Gracie in the crook of his arm.

"That doesn't matter, Robert," Jimmy said. "You got to have that registration. They can fine you up to a thousand dollars and then you're going to have to get it anyway. It isn't but…how much would it be for a boat Robert's size?" he asked JV, who stroked his white beard and said he wasn't sure but it couldn't be above thirty five dollars.

"But I never did pay the sales tax on that boat," Robert explained. "They're going to get me for that too."

"I don't even have no holding tank," John said. "Down, Sandy," he grabbed the big lab's collar. "You behave yourself. Leave Gracie and Sammy alone." Sandy settled down at his feet. Near the snack table there was another large dog, a beautiful German shepherd that raised its head hopefully whenever someone approached. "You mean to tell me I got to buy me a holding tank?"

"You've got to have a holding tank somewhere on that boat, John," Jimmy insisted.

"No, I don't. Any fool ought to know if he got a damn holding tank or not. I got me a extra fuel tank instead, is what I got. Previous owner done that."

"Maybe I can help you put one in, John," Sailboat Dave offered, his arm around a new girl whom he had introduced as Cindy. Where did he find these girls with the long ponytails? This one had a beer bottle in one hand and a cigarette in the other, clearly not born again yet.

"Fuck that," John said.

"Watch your tongue, boy," Vernon said, but John just scowled at him, he was that pissed.

"All right, all right," Jimmy put his hands up. "For now, John, you tell the police you are using the marina head and are putting in a Lectra/San. They'll give you ninety days until they fine you. I'll smooth it over for you the best I can." John mumbled something. "What?" Jimmy said.

"I said I don't have no thousand dollars for no Lectra/San or Purisan or whatever."

"Well, have you got a thousand dollars to pay the fine first and then buy one?" Jimmy asked.

"You throw that thousand dollars stuff round like it was nothin," John grumbled.

People began to break into smaller pools of conversation and music started on the outside speakers. "We better enjoy this while we can." Georgie Lassiter motioned toward the sun already low in the sky at 5 o'clock. "Have you met Randall and Marlene?" She introduced them and Dorie shook hands, glad the woman wore sunglasses so she wouldn't have to try not to notice the mismatched eyes that Sylvia had told her about. "They live aboard a Hatteras that is drop-dead beautiful. Randall does the best wood working around here," Georgie said and Randall smiled shyly, hanging his head.

"You weren't at VJ's party," Dorie said to make conversation with the quiet couple when Georgie had moved on.

"We don't go to too many to these things," Marlene said. She motioned toward the shallows where hundreds of coots were gathering as they did each evening, one bunch flying in and setting the others to their strange clucking as they argued about room. "They'll be leaving soon. Did you notice that the gulls have gone and the purple martins have arrived?" Dorie hadn't paid attention.

"Yup," Randall shifted uncomfortably in his struggle to make small talk.

She smelled the sandalwood first and then felt his chest against her back and she shivered. "Cold?" Matt whispered into her ear. She shook her head no. "Hey, Marlene, Randall," he greeted them before they wandered off. "I can warm you up," he said. His voice was so sexy that Dorie found herself as tongue tied as Randall had been.

"You look real nice tonight, Dorie," Ronald the Mooch came up to them. He wore the same outfit as before, she noticed, baggy gray sweat pants and gray sweatshirt but without the utensils around his neck this time. He was clean though, and clean shaven, a nice looking man, probably mid-forties. "Matt, how you doing?" he asked politely and Matt backed off a bit to shake hands. "Dance with me, Dorie?" Ronald asked. "I have always liked this song."

"I'll hold that for you," Matt offered and took her cup, smiling at her, and she found herself in Ronald's very capable arms dancing to "The Lady in Red." She could scarcely remember when she had danced last. It was before Fred's retirement party, she knew that.

"So, what do you think of all this?" Ronald asked.

"I think it has to be done. I assume you're talking about the new sanitation law," she said.

"I was thinking bigger. About the whole marina lifestyle. Oops, hold on." Ronald let go of her to prop up Yolanda, who was careening around again and had bumped into them.

"S'cuse me," Yolanda said.

"Foster Brooks!" Dorie laughed.

"Who?" the young woman asked the sky.

"We've got to stop meeting like this," Ronald said as he smiled an apology at Dorie and moved the tiny woman toward a chair while she grinned up at him blindly, silly putty in his hands.

"Let's finish this," Matt moved in smoothly and enfolded her tight against his chest to dance. Dorie felt small and desirable in his arms, a dramatic sunset of mauve and pink providing a romantic backdrop, and she shivered again. Now Willie Nelson sang "Harbor Lights" and she thought how perfect that was with pinpoints just becoming visible across the lake. But mostly she didn't think at all, just felt this man's solid body moving slowly with hers. His legs were tree trunks and she could disappear inside those thick arms, against that muscular chest. She was floating on a sea of vodka and sandalwood, a teenager with hormones amok, and she thought she would die if couldn't dance like this forever. The crowd around them was thinning out, driven into the boat by the cold, but Michael Bolton belted out "When a Man Loves a Woman" and she wanted to lick Matt's fragrant skin, all of it.

"C'mon in now, you two," Vernon called from the top of the stairs. "But you probly ain't in no danger of freezing to death, entwangled as you is together out there."

They were alone with the two dogs that had curled up together under the table for warmth. "Guess we have to go inside, Dorie." Matt sounded as reluctant as she felt, but it was dark and cold now that they weren't "entwangled," and they climbed up to join the others, Matt's hand still on the small of her back where it stayed pretty much the rest of the night. "Is your husband the jealous type?" he asked at some point.

Neither Fred nor Sarah was with the others crowded into the main salon, the galley, and the back deck. "I don't know," she had said. "I don't know what type he is."

CHAPTER 7

❀

For as many boats as there are in the U.S., there are few arrests for BUI, Boating Under the Influence, but that's probably because there are so few marine police. For many folks at Sunset, getting wasted, schnookered, loaded, high as a kite, drunk as a skunk, however you want to describe it, is as commonplace as it is in a frat house on Saturday night. In the hot summer, it is not unusual to see a boat-load of these folks go out for a night ride and then try to come back in sideways. It's quite entertaining if it's not your boat, and it keeps the local repair people in business. While drunk, you can get away with anything except surliness or mean-ness. The rule is you must be a happy drunk and try not to puke on anybody. A certain amount of marijuana smoking goes on too, and not very discreetly consid-ering it is illegal, but there it mostly stops.

Methamphetamine is a huge problem in northern Alabama because it can be made so easily in mountain hideaways. You can't even buy the precursors such as Actifed or Sudafed here without asking for them behind the counter.

According to experts, "Ice," the most pure and potent form of crystal metham-phetamine, began showing up here in 2004. You are addicted to it after using it just once because meth stimulates and then restructures the pleasure center of the brain. For a short while, six months or so, meth can boost sexual appetite and per-formance. You lose weight and have great sex as meth revs up the dopamine ner-vous system in the brain. Some users say an IV hit is the equivalent of ten orgasms all at once with a feeling of arousal that lasts for 20 hours, ten times longer than cocaine. But then the downward spiral begins as users try to recapture that initial high and then they can't reach fulfillment even when they are high. They begin to lose their hair and their teeth fall out. "Meth Mouth" is what they call it in prison.

Here in Marshall County, 80 percent of all drug arrests in 2004 were related to meth.

—A Genuine Liveaboard

Well, she must have walked home because here she was in her bunk with her nightgown on and a plastic glass of water, as usual, on the vanity that separated their two bunks. It was after ten, practically the middle of the day, and that was not at all usual. The boat was very quiet except that the north wind had come up and waves were slapping the aft end, tossing them around in the slip.

"Fred?" she called. Nothing. Suppose he was so mad at her after last night that he had left her? Dorie didn't remember him being mad but she didn't remember much. Matt kissing and then touching her when they had sneaked out to the front deck, this she remembered very well. She grimaced with guilty pleasure. Not once had she felt ashamed of her body, worried that Matt's huge hands would find it unlovely. And she had forgotten the thrill of exploration, the tastes, deliciously delicate sensations that could be derived from just kissing. She was being silly. Kissing and a little petting. No big deal. Well, it was a big deal to her because she had never done that before, hadn't even done it with Fred for a hundred years, but to most people, it was a small, drunken indiscretion. The boat was awfully quiet except for the creaking lines and the crackling sounds of the metal roofs being attacked by the wind. She padded barefoot up the stairs, clutching the handrails for dear life, and found a note on the galley counter. Her head hurt more than a little.

Hey, Party girl! Gone to hardware 9 a.m. Aqua called. We can go first good weather. Me.

Oh, boy. She hung on to the counter and heaved into the sink, a couple of dry retches before some ghastly yellow bile and other stuff came up. She hadn't gotten tipsy in years. Drunk. She had been really drunk, not tipsy. She rinsed her mouth with orange juice and felt slightly better, but then she looked out the window at the other boats bobbing and bouncing in their slips, and she heaved again before groping her way down to the aft cabin and crawling back into bed.

"Here, drink this, honey. It will make you feel better." Fred had propped an arm behind her and offered her an Alka-Seltzer in one of their four good wine glasses. "I'm glad we have some real glass on board because I have discovered that Alka-Seltzer doesn't fizz very well in plastic," he cheerfully informed her. As if she cared, but her stomach did feel better after a few minutes and she thanked him. My God, it was two o'clock in the afternoon. He laughed at her expression. "You were due a day off anyhow, Dorie. All you've done is work. Whatever happened to the flower committee and bridge and kung fu? I didn't expect you to drop everything you enjoyed, you know."

"It's Tai Chi, Fred, and someday I'll go back to it. The flower committee expects you to have flowers, I believe, which I won't have when we sell the house." It was her turn to look sideways at him. "I did promise my bridge club we would play on the boat one afternoon and then take them for a cruise when the weather got better." He nodded okay. "I also promised them margaritas made with hundred proof Jose Cuervo, homemade guacamole, and bulbs from my day lily beds if they would put up with Mildred's mother as a stand-in for a few months until we get *Spot* in hand."

"That was smart," he said without being sarcastic. Years ago she had begged him to learn bridge so they could play with other couples, but he had refused. Card games were not his thing.

"Well, they've been good friends for almost twenty years, and I don't want to lose them."

"Of course not."

"Why are you being so nice?"

He threw up his hands. "I'm always nice," he said in a hurt voice.

"You're always nice as long as we're doing what you want to do." After she said it, she realized the real truth of it. Maybe if she had gone back to work full time, taken Teddy to daycare, then she would be more forceful about her own needs, would have kept her figure better, would be more respected, happier.

"I'll make you some soup," Fred said with pinched lips and narrow eyes and left her. Her mood as sour as her stomach, she counted her grievances against her husband. All those weekends and evenings he had to work and she was stuck with baseball, soccer, dance lessons, yard work, birthdays, cookouts that he had promised to be home for, endless homework. Now she wondered just how much he really worked. They had spent so little time together the last years before his retirement. Maybe there were "Sarahs" on the side that made him so busy. Maybe he was repairing their garbage disposals instead of watching the grandkids in their tutus and ballerina slippers.

And what kind of man didn't even notice that his wife had been admired and made love to by another very attractive man right under his own nose? A man who was too busy with his own lovemaking to pay attention or care, that's who.

"Did we hear from that last couple about the house yet?" she called up in a loud voice shrill with anger.

"No. Well, they haven't made a offer, if that's what you mean."

"Good," she said with conviction.

"Good?" He brought the chicken soup down using the breadboard for a tray and set it carefully on her lap. "It's hot," he warned, but she burned her tongue on it anyway and shot daggers at him. He threw up his hands again and turned toward the door.

"Don't you turn your back on me when I'm talking to you!"

"Dorie," he turned slowly and spoke in that patronizing tone that if she never heard again would be fine with her. "I'm sorry you overdid it last night and feel rotten today. I had a little too much myself and was feeling no pain, and if I did something to offend you, I'm sorry, but I don't know what I did."

"Maybe it's something you didn't do." He rolled his eyes and that was the last straw. "Maybe we'll rethink this liveaboard business. It's not too late. You made the decision that we can't have the boat and the house, but I'm not so sure. I have to look at those numbers of yours more carefully. I'll bet a lot of people get along just fine without a twenty-two-hundred-dollar battery charger. And the house…take this away, will you please?" she waved at the soup and he removed it, clearly humoring the nut case. "The house might not be as nice as the Andersons', but it's my home, and I love my garden and my kitchen and my friends, and I can live without a new roof for a long time yet, I'll bet." Her voice was rising hysterically but she didn't care. "You say you want a change, huh? Well, you might get more than you bargained for, old salt. Move," Dorie commanded and made a dash past him for the head where she closed the sliding door just in time so he wouldn't see her throwing up again. She decided to take a shower while she was in there and felt almost human after she put on clean sweats only slightly tainted by "eau de diesel fuel."

While she was attempting to repair her blotchy face, she heard knocking on the side of the boat and a familiar "Hello the boat, y'all!" Sarah was seated on her lumpy deck furniture gazing raptly into her husband's blue eyes, one hand propped beneath her chin. Sarah looked as bright as a new penny, disgustingly perky in painter pants and a coral colored twin sweater set. "Hey, Dorie," Sarah gave her the once over. "Did you have a good time last night?" she asked sweetly.

"I had a wonderful time," Dorie said. What the hell, she could be perky too. "The best time I've had in ages! I haven't danced like that in I can't even remember when."

"Well, that's good." Sarah wrapped her cardigan more closely around her as a gust of wind pushed them from side to side. "Brrr. I should have worn my coat but who would believe it's so cold today! Even in the sun! I know you sure had a ball, didn't you, Freddy? You were feeling no pain from that Mexican grass, huh?" Freddy just sat there with a goofy smile on his face as he contemplated his sneakers. "Those spics sure know how to grow the stuff. I'll let you know the next time Bobby Ray gets another good batch. Oh, we had a big deal with Yolanda after you left." Sarah shivered and moved to the edge of the seat.

"Just a minute." Dorie went down and retrieved her shawl from the chair where she had tossed it the night before. "You got chilled through walking over here," she said as she wrapped it around Sarah who accepted it gratefully and curled into it like a kitten.

"Thank you so much," she said sincerely, and looked intently into Dorie's eyes as though searching for something and shivered again.

"Do you want some hot tea?"

"No, thank you, Dorie, but that is very sweet of you." Sarah smiled so guilelessly that Dorie had to smile back just a little in spite of herself. Fred Jr. was two years younger than this pretty woman and twenty years more mature. "Anyway, about Yolanda, Phillip pushed her down the stairs. Not all the way, just the last two. He says he didn't, but Ronald and I both saw it. Most everybody else had left already. She bashed her face up pretty bad and Ronald and us took her to Marshall North Emergency, but they said nothing was broke and just to keep putting ice on her eye. That girl is high on crystal meth most of the time, you know?" She looked at them expectantly. They hadn't known. "Oh, yah." She shook her head vigorously, her brown curls dancing. "She got hooked when she started going with Phillip and I think he's selling but he never offered it to any of us. That stuff is awful! I read where you can get hooked the first time you use it. It changes your brain cells or something. Course you also have the best orgasms of your entire life." She paused to let that sink in and seemed satisfied that she had shocked them.

Southerners know that the secret of a good story is timing and Sarah was into it now, her eyes shining. From the mesmerized look on Fred's face, she had him but good. "Oh yah. She goes like a maniac for days, and then when she has a couple of drinks, she just collapses. And I've read where after a while, you can't have an orgasm at all even after you take the crystal meth so how great is that? Anyhow, after we saw Phillip push her, VJ told him not to come around here no more. And Phillip says he'll go wherever he damn well pleases and to stay out of his way or he'll fix the other side of VJ's face for him. You know how Phillip can be. Bobby Ray had to step between them and even Lady started hollering from the top of the steps. That's when Phillip left. VJ is going to get Jimmy Lassiter to tell him to stay away from Sunset. Can he do that?" She turned to Fred.

"Huh?" Fred said, startled. He was probably still pondering the "orgasm" part.

"Can he do that? Tell somebody they can't come to the marina no more?" Sarah looked at him in that childishly expectant way she had, as if his answer were the most important thing in the world to her. The girl was adorable, Dorie had to give her that. "VJ and Bobby Ray don't know."

"I never thought about it. It's a good question, isn't it, honey?" Fred looked at her so helplessly she had to smirk. She might not be as young and sexy as Miss Alabama, but at least she could still rub some brain cells together.

"It is a good question," she said. "We own our boats and should be able to have anybody we want on our property, but to get to our property, unless he goes by boat, a guest has to use Jimmy's property." Dorie thought for a minute. "I suppose it would be close to living in a condo group where you own the space you live in, but the condo association owns the common land. It isn't the exact same thing, though, because we can move our property at any time."

"Maybe it's more like a mobile home or an RV," Fred suggested, his voice back to normal. "They can move too."

"Yes, but I think the mobile home park or the RV park would have to be located on state-run land to be the same because Jimmy doesn't own the water under us. He just has permission from the TVA to use the harbor space. I think if I invited Phillip to come on my boat, Jimmy couldn't stop him," she decided, "but I would be responsible for his behavior. If Jimmy didn't like that, I guess he could ask us to leave at the end of the month, the same as we could leave if Jimmy did something we didn't like."

"You are so smart," Sarah gushed in guileless admiration.

"Maybe book smart sometimes," Dorie snorted, "school teacher smart. When it comes to common sense, I'm an idiot."

"No, you're not!" Sarah leaned over and affectionately patted her knee. "I never saw Matt come on to any woman and he's a brain and a hunk." Again she gave Dorie that searching look, tinged with sadness, before she shook herself and smiled brilliantly. "You definitely have an admirer, you lucky duck. Well, I just stopped by to say hello." Sarah rose to go. "Bobby Ray and me are real happy you folks are here at Sunset. Y'all give some class to a party."

Fred fought with the door to get it shut against the wind after he let Sarah out and then turned on her, hands on hips. "Did Matt Thompson, or whatever his name is, come on to you last night?" he demanded.

"It's Thomas, Matthew Thomas."

"Is that so?" He waited for more but got only silence. She decided to let the green-eyed monster work on Fred for a while. It certainly had done a job on her. "It's gotten too cold up here. Let's go downstairs and talk."

"Sure." She headed for the refrigerator. "I'm going to have a Bloody Mary. Hair of the dog. How about you? Or do you want to toke up just a little to ease on through the afternoon?"

"Don't be a smartass. I'll have a drink with you, but I don't think marijuana is as bad for you as alcohol."

"That certainly isn't what you told our kids."

"I'm not talking about our kids, Dorie, or any kids, for that matter. And our kids aren't kids anymore. They're adults. They can do what they want. You got just as wasted with this Matt Thomas as I did, but I don't have a rotten hang-over today."

"That's true. But what's worse, a hangover…" she handed him the drink, "or a jail sentence? Regardless of what you think or of what Sarah and Bobby Ray think, pot is illegal. It's a crime." She sat down across from Fred and really looked at him. His face showed every bit of his fifty-seven years this afternoon, the two grooves on either side of his mouth looking especially deep. When his light blue eyes were sad like that it always got to her. "When did you start doing this?" She tried to sound softer, less judgmental.

"I don't know that I have 'started doing' pot at all." His tone was belligerent. "I did it last night and I had a ball. I felt like a kid again. Maybe I didn't have as much fun as you and this Matt seem to have had, but a good time."

"Why are you so angry? Because I'm objecting to the marijuana or because I had fun?"

He ran his fingers through his hair, which was long overdue for a cut, she realized. Or was he going to have a ponytail to go with the weed? Maybe an ear-ring? "You're entitled to have fun, Dorie, and so am I. Nobody's going to turn anybody in around here for smoking a little pot at a private party."

"What about somebody like Phillip?"

He thinned his lips in annoyance. "Phillip isn't likely to tattle on anybody, especially if he's dealing dope worse than marijuana."

"You don't know that for sure. I'm afraid of him," she said.

"You're afraid of a lot of things," he spat. "You're afraid to leave your home and garden, and afraid to talk honestly with me, and afraid to let me touch you, although you let some stranger put his hands on you last night, I reckon."

Dorie clenched her fists in anger. "You have some nerve, Fred. You talk a good line but we haven't made love in months. You couldn't get far enough away from me at that party, but when someone else shows a little interest, you get all excited. And where were you while this "putting on of hands" was supposedly taking place? Off smoking pot with your girlfriend, the beautiful young Sarah?"

He leaned toward her, elbows on his knees and palms together, fingers tapping his lips for a few seconds as he calmed down. "That's fair, Dorie," he said quietly. "I know that's probably what it looked like, but Sarah is so..." He searched for the words and she didn't attempt to help him. "She's like a child..."

"Lolita?"

"I was going to say, she's like a child in many ways that are charming, and I enjoy her company to a point, but..."

"And where does this imaginary "point" begin? Does it begin before or after the putting on of hands?"

Fred laughed. "Touché." He spread his arms wide. "Let's forget about last night, honey. Let's start fresh. I have a..."

"Not so fast, Fred." His arms and smile dropped at the same time and he shifted uncomfortably in his barrel chair. She took a measured sip of her Bloody Mary. "You spent a lot of time on the road, especially toward the end but also for most of the time I was pregnant with Teddy and a long time after. Do you remember that? In fact, you missed most of Janie's early years and didn't really get to know Teddy until he was in kindergarten."

"I went where the work was, Dorie. You know that. What the hell was I supposed to do with six mouths to feed and four kids to put through college? And what has this got to do with the price of tea in China?"

"Why are you so defensive, Fred? I know you've always worked hard. I haven't accused you of anything, have I?"

He jerked angrily up from his chair. "If we're going to dig up old bones, I want another one of these. You?"

She shook her head no and looked at him speculatively. "Teddy is one 'old bone,' I suppose, but I thought we had buried it pretty deep. Maybe not."

He set his refilled glass beside his chair and plopped down heavily. "We don't really have to talk about this again, you know. I love Teddy as much as I love the others."

"I know you do, Fred, but let's do this anyway. Humor me."

"It was just too much at the time is all." He ran his fingers through his hair, always a sign that he was agitated. "We were thirty-one years old and had three little kids and that big house to pay for. Health insurance was starting to go through the roof and I was already working so damned hard I couldn't see straight. And then you announce that you're pregnant again, that you must have forgotten to take a few pills, and so there was Teddy. End of story."

"And then you had to work even harder." She tried to keep her tone neutral and her green eyes studied him solemnly while she dropped her bombshell. "And that's when you began to be unfaithful to me when you were on the road?"

"Jesus H. Christ." He almost spilled his drink as he leapt to his feet and towered over her. "Where the fuck did that come from? So I smoked a little pot and enjoyed the company of a pretty woman last night and that makes me unfaithful to you? Give me a break, Dorie. Or is this some kind of smoke screen to cover up for what you and that Matt had going?"

"Sit down and stop shouting, Fred. Were you unfaithful to me when you were on the road? Yes or no."

He did sit back down but his blue eyes were bloodshot and wild and he dragged at his silvery brown hair as if he wanted to pull it out by the roots. "That was twenty years ago, Dorie! Twenty years!"

"So that was right after Teddy was born," she said calmly. "Was that the only time?"

"Yes. And it was a big mistake."

"Was this in Houston?"

"Yes, it was, and it was a mistake I never, ever repeated anywhere, Dorie, I swear." His eyes were pleading with her for understanding, and the funny thing was that she wasn't really upset. She should have been, but especially after last night, she did understand. "It's a mistake I never will repeat no matter what you think of me now, not with Sarah, not with anybody."

"I believe you, Fred," she said simply but he didn't seem to have heard her because he began pacing around the small salon in his agitation, his hair standing up in spikes.

"I vowed you would never find out, never be hurt by my stupidity, and now this," he groaned.

"Fred, it's all right. I believe you and it's all right. Sit down, please, Fred." He sat down again but looked at her so bleakly, his shoulders hunched over in such misery and his eyes even more bloodshot than before, that she forgave him completely. "A woman can get so wrapped up in the kids that she puts her husband in the background sometimes. I forgive you if you can forgive me for not knowing how you felt and what you needed, Fred." She wanted to go to him and wrap him in her arms, tell him that she loved him as much as she always had, but she realized in that moment that he hadn't said he loved her for longer than she could remember. Maybe he didn't anymore. Maybe their marriage had become one of convenience, a trusted friendship, companionship.

He sat looking at her balefully for a long time and when he spoke, it was so quietly she had to sit forward to hear him. "If the husband is an adult, he should be able to accept that. Raising four kids wasn't easy for you, either, I know. And then you end up with a man who...." He cleared his throat noisily before resuming in a more normal voice. "You remember my mentioning Viagra? Well, I've got some. Bobby Ray let me have some of his and I'd like to try it, if you're willing. Dorie, I've felt so bad about us not being together. It isn't you, honey. It's me. Even when I have those old feelings, when I get horny, nothing much happens down there anymore. I don't know why but if I tried, I'm sure I would just embarrass myself. I've thought about seeing a doctor, and I will if this Viagra works. There are other pills you can take now too. You've seen them advertised. I'm willing to try if you are, Dorie, but..."

"Does this mean you still love me, Fred?"

"Love you! Of course I love you, but every time I try to touch you, you pull away and hide or make some joke about it and I..."

"I feel old and fat and uninteresting, Fred. I look at myself in the mirror and I'm not the girl you married and..."

He snorted and went down on his knees beside her chair, his arms around her legs. "You still look wonderful to me, Dorie. You're beautiful and smart and you're my wife. In case you haven't noticed, I'm not exactly a kid anymore myself." He patted his slight paunch and smiled into her eyes, his first genuine smile of the day. "You're the only woman I have ever loved. You think I would let a little extra weight change that? I'm so sorry about Houston, sweetheart. I really am."

"Let's bury that one too deep to ever dig up, shall we?" Fred kissed her, and he held her hard and kept on kissing until she opened her mouth and let his tongue inside. She put her arms around his shoulders and gave in to the wonderful sensations that Matt might have resurrected last night but that her dear husband Fred made so much sweeter today. When they finally came up for air, Dorie felt dazed and even a little dizzy. "Wow," she gasped.

"You ain't seen nothin' yet, babe," he leered before pulling back to look straight into her eyes again. "I'm sorry about last night too, but that was nothing to me. Tell me that Matt guy was nothing to you, Dorie. That I haven't lost you." She wrapped her arms around him and squeezed him so tightly that his breath came out in a whoosh and he lost his balance and they toppled onto the couch, laughing.

Later, when they had kissed some more, he said, "Let's wait until we get back from Aqua to really decide about selling the house and living aboard. Even if we do get an offer on the house in the meanwhile, it probably won't be our asking price so we could turn it down." He very gently took her hands in his. "I realize that I've been rushing into this, and that's not fair to you and maybe it's not what I really want either. I want us to be together, like we used to be. That's more important than anything to me."

"Okay," she breathed. Maybe there was a God.

CHAPTER 8

✿

The Tennessee River has its headwaters at Knoxville, Tennessee, Mile Marker 652, which tells you that's how long the river is. Sunset Marina is at Mile Marker 361.2, between Signal Point Marina and the State Park Lodge. The Tennessee River ends when it feeds into the Ohio, Mile Marker 0, at Paducah, Kentucky. If you've ever traveled on other major rivers in the heartland, such as the Ohio or the Illinois, for example, you know that the Tennessee River is a treasure; beautifully set in the foothills of the Appalachians, very little industry to mar its shoreline, easy to navigate if you follow the markers, generally benign, and relatively clean. Of the major lakes formed by Tennessee Valley Authority, and these include Pickwick, Wilson, Wheeler, and Guntersville, the last is the cleanest and has wonderfully protected coves all up and down the shoreline.

Some liveaboards, like Robert Marvel, never leave the dock. Robert may not even have a viable engine on that houseboat. Some like VJ and Sylvia take day trips but now feel too dependent on land resources to go away from the dock for long. Others love to go into a cove and throw in the hook over night or "anchor out," as they call it here. Groups of friends sometimes raft off and you'll see five or six boats hanging from one or two anchors, kids and dogs jumping in off swim platforms, a Jimmy Buffet CD on the stereo, adults climbing from boat to boat with their paper cups. Others like to be away from everyone else for days at a time and get naked, or so they say. They might just mean divesting themselves of those dock lines, which can be a very freeing experience.

—A Genuine Liveaboard

Dorie stood on the bow as Fred handed the heavy power cord, telephone and cable lines up to her where she neatly coiled them on the deck. They left the water hose behind on the pier. She was so excited to be going out on her boat at last, and the day was perfect, cool but calm and sunny, as predicted. She held on to the last line that attached *Sun Spot* to the dock until Fred yelled, "Let's go!" and she released it and draped it over one of the hooks that Fred had installed high on the roof supports so she could pick it off easily by hand or with a boat hook when they returned.

The 8V71 Detroit Diesels roared as he put her in reverse and backed slowly and smoothly out of the slip and out of the marina into open water. She saw someone waving from the other dock as they cleared the breakfront and she waved vigorously before seeking the safety of the enclosed back deck. Dorie closed the side door on the aft deck and snapped the Isinglass down to keep the wind out and held on to the railings as she went below for a quick look around. Fred had accelerated to 2000 rpms and they were making a good wake with *Spot's* nose in the air, her trim tabs adjusted to get the most speed for the effort. She had been concerned about the refrigerator door opening as the bow tilted up but saw now that the frig wasn't a problem because it sat with its back tilted aft so the door was kept shut by gravity. The problem was with the storage under the sink, and she retrieved the dish soap, kitchen cleanser, and a few other cleaning supplies that were rolling on the floor before using a bungee cord to hold the cupboard shut. The restraining metal band in the front of the stove rattled so she wedged a toothpick in the groove to stop that. So did her flatware hanging in the little box that Fred had made for it but she'd have to think about what to use to stop that. Maybe a thin sponge cut to fit.

In the aft cabin, the biggest problem was the tall reading lamp. It had fallen over, flattening one side of its new shade, dammit. She propped it up in a corner of the bed. Fred would have to bolt it to the vanity counter. The sliding door to the head had shut because she had forgotten to push in the button that would hold it open, and the toothbrush holder had slid down the shelf and overturned on Fred's shaving things. She secured it in the sink and made a mental note to put rubber liner on that shelf too. She had it just about everywhere else and was gratified that their knickknacks and books, sparse as they were, seemed to hang on sideways quite well. She returned up top.

"Everything shipshape, matey?" Fred yelled and mock saluted her.

"Aye aye, captain sir. All's well below!" she yelled back and returned the silly salute before climbing up on the wide helm seat with him. The noise from the engines was loud enough to make normal voice levels inadequate, and they felt as if they were shouting at one another until they got used to it. The air coming in the front window, which operated on a little automatic gizmo, was sweet and played with her hair. Other than a towboat far upriver, they were alone on the water as they headed for the high bridge on Highway 431. The water was a lovely dark blue today with bands of jade green, flat but with swells left over from the high winds. Already the marina looked small in the distance, its geometric configuration unfamiliar and foreign. "Not much of a muffler system, is there?" she hollered to make conversation. Fred looked so happy at the wheel, a little nervous but obviously happy, his eyes constantly checking all the gauges and the horizon.

"No, not good at all," he said. "I thought about putting in more modern, quieter ones, but the cost isn't worth it. One of the mufflers is under the vanity, you know, so we have to figure that in when we remodel." He didn't sound one bit disheartened to have to shout and smiled at her in delight. Must be a guy thing, that engine racket. He said he'd had people tell him they loved that sound, that they'd know those Detroit Diesels anywhere. Good for them. Personally, she'd like better mufflers.

Dorie knew enough to know that they had to stay within the green and red buoys because there were areas shallow enough to run aground, but they soon came to a section where there was only one buoy. How did you know which side to go on?

"'Red right returning' is how you remember," Fred explained.

"But we're not returning anywhere! In fact, we're going away."

"No, returning is going upstream. Right now we're going downstream, with the current, so the red buoys should be on our left and the green on our right. See that red one there?"

"That's the one I mean, Fred. There's no green one."

"Then you figure you are safe from the buoy to the shoreline as long as you keep the red buoy on your left going downstream and on your right returning upstream." They practiced with the markers for a while until she got the hang of it. She got better finding them on the horizon too. The red ones had pointy tops and the green ones had flat tops.

"But how can you tell if you're going upstream or downstream?" she wanted to know.

"You make it your business to know," Fred said. "You study the charts. We'll practice with those when we go to Aqua. By the way, there's an easy way to remember port and starboard too. 'Port' has four letters and so does 'left.' So port is always left. Captain Larry taught me well," he said smugly when she looked impressed at all of his nautical knowledge.

They slowed down to go under the bridge, although they didn't have to slow down under this bridge because there weren't any "No Wake" signs posted, but it was neat to watch the semis and cars going over them and to hear the whish of the tires and feel the structure shudder.

They passed three small islands on which dead trees were dotted with black exclamation points, the cormorants that Vernon had told them about wheeling up into the air from time to time. As the trees had died, smothered by cormorant waste, the roots around the shoreline were becoming exposed and many of the trees were leaning, ready to fall. Kind of ugly and sad, Dorie thought, like those moss-choked sections of forests in Florida. No wonder Vernon was concerned about cormorants.

Parts of the shoreline reminded Dorie of the Wisconsin Dells, high cliffs of variegated rock with pockets of water more than sixty feet deep along the cliffs. Remnants of ropes obviously used by youngsters to swing out over the rocks and into the lake on warm summer days dangled down from trees and bushes. She spotted a few fishing boats tucked into coves and twice bass boats buzzed around them, up on plane and flying over the water, barely touching it. She waved and they waved back and smiled. She was sorry when *Sun Spot* turned into Honeycomb Creek behind Goat Island. "How far did we go?" she asked.

"About thirteen miles. Not quite an hour and a half, I figure, doing ten miles per hour on open water, which is pretty good for us, but then we have to go slow getting out of the marina and into the creek."

They found a good place off the shore marked with the white cross that designated a safe anchorage and, as they had discussed, took their time in setting the Danforth anchor. They checked the depth and followed the seven to one ratio suggested which meant letting out about 125 feet of line because they were in 18 feet of water. Since they were alone and had plenty of room to swing, Fred let out 150 feet just to be safe. He could tell how much was out because of the little yellow numbered tags he had intertwined in the anchor line. They waited for the anchor to settle and the line to pull taut and then put the engines in reverse a couple of times to suck it in deep and looked at each other for conformation. "Feels good to me," Fred shrugged. He put the headings in the log they had started. "We'll watch it for a while, see how much these last two numbers change, but I think we're in good." He turned off the engines and the generator.

The silence was stunning. They sat at the helm and rocked gently in the easy wind, feeling the mountains soar up all around them, dressed now in various shades of green. The darker pines contrasted beautifully with the lime green of the hardwoods just opening. Here and there a pink flowering bush was set against an oak tree still locked in winter. No homes had been constructed on this cove in the Appalachians, at least not yet, and soon they heard birdcalls and heard fish jump, making concentric circles which spiraled out. A young heron stood stock still at the edge of the water waiting for breakfast while an eagle doing the same thing silently soared high above.

"Let's get comfortable," Fred smiled mysteriously and disappeared below for a few minutes before emerging barefoot in a long, flowing caftan striped with bright red, yellow and turquoise. "Ta dah!" he crowed as her mouth dropped open.

He looked magnificent but her Fred thought bathrobes for men were too fussy. "What have you done with my husband?" she teased as she stepped back to admire him.

He held up a finger and smiled that goofy smile again. "Just you wait," he said, and making a great show of holding up his skirt before negotiating the curving staircase, he disappeared below again and reemerged with a matching caftan for her. He spread it out and fanned it back and forth like a bullfighter's cape, and it was her turn to disappear below. "You can't wear anything underneath," he called down, and then added, "captain's orders," for good measure. He was probably rechecking all the gauges while he waited because she could hear him humming tunelessly, a contented murmur from a contented man.

The material was polished cotton with three-quarter length sleeves and a rounded neckline with buttons down the front. It was plain but cut so generously that the voluminous folds fell satiny smooth against her skin. She loved it. She couldn't remember when Fred had bought her clothing. Of course, when he had last attempted to surprise her with an outfit, he had bought it two sizes too small. "Where did you find these?" she asked while she twirled barefoot for him on the back deck, the colors flashing. "I love them, but where on earth did you get them?"

"Sarah found them in Atlanta."

"Sarah!" She stopped in mid-twirl. She hadn't seen the pretty one in over a week and had assumed she and Bobby Ray were traveling again.

"Yes, the beautiful Sarah. It was her idea." He put his arms on her shoulders. "She wanted to atone for her behavior to you, she said. She was jealous of you and…"

"Jealous! Whatever for?"

"Never mind about what, she said to tell you. She was jealous and thought she could hurt you by flirting with me and she's sorry."

"She actually said all of this?"

"Yup."

"Not very flattering for you then, is it?"

"Nope." His caftan was cut much straighter than hers and he had it unbuttoned part of the way down so his chest hair peeked out. She thought how manly he looked in something that made her feel completely female. "They're made in Egypt," he said, as if that were significant in some way.

"That was very honest of her," she said.

He put his arms around her and drew her against him. "To find something from Egypt?" He nibbled softly on her ear.

"To tell you," she laughed and turned into him so he could nibble more comfortably. "Aren't you just a little disappointed that it wasn't your manly charms that attracted the pretty one?"

"How in the world could I be disappointed when I have you alone at last floating at the end of a hook in a beautiful cove, just my honey and me." And he stopped nibbling and kissed her so sweetly she thought she had died and gone to heaven.

"So, how does this Viagra work, anyhow?" she inquired innocently and reached down to stroke the caftan at the critical place in question not at all innocently.

"Well," Fred cleared his throat, looking a little alarmed at her forwardness, "you take one and then fool around until you feel like getting down to business, I think. Should I do that and see what happens? Do we, by any chance, have champagne to wash it down?"

"No, but we have the makings for screwdrivers," she grinned.

"My clever girl. I'll get the Viagra and you get the screwdrivers. I'm sure we can come up with something."

Matt watched the Langfords going out and called to Shirley. The front patio door was open and he was on the front deck of his 60-foot Monticello, shirtsleeves rolled up over thick arms. It was going to be a beautiful day on the water for them. Not for him, though. Shirley didn't like to anchor out. He was lucky if he could talk her into taking a boat ride. He jammed his hands into his chino pockets.

"Who?" Shirley hollered from the galley.

"Dorie Langford and her husband, in that 45 Chris named *Sun Spot*. They're going out!" He would give anything if he could be on that boat with her, just the two of them away from everything.

"Oh ya." She joined him on the deck, drying her hands on a dishtowel. Her hands had gotten so thin that she had to be careful she didn't lose her rings in the towel. "Pretty, isn't it?" Her dull gray topknot used to be a rich brown that had picked up red highlights in the sunshine.

"The day or the boat?"

"Both. The air smells so sweet with all those blossoming trees and bushes, it kind of makes you lightheaded, doesn't it?" She smiled but the smile never quite made it to her eyes these days.

"Yup. Supposed to hit 60, maybe even 65 this afternoon." Matt shifted restlessly, jingling some coins in his pockets. The Langford's boat was pulling away toward the big bridge, the throb of the engines fading. He closed his eyes briefly and with all his might willed himself on that boat, pictured himself at the helm, his arm around her.

"I'll bet that Bradford Pear we planted for Ann is blooming this week."

It was no good, of course. They could never have more than two minutes of conversation without the dead babies coming into it. "I suppose you would like to visit the graves today," he said dully. Sometimes he could escape if he were going to be traveling a lot, but this week was light. He wouldn't be flying out until Wednesday morning and this was only Monday. Two whole days. "Decoration Day is May 1 at the church this year. Can't you wait until then?"

"You don't have to come if you don't want to, Matt." She was wringing her hands in the towel and her gray eyes had that martyred look. "I can probably get Sylvia to come with me. She's kept me company before." Shirley stopped twisting the damned towel and stood very straight, so slight that a strong wind could literally blow her over. The woman ate—he saw her eat. "Or I can go alone. I surely do know the way."

Like he didn't. Like he hadn't visited his two baby daughters dozens of times over the last three years. Fat lot of good it did to have the best-tended graves in Georgia. He was damned if he was going to ruin another day mooning over those poor children, reliving the misery of losing them, speculating on what they would look like or be like now. "If you can't get Sylvia or someone else, I'll drive you, Shirl. I don't want you driving all that way alone when I'm here." She turned away from him and he followed her through the patio door, determined to explain but not to apologize. "I want to change the generator oil today and get somebody's opinion on the stuffing around my shaft logs. I've got a leak somewhere. Not a bad one, but enough. Haven't you noticed the aft pump running more than usual?"

She didn't answer but kept her back to him as she punched in numbers, her angel bones sticking out sharply as she cradled the cell phone. He went to the aft deck, opened the engine hatches, pulled up his bag of work clothes, and slammed it angrily on the deck. God damn it! Were they supposed to mourn for the rest of their lives? Was that the only way to satisfy her? They had done grief counseling with Brother Clay from the church, had seen a psychologist together for a year, had prayed on it in groups and alone. Matt had really thought that if they could get out of that house, out of that town with its constant reminders, Shirley would start to heal. But, hell, Instead of a boat, he should have just bought the neighboring burial plots and set up house there! Time heals all things, but how much time? Ann had died two years ago, Maggie the year before that.

Shirley startled him by appearing suddenly at the screen door. "You can stop slamming things around," she said coldly. "Sylvia will go with me."

"Good."

"And we'll stop at the outlet mall on the way so we'll probably be gone all day."

"All right," he agreed, trying to think of something pleasant to add to defrost the chill, but she was already down the hallway, her back rigid, gray topknot jerking with angry movements. As he climbed into his work jeans and shirt, he couldn't help thinking how Shirley had aged prematurely because of all this. She was only forty-three but looked older than Dorie, for instance, who had to be much older, judging by the age of her kids. Holding Shirley now was like holding a bag of bones, brittle and sharp and so fragile he was afraid to touch her.

For various reasons, neither had wanted children with their first spouses. Matt and Shirley had been married for nine years now and they had planned to have children together from the first, but in spite of up-to-the-minute fertilization techniques and modern health care, Shirley took forever to become pregnant, that famous biological clock ticking, ticking. She had two miscarriages before Maggie was born prematurely. Both girls had been born premature, not deformed but weak. They were finally allowed to take the babies home from the hospital, but neither survived beyond six months, their livers and kidneys unable to function properly as their tiny bodies tried to grow. A congenital defect. Nobody's fault. Just one of those things. Some day there would be gene therapy to correct the problem in the mother's womb but not quite yet. No one had ever said it, but Matt thought Mother Nature was showing him that they were just too old to start a family. In fact, he was sick to death of the whole thing, sick of sickness and death.

"Shirley? You still here?" he cupped his hands and called through the screen. He didn't want to go inside with his oily clothes. Big as he was, he always brushed up against something.

"What?" she appeared, purse in hand, impatient to be gone.

"If I'm out of the slip when you get home, don't worry. I may want to run her a little, get the winter cobwebs out. I'll look for you at Lady's, okay?"

"Whatever."

"Be careful driving, now!" he called.

"What for," he heard her mutter and he climbed down into the open hatch. Well, she could wallow in guilt, anger, depression, whatever it was she was wallowing in, but he'd be damned if he would live the rest of his life that way. He closed his eyes again and saw himself dancing with Dorie Langford, feeling those rounded breasts pressed against his chest, envisioning that warm glow in her green eyes as she looked up at him. By God, he hadn't felt this way about anybody in years. She was so robust and healthy, so wholesome and alive. That was it, wholesome. That's what he needed. Well, maybe sexy too.

It was hot in the engine room, and Matt was sweating hard when he had finished with the oil change and lugged the dirty stuff up to the big barrel beside the office for proper disposal before heading over to the next dock for advice.

"Hey, VJ," he yelled outside of the houseboat and pounded on the hull. VJ would know who best to ask about the shaft logs. Country western was blaring inside and it wasn't even noon. You could always tell when Lady was gone. Vernon stuck his head out the curtain door, his right cheek so swollen and inflamed it was purple in places. Even his good left eye was puffy and watering. "You need to see a doctor, boy!" Matt said.

Vernon took a sip from the straw he carefully inserted into the left side of his mouth and waved his glass. "Don't tell Lady, but…"

"Turn that damn music down so I can hear you, VJ."

VJ held up a finger and went inside to turn it off. "I said don't tell Lady but I already seeing Doctor Daniels." His voice was so soft and breathy that Matt could hardly understand him. "I hurt so damn bad." Vernon seemed on verge of tears.

"You call your dentist and tell him whatever he's giving you for the swelling and the pain isn't working, VJ." Vernon asked him something but Matt couldn't understand him. "I'm going to take you to see him right now," he decided. "Let me change out of these work clothes and you meet me in the parking lot in ten minutes. And no more Jack, VJ. I mean it." He ran back to his boat.

They had to go to nearby Guntersville but the dentist took Vernon right back and Matt prowled the waiting room, hating to be inside on such a gorgeous day. The young receptionist who signed them in was making goo-goo noises behind the desk and Matt went over to see what was eliciting the baby talk. If Shirley had been here, he would have ignored it because she hurt so much to see a child that wasn't hers. Grandchildren visiting on the dock were a source of anguish for her, and she would disappear inside the boat or take the car and go shopping if they were around. She wouldn't even discuss adopting as an alternative, assuming they weren't too old for that. You'd think she would behave the opposite way, but her bitterness was that great.

Behind the reception desk was a box with a mother dog overseeing four of the cutest puppies Matt had ever seen. "Ain't they just darlin?" the receptionist cooed. "Doctor Allen's wife had to tend to her sick daddy so he brought them to the office so Candy wouldn't be alone all day. Ain't they something?" Candy's ears perked up at the sound of her name and she delicately touched a pink tongue to her black rubber nose and looked at him calmly with enormous brown eyes fringed with long lashes.

Matt hunkered his big self down beside the box and wanted to crawl in with them. They were multicolored but mostly black and white with short little legs, squashed button noses, and curling pig tails. The fattest and biggest of the puppies waddled over to investigate his hand, which he offered gingerly. "Does Candy mind if I touch them?"

"Not if you move slow. She's not scared but she's jumpy, being away from home."

"Sure." The puppy sought the warmth of his palm and he curled it around the soft, squishy body and it squeezed its little eyes shut in contentment and curled up to sleep just like that, in his palm. He was so charmed, he felt silly and was sure he blushed with pleasure. "What kind are they?" he whispered.

"I forgot," the nice girl whispered back. "Some kind of Chinese dog. Doctor says they don't shed. They're not Pekinese. My auntie has a Peke and they got pointier noses and skinnier bodies. Just a minute. I'll ask." Matt carefully stroked another, much smaller bundle with his free hand, and while Candy watched him closely, she seemed satisfied that he wouldn't harm her offspring, and Matt ran a gentle hand over her head too, which she seemed to enjoy. "It's a Shih Tzu, but don't ask me to spell it," the girl giggled.

"Do you think the doctor might be willing to sell one?" Shirley was allergic to dog and cat fur, so what did he think he was doing? But they were just so appealing. The fat one wriggled in his palm and then wet it, which made him laugh, before it waddled off to snuggle next to its mother.

When VJ came out, he didn't look any better but nodded when Matt asked if he felt better. The doctor explained that he had given him a different antibiotic. Seems that Vernon was probably allergic to the first kind and should have come in right away. "If this doesn't work, you be in Wednesday, Vernon," the dentist shook a finger at him. "No fooling around." VJ just nodded, his mouth so crammed with packing he couldn't talk at all. The dentist had also given him stronger pain pills and he was beginning to feel woozy.

"I'll see he gets here if he needs to," Matt said and asked about the puppies. They were purebred and had AKC papers. When he found out they had hair instead of the fur, which was the troublemaker for most people with allergies, he gave the dentist a check for $200 with the rest due when the puppies were ready to leave Candy. Two had been spoken for but not fatso, thank goodness.

He ushered VJ back to his boat and tucked him into his recliner, the poor man so grateful to be out of his misery that he fell asleep before Matt was off the front deck. Why VJ hadn't told Lady how sick he was, Matt couldn't figure out. Lady was always ready to help, a fine woman.

He should have been tired too after all that but instead he found that he was exhilarated, his step light as he returned to his own boat. He had made his decision without consciously thinking about it and he knew it was the right one. He would come in off the road and take that desk job in Huntsville. Burns Heating and Cooling, Commercial and Residential, where he had worked for over twenty-five years, was based in Atlanta but had generated enough business in north Alabama to set up an office here, and he was going to take it. The pay was a little less to start, but it was time to stop running away from his life with Shirley. He knew that he was being stupid. What could a goofy puppy do to replace a real child? But still, it was so adorable. If Shirley didn't grow to love it, he didn't care. He would. He'd train it to use those puppy pads to piddle on the boat when they were out on the water or just couldn't get to land conveniently. They were scented with something, other puppy pee, probably. He would love that fat, sweet little thing to bits.

He warmed up the engines and watched the generator carefully for problems but after a little initial smoke, everything seemed fine, and he backed the Monticello out of the slip and headed for his favorite place, Honeycomb Creek. The aft bilge pump went on for a while when he revved her up to 2800 rpms but then stopped. Maybe the packing around the shaft logs was just dried out from the inactive winter.

Matt spotted the Chris Craft after he made the turn around the rock outcropping on Goat Island into the creek and he decided to edge up to them to just say hello. That was all. He didn't want to bother them but he had to see Dorie just for a second. He made out two flashes of color on the back deck before he realized they were in matching dresses of some kind, something with skirts. Caftans. "I'll be damned," he muttered aloud without realizing it. Dorie had said she didn't know what type her husband was but he would have sworn that Fred was straight. You just never knew these days. They were in matching caftans, by God. He slowed the Monticello, put her in reverse to stop her, and then in neutral so he drifted gently in their direction.

"Hey, Matt!" Dorie waved enthusiastically and laughed as she twirled on the deck so the colors were a blur around her. "How do you like our outfits?" Fred stood behind her and waved too but not nearly as vigorously. Well, of course not.

"Just awesome, Miss Dorie." He smiled and hung out the side window to get a better look. "Those must be your 'anchoring out' clothes."

"That's exactly what they are, Matt." She laughed in her delightful way again.

"I've got an outfit too. It's called my birthday suit!" Now what on earth made him say that? He and Shirley never anchored out at all, let alone got naked doing it.

"We've got those suits on underneath, haven't we, Fred?" She smiled that warm smile at Matt and then turned to her husband with such obvious affection and love that it just about broke his heart.

"I bought a puppy today!" he hollered as he began to pull away slowly. "Y'all have fun now, and be careful." Fred was a damned lucky man.

CHAPTER 9

❀

The Monticello that Matt and Shirley live aboard is a highbred, part houseboat and part cruiser; they call it a river yacht. Its name is Lucky in Love. *Kind of ironic when you think about it. It has a houseboat layout, very spacious and on one level except for a cuddy cabin down, which some people use as a computer room or for storage. But it isn't flat-bottomed like VJ's boat; it has a five-inch keel for some stability and V drives for better control. Most everyone at Sunset agrees that the Cadillac of river yachts is a Pluckebaum, but the Monticello is a close second and some folks prefer it.*

There are nine locks and dams on the TVA system. If you've never been through a lock, it's an experience. Going downhill, when the water runs out of the lock to match the level below, is a much easier ride than going uphill, when the water is forced into the lock in torrents until it reaches the level above.

The start of the Tennessee-Tombigbee waterway, which runs parallel to the Mississippi River and caters to recreational boaters who want to get to the Gulf of Mexico, begins at Iuka, Mississippi, so lots of boaters pass by there one way or another and there are several large marinas in the area. Aqua Yacht Harbor is the largest with more than 600 boats. The trip from Lakeside is about 150 miles and three locks; three hours by car and at least two days, probably more, in an old Chris Craft.

—*A Genuine Liveaboard*

Dorie invited Bobby Ray and Sarah for dinner, their first official guests, and she was a little nervous but excited too because the seasoned boaters were going to help them plan their trip to Aqua for their lift out. They had decided to take it easy with the old girl until the problems were solved. No rush at all.

She was going to start with Brie softened in the microwave and topped with toasted almond slivers, and asparagus with cream cheese rolled in Flatbread and sliced into rounds. They would have the hors d'oeuvres on the back deck and then squeeze around their table in the main salon, which she had set as nicely as she could, considering the paper napkins. She would serve her home-made lasagna, a salad from a bag, and those crusty sourdough rolls she could take from the freezer and pop in the oven while the lasagna was setting. For dessert, ice cream and strawberries with Grand Marnier. They had plenty of red wine, one of those smooth Australian merlots and a cabernet, and a bottle of Leipfraumilch to go with dessert.

"I was really tempted to cheat and make the lasagna at home." Dorie slid the biggest pan that would fit into the tiny oven. There was room for nothing else.

"Sweetheart, you've worked too hard already." Fred had finished his projects for the day, had showered, and looked tanned and relaxed in one of swivel chairs as he had started a cocktail, his long legs stretched out across the salon. Since their lovely anchoring out evening, the lines in his face had softened, she noticed, and he looked almost dreamy at times. He smiled more too, just as he was doing now at her. "Beans and weenies would have been okay, you know."

"Now you tell me" she laughed and gave him a kiss on the forehead while he snuggled against her breasts. The Viagra hadn't worked the way Fred had wanted it to, but she wasn't concerned. Maybe he would try that new Cialis advertised on TV or something else when he saw a doctor. Maybe not. There are many ways to get sexual satisfaction and Dorie was so happy to feel desirable and comfortable with her own body again that the relief was palpable. They would work it out as all lovers did.

"Hello the boat, y'all" heralded the arrival of their guests and Fred gave her a quick smooch before they went up top. Sarah looked gorgeous as usual in tight jeans cinched with a big silver and turquoise buckle topped with a simple white blouse in some fabric that draped fluidly. Wherever did she get such lovely clothes? "Oh, I can shop, honey, just ask Bobby Ray. I understand you know how to sew, Dorie. I wish I knew how. I could save a bundle, I bet!"

Dorie thought for a minute. "I could teach you the basics"

"Really! That would be so neat!" The not-so-young teenager clapped her hands in excitement. "I had home economics in middle school, and we got to sew for one semester and I loved it. I made a shirtwaist dress that was real pretty, but we never had a sewing machine at home and I forgot about it"

Dorie turned to Bobby Ray who was huddled with Fred over a copy of the *Tennessee River Navigation* charts prepared by the Army Corps of Engineers.

"Would you have room on your boat to set up a sewing machine where we could leave it up for a while? Sarah could help me make the new cushions for back here as a way to learn, and then I'd help her make something she wants"

"You tell me what kind of machine to buy and I'll buy it tomorrow," Bobby Ray beamed at the two of them. Dorie said they'd use hers and then Sarah could decide if she wanted her own. Bobby Ray smiled affectionately at his girlfriend and reached for a cracker, which he loaded up with Brie before offering to her.

"Bobby's good to me," she said sweetly.

"How bout you learn to sew a wedding dress, lambchop?" Bobby Ray reached to caress her silky brown hair, and his diamond rings caught fire in the afternoon sun. Dorie hadn't noticed the pinky ring before but it was a sparkler. In his western style shirt he looked a little bit like Johnny Cash, she thought, attractive but world weary, lines of experience etched hard and deep.

"We'll see, Bobby Ray," Sarah said, her perfect face a perfect frown. "He gets bored with stuff real easy," she explained, waving the cracker and cheese as if to throw it overboard. "Then he just throws it away and gets something new." She took a big bite, reconsidered, and jammed the rest into her mouth. "I lub Brie!" she said, spraying them with cracker crumbs and started to laugh until she choked and laughed harder, and then they all did. "Sorry. I clean it ub," she gasped, and Dorie found herself on the floor with her, laughing and brushing at crumbs.

"I lub Brie too," she said, and that set them off again. It felt so good to laugh at nothing, and the rest of the evening was fun and easy because she didn't care if something went wrong. She burned one corner of the lasagna and all but three of the rolls but they had plenty to eat and it was good. She made a mental note to get an oven thermometer.

With Bobby Ray's advice, they decided to make the trip to Aqua in four days. This would allow them to check out three marinas along the way and not push *Spot*. They wouldn't need reservations so early in the year. It would also allow them plenty of time to get through the three locks involved if towboat traffic was heavy. You never knew. Lockmasters tried their best, but towboats pushing barges had the right of way and might take hours to move through.

"And never get into a lock with a towboat load unless you are at the front of the lock," Bobby Ray said after they had resettled on the back deck with a space heater, candles and more wine to keep them warm. Then he told a story of how he was almost blown off the wall behind a towboat when it had to put on its side thrusters to get out of the lock. "The lockmaster had warned me that it might be rough but I was in a hurry. We actually did a three-sixty right in the lock and almost took the bow pulpit off. Missed by inches. Less. And don't ask me which wife was along that time, Sarah, because I don't remember," he finished with a sharp look in her direction.

"Did I say anything?" The big brown eyes were wide.

"No, but you were going to."

"Pish tosh," she thumbed her nose at him. "He doesn't know," she said in the lofty manner of the slightly inebriated and took another sip. They had had plenty of wine with dinner.

They talked for a long time after dinner, and as the evening drew to a close, Sarah pulled her down the steps and onto the couch in the main salon. "I wanted you to know something," she whispered conspiratorially, her arm draped around Dorie's shoulders. "It's about those artificial flower arrangements."

Dorie thought for a moment. "I don't have any here."

"No, the ones on Bobby Ray's boat! The ones I made in that class!"

"Oh, yes," she said carefully.

"See, that's the thing. I know they aren't very good, except that one. I don't know, there was just something about that teacher that made me want to do this mediocre stuff in all the wrong colors and then wait for her to gush over it, you know? Like we were two-year-olds making cool mud pies. I'm going to give them all to the Goodwill tomorrow. Except that one you said you liked. That's the only good one. What do you think?" Dorie thought it was a fine idea. "I knew you'd say that! See, I'm bringing this up now because I want to apologize to you for how I acted toward you at first. When Lady told me you were a school teacher, I decided certain things about you."

"What things?"

"Oh, you know," she gracefully waved her hand, "fake-nice school teacher things."

"I taught for only a few years when Fred and I were first married and where did you go to school to get such ideas, Sarah?"

"Oh, I been to a lot of different schools, lots of em. But you're not like those teachers at all. You say things how they are. When you called me 'darlin' I about fell down! I really did deserve that. See, the thing is I want you to trust me to pick out the fabric for your cushions, and I want you to teach me to sew really good. I want you to tell me straight out if I'm doing shitty work." Dorie promised she would.

She gave Dorie a hug and a sweet kiss on the cheek before leaving. "Oh, and Matt is really in love with you," she whispered into her ear. "You should have seen his face when you guys were leaving the harbor." She made a sad face before allowing Bobby Ray to drape a huge woolen shawl around her. "He's got it bad"

"Who's got it bad, little girl? Somebody besides me?" Bobby Ray wrapped his arms around her from behind over the shawl and held her against him. "Somebody else has got it bad, huh?" he chuckled before kissing the top of her head but she didn't smile.

"Never you mind, now, Bobby Ray. I can see where Matt is coming from," she told Dorie. "And Freddy too."

"So big hunky Matt is back in the picture then?" Fred teased as they were doing the dishes later.

"Big hunky Matt never really was in the picture, sweetheart, but you can just keep worrying about him if you want to. Hurry up and dry so we can get to bed. Tonight, your sleep number is my sleep number."

They left for Aqua Yacht Harbor two days later. The round orange fenders were very heavy but she learned to adjust the length of the lines and secure them to the rail before heaving the fenders over the side. They had been instructed on Channel 14 by the Guntersville Lockmaster to use the starboard or right side and go to the bollard second from the front. They would be alone in the lock. Fred had shown her where to place the big fenders, one forward where the gunnels just started to curve and one between the windows of the aft cabin. The end of the special bollard loop was secured loosely through the amidships cleat, and she had her serrated knife close by in the rare event that the floating lock bollard hung up and she had to cut the line. She also had a telescoping pole ready in case they couldn't get close enough for her to lasso the bollard with the loop. They were idling outside the Approach Point waiting for the green light to enter the lock southbound, or downstream, and drop 40 feet.

"Captain Billy should have made me do this!" Fred called and danced in place, too nervous to sit at the helm.

"You handle the boat beautifully, honey. Don't worry," she said with assurance she didn't feel at all. "Just take a deep breath,"

The lock doors were open now and the light turned green so they began their approach, Dorie in her life jacket holding the loop ready with both hands. Fred swerved to miss a tree trunk and other debris that emerged from the swirling waters, and then they were inside the metal doors where the water and wind were calm. "Is that the one?" he pointed to a bollard recessed in the wall and she shouted that it was, and he got close enough for her to loop the bollard and secure the line with no trouble at all. Fred put the boat into neutral and the fenders scraped the sides of the slimy lock as they settled down. So far, so good. The horn blew and the lock doors creaked and groaned to a close and down they went, dropping maybe two or three feet and then there was a lull before they were dropping again. When they reached bottom, the walls made a canyon and they felt small as they waited for the doors to open. The big horn sounded again and Dorie used the pole to lift the loop from the bollard and push them off the wall as Fred carefully edged forward. He had to plow through the debris this time as there was no maneuvering room, but they emerged unscathed from their first lock. Fred gave four short blasts of the horn to thank the lockmaster. The relief and satisfaction on his face were delightful. "You did that like a pro!" he told her.

They had only 24 miles to go to get to Ditto Landing Marina, but the next one, Bay Hill Marina, was almost 50 miles farther and that was more than they wanted to do in one day. Joe Wheeler State Park was a good place too but they were saving that for a longer stay on the way home so they could sample the lodge's seafood smorgasbord. They chugged along at trawler speed, about seven miles per hour, and were so engrossed in watching the scenery and talking that they missed the narrow marina entrance entirely and had to double back. Some navigator she turned out to be. Anyway, they tied up to a transient dock as instructed by the dock master, paid their fee, and stretched their legs a bit.

Ditto Landing is a public marina operated by the city of Huntsville and is in a very shallow basin next to a golf course and a campground. In fact, someone was operating a riding mower in the distance. It has two pavilions, which groups can rent, but no restaurant and no convenient way for transients to get into town. The city was working on a grant to upgrade the place, they were told, but Fred and Dorie thought it was charming just as it was, and they sunbathed on the front deck most of the afternoon. There were few people around this early in the season mid-week, but two retirees like themselves who were working on a Bayliner said they loved it at Ditto except for the hot summer when the place was buggy and the water was stagnant and smelly. That night they slept with the windows open and reveled in the smell of newly cut grass.

They left mid-morning and enjoyed an uneventful trip to Bay Hill, a small marina set among steep hills with a barge anchored in front as a break wall. The river is very wide here with reedy shallows off to the sides forming islands out of the current. The narrow entrance around the barge was just wide enough for two boats to pass. They were given a slip with their bow pulpit nosed up to the dock that was built right behind the barge and discovered an entire little community there. Patio furniture, grills and fish cleaning stations were everywhere, even on top of the rusty barge. There were several additional docks deeper inside the cove, a restaurant with a patio nestled into a hillside, and a nautical store and repair shop way around to the back.

More people talked with them, several liveaboards, and they chatted and swapped marina and boating information. One couple had a Chris Craft Commander like theirs except that it was the three-stateroom model and a 1977, two years newer. They toured each other's boats and Dorie got lots of ideas, especially for storage. They swapped names and vital information and said they would keep in touch. Another fellow gave them his cell phone number and said to call him first if they ever wanted to sell *Spot*. Fred got a few inches taller after that. Not much of a river view unless you climbed up on the barge, Dorie thought, but certainly well protected and a close-knit group.

The following day was the biggie; only about 30 miles but a 48-foot drop at Joe Wheeler Lock and a 93-foot drop at Wilson Lock, one the biggest in the world, just before Florence City Marina or Mystic Harbor, as it was about to be called when new owners took it over. They weren't nearly as nervous as before, of course, and the Bay Hill folks had said both locks were in good repair and moving boats through smoothly. Still.

Wheeler was almost a duplicate of Guntersville except that they were farther back in the lock behind a 42-foot Carver named *Rascal*, but everything was fine, and there were only about 15 miles between the two locks so they expected a clear shot at Wilson. Then they noticed that one towboat had a big load of fifteen barges pinned up against the bank and called the Wilson Lockmaster, this time on channel 13, as the charts directed. He said that they would be backed up for several hours because a barge had just damaged a gate while exiting. They were using the two smaller auxiliary locks but that was slow going. They already had a crew working, but he couldn't say how long this would take. He was very sorry for any inconvenience. He asked the size of their boat and the name and said he would keep them informed and to wait on channel 16.

They looked at each other. Okay, time to punt. There were two large creeks and a small yacht club on the map within hailing distance from the lock. They needed to get out of the channel because other towboats would begin to pile up along the sides eventually.

They heard *Rascal* trying to raise the Wilson Lockmaster on 16 and not having any luck, so they responded and switched to channel 68 to talk while they paddled around. Fred explained the situation and suggested *Rascal* call on 13 to get on the list, or whatever. "I am so fucking-A sick of this shit," snarled the voice back loud and clear.

"Can he do that on the radio?" Dorie asked.

"Guess he just did," Fred said and pressed the speaker bar. "Sorry for your trouble, *Rascal*, but we'll be standing by on 16."

The captain's voice was deep and gravelly and slightly slurred. "Stay on 68 a minute there, *Sun Spot*." They heard other voices in the background, arguing and scuffling sounds. "What you going to do while you're waiting for the fucking Army Corps to get their fucking act together?"

"He said 'Army Corpse,'" Dorie said in amazement. "Do you think he was making a pun?"

"Not a chance," Fred laughed. "I'm going to take a look at throwing in the hook in McKernan Creek if it's deep enough, *Rascal*. Do you know anything about that creek?"

"Sorry, captain, I'm from Chicago and if I ever get back there, by Christ, I'm sure as hell going to stay there!"

"That's a roger, *Rascal*. We'll go back to..."

"Wait!" More scuffling in the background. "I'm having a little trouble with my anchor, *Sun Spot*, and I wonder if we could raft off you in that creek until the son-of-a-bitches fix the fucking lock?"

Fred rolled his eyes at her and mouthed "no way." "*Rascal*, I cannot offer you a raft-off in unfamiliar water. What exactly is the trouble with your anchor?"

"The trouble is I don't fucking have one anymore! Damned kids got it stuck on a log or something...shut up back there!" Slap and the sound of crying. "Brats cut it loose without me knowing." Dorie started to giggle and Fred couldn't help it either and soon both had tears running. "Hey, you still there, *Sun Spot*?"

"That's a roger, *Rascal*." Fred wiped his nose. "I suggest you try the Turtle Point Yacht Club over on the other shore, right next to Shoal Creek. Do you see it?"

"No. I got a pretty old map, though. Which way from this Shoal Creek is it?"

"It's upstream in the first deep cove you come to. Before Six-mile Creek."

"Okay...Shut the fuck up! Not you, *Sun Spot*."

The creek was plenty deep in the middle and that's where they threw in the anchor to wait. Three more tow boats pushed into the bank or hooked up to the mooring cells during the afternoon and still they waited. When the lockmaster finally hailed them that the lock was operational again, it was after five and they agreed to wait until morning rather than run at night. The lockmaster thanked them for their patience and said he would call at first light and take them right though.

Rascal had been listening and broke into the conversation. "No way I'm paying god-damned dockage for another night here, Lockmaster. You take me whenever you can." He was told, and not very politely either, to stand by on 16. They heard *Rascal* call the lockmaster several times before they set the alarm for six a.m., turned off the generator, and went to bed. As promised, at first light the lockmaster called, and they entered Wilson Lock with a furious and probably exhausted *Rascal* behind them. Seems the lock was just too busy with towboats to get the foul-mouthed Chicagoan in during the night.

The 93-foot drop went as smoothly as the others and, instead of docking as they had planned at Florence City Marina, they decided to go the 44 miles to Aqua Yacht Harbor so they really lost no time at all. *Rascal* had passed them up immediately out of the Wilson Lock, making such a big wake close to them that they had to turn into it to avoid being rocked severely. They heard him calling the Pickwick Lockmaster as they got closer to the Yellow Creek turnoff that led them back into Aqua. Good riddance, they agreed. "Good fucking riddance," Dorie amended.

CHAPTER 10

❀

Water, which is city water and quite good, is included in the rent at Sunset Marina and comes through PVC pipes along the sides of the docks in the summer and through under-water hoses in the winter. Clean water is not so abundant everywhere. In some areas in Florida, for instance, dock water is metered and expensive. Some boaters have found that potable water can be traded for many things, even fuel, in the Caribbean. But here water is still plentiful and probably cheap or Jimmy Lassiter would be metering it.

Marina water pipes and hoses break fairly often. Piers flexing in high winds, expansion and contraction from extremes of heat and cold, and muskrats are the biggest culprits. And in the deep winter, water lines sometimes freeze at night. Not the hoses running under the water, but the exposed water line going into the boat, even though you wrap it with foam for insulation. It usually thaws in the daytime but not always so you might be on your own boat water for days even at the dock. Most liveaboards are careful to keep their fresh water holding tanks clean and full and their pumps in good repair.

Other amenities, like power, telephone, and cable or satellite dishes, cost extra and like the water supply, these fail just as they do in regular neighborhoods, only more often. Some boaters use cell phones and buy battery operated satellite dishes, but you've got to have electricity for heating and cooling. Alabama isn't in the tropics and there's no way around it. Liveaboards here make sure their generators are working and their fuel tanks full enough to support the generators.

—A Genuine Liveboard

"Want to take a little ride with me?" Matt had waited until she got off the phone with her mother, a vivacious, seventy-year-old widow who lived in Florida year round now. Shirley had not been particularly close with her mother until the last year or so. Now they talked every day, Shirley huddled over the cell phone out of earshot. Matt suspected that he was the topic a good share of the time, as Marlene hadn't approved of him from the start. She hadn't liked Shirley's first husband either but that was small comfort.

"Not particularly." She had been cool before the Sunday he wouldn't visit the graves with her, but since then she had been downright cold and overtly nasty. He told her he would go with her on the first Saturday in May, Decoration Day at their church, and he'd help her pick out new plastic flowers and throw out the old, faded ones and clean up the graves, but that got no response. She had insisted he move into the guest bedroom several months ago, and of course he was on the road several days a week, so he was used to sleeping alone. They never ate together now although she did keep the refrigerator stocked, and she had begun separating their clothes and washing just her own, leaving his in a pile on the floor. Since he had his work shirts and suits dry cleaned anyway, this wasn't much of a hardship. Sometimes he stayed on the road an extra day on some excuse or another just to avoid this atmosphere. But no more. No more.

"I want you to come with me," he said firmly and moved to face her wounded gray eyes. "I have a surprise for you, Shirl. A couple of them really." She turned her body away from him, so thin he could almost count her vertebra through her light blouse, but he moved with her. "I'm going to run that new office Burns is opening up in Huntsville. I start on Wednesday." She refused to look up and studied her tennis shoes. "I'll be home every night, Shirley, and we can live like normal people."

At that she did look at him. "Hah!" The ugliness in that one syllable made him step back and he thought for the first time that maybe she hated him. Maybe it wasn't just grief over the babies but hatred for him that made her like this.

"I bought something for us and I want you to come with me to get it," he said, determined to try anyway.

She folded her arms over shrunken breasts. Shirley had had a nice figure when he met her. "There's nothing you can buy that I want, Matt, so I don't see the point."

"Just come with me."

She said nothing in the car during the ride to Guntersville but looked mildly curious when he pulled up to the dentist's office.

"Oh, Mr. Thomas," the young receptionist grinned, "he's all ready to go!" And there he was all alone in the box with his funny rabbit's-foot hind legs sprawled out in different directions and front paws exactly aligned, looking expectantly up at them with big brown eyes.

"You know I'm allergic!" Shirley shook an accusing finger at Matt but he could see that she thought the puppy was cute and was already bending down to touch him. "Oh God," she sighed when she stroked his silky back and the puppy tentatively stuck out a pink tongue to lick her finger when she reached to smooth under his little beard.

"He's got hair instead of fur, like a poodle, so he doesn't shed, honey. Fur is what most people are allergic to. And he won't get real big, although fat as he is, he'll probably go eighteen, twenty pounds. He's got papers, don't you, buddy?" and Matt had to pick him up and hold him in one hand where he looked right at home, his curled piggy tale waving with happiness. "A pure bred Shih Tzu, aren't you, sport?" he nuzzled the squashed black rubber nose before offering him to Shirley who gingerly cradled him in both hands, sliding down to sit beside the box.

"He's so tiny and wobbly," she exclaimed as she set him down and let him climb around and over her ankles, his soft belly dragging as he struggled to conquer these mountains. He was variegated but mostly black and white like his mother. The darker parts would become more pronounced as he got older so he looked gray and white now, his body squishy and round. Of course he had to squat and pee on the floor just then and she pulled her legs up and made a face at the little puddle.

"We'll train him right away. I've got the puppy pads and everything in the trunk. I bet he'll learn fast," Matt hasted to assure her as fatso blithely padded through his own mess.

"Oh, they're real smart dogs," the receptionist said and bent over to wipe up the pee with a paper towel. She flipped him over and gently wiped his tiny bear-track paws. "Course they are dogs," she laughed before she kissed the top of his head and set him back down. He made a dash, so to speak, for the office door, determined to explore now that he was finally out of the box.

"I don't know." Shirley watched his progress, his adventurous nature asserting itself as he headed for the small step down into the waiting room. Matt picked him up again before he could tumble over it. The dentist came out to hand a form to the girl and Matt made introductions. "He's adorable but I don't know," she said again, shaking her head. "He could fall off the boat so easily. Are they good swimmers?"

All dogs could swim but Shih Tzus weren't designed very well for it, the dentist said. Their short little legs couldn't propel their square bodies efficiently. They didn't require a lot of exercise, though, so that would make them good boat dogs and he too thought they were smart. "I may be biased," he laughed. "I absolutely love the breed. And they're good with kids," he said before returning to his patient, "although they do tend to hide from the toddlers."

"Nothing to hide from on our boat," Shirley said and he was gone but her sour tone wasn't lost on the receptionist who half turned from her computer to better catch the exchange. "I don't think so, Matt," she said with finality and picked up her purse.

"Well, he's ours, Shirley. I bought him already." He tried to keep the desperation from his voice. The puppy was tired out and curled against his chest, his eyes meeting Matt's in a long searching gaze before seeking the warmth of an armpit. "Let's discuss this outside," Matt said.

"No, Matt." She wouldn't take the puppy while he drove, so he handed her the keys and got into the passenger side. "You seem to be making all the decisions so I'm afraid it's all yours," she said. "I won't be responsible for it while you're gone all day either. I hope you bought a crate or something for it." Shirley pulled into the marina lot. "And while we're having all of these surprises, this is a good time to tell you that I've decided to spend some time with my mother. I'll drive my car down and at this point, I don't know how long I'll be gone."

"You're leaving us."

She laughed in a sarcastic way. "I'm leaving you, Matthew. You left me some time ago."

"That's totally unfair and you know it." Now he was mad and he slammed the car door hard. He had done all he knew how to do for her. The babies just died, God damn it. The puppy never moved but Matt soothed him anyway. Poor little guy.

"You think I didn't see you with that fat Dodie or Dorie or whatever her name is the other night? Your hands were all over her. Everybody saw it, especially little Miss Sarah."

"She's not fat," he protested but then he didn't know what else say. She was right, probably. Thank God there wasn't anyone else in the parking lot because Shirley was not speaking softly.

"And you think I don't know there are other women too, Matthew? Sarah moons over you like you're some kind of a hero and now that Dorie. And what about all those extra nights 'on the job' in Tallahassee or Beaufort or Savannah?" Her hands were fists and he thought she might punch him and reflexively shielded the little one.

"There are no other women, Shirley, I swear." And she did punch him then, a good one in the shoulder, before she started to cry and stomped off toward their dock. Where in God's name had that come from? She hadn't hit the puppy but it was startled and began to tremble in his arms. "Fine. Let her go," he stroked the sweet, warm floppy ears with a big hand as he watched her storm down the pier. He couldn't make her enjoy life and maybe her mother could do something for her. Maureen was a pistol. "Happy," he said to the pup, "I'm going to call you Happy because that's what we're going to be together."

He decided to avoid his boat for a while, let her cool down. Maybe he was just no good with women, not meant to be married. He had been the one to initiate the divorce the last time, though, and he wondered how it would feel to be the one left behind. "Hey, Lady, look what I've got here," he called and saw the enormous woman heave herself out of her chair and call to VJ who was somewhere in the back.

"Well, now, ain't that the sweetest thing I seen in a long time." Happy's eyes never even opened when she cradled him against her cushiony bosom; in fact, he made a noise very close to a snore, and they looked at each other and laughed. "Happy is a good name for this one," she agreed when he told her.

"How you, Matt. What you got there?" VJ joined them on the dock. He had had the infected tooth pulled and was back to normal, even to the cold cigar in his mouth but this time on the left side. He spat into the lake and beamed at the puppy in Lady's arms. "Ain't that something?"

"What are you doing with a that, VJ?" Matt demanded. "You want to start that misery all over again?"

"I know, I know," VJ waved his cigar, "but I got somepin wrong with my generator and my pump back there keeps runnin too. I don't know what's wrong and I got to chew on somepin, you know, when I so worried and all. You know that the power done gone out twict last week."

"It did? I didn't know that," Matt said.

"Yahuh," Lady confirmed it.

"I think they fixing the highway up the mountain to the lodge. Must be when you was gone. Didn't but last a few minutes the one time but then the other time it was maybe couple hours. Didn't Shirley say nothing?"

He sighed and decided to bring it out into the open. "Shirley hasn't been speaking to me lately, VJ. She's got some crazy idea that I've been cheating on her when I'm on the road." He looked from VJ to Lady. "I haven't been except that I did dance with Dorie Langford a lot at the party. I do admit that. I got a little carried away with Dorie that night, but otherwise, I don't know where that idea would come from." He waited for a moment but when there was no response from either of them, he shrugged. "Well, let's take a look at that generator, then. You've got to have it."

"You come in and sit down first, Matt," Lady said and grunted with the effort of lifting herself up the small step and onto the boat without jostling the sleeping dog.

"He's due to piddle again," Matt warned her.

"Shoo. Little puppy pee can't hurt a thing on this old tub," she said. "Vernon, you go look into that leak some more. I need to talk to Matt here."

"I done looked at it all I can, Lady," VJ protested.

"Vernon, get you a little Jack first," she said and he stopped grumbling, got his three ice cubes in his glass and went aft. They could hear the pump go on and water splashing when he opened the patio door.

"She said she was going to do something," Lady looked at him sympathetically after he told her, her beautiful eyes warm with concern. "It's too bad this little guy didn't change her mind." When Happy woke up and began to twitch and wiggle, she reached for a dishtowel and set him down on it until he peed on it, and she gave Happy a shallow plate of water to lap at before he settled down to chewing on the toe of her slipper. "Shirley's troubles are bigger than we know about. Let her go for a while, Matt," she said after she sank back down into her chair.

He snorted. "Like I have a choice. I just wish her mother liked me or at least respected me."

"Why?"

"Well…" Why indeed. He sat back on the couch, his big legs thrust out in front of him. "Well…" he began again and made a steeple of his thick fingers, "Shirley wasn't like this when I met her. She was always a serious person but we had fun together and she traveled with me lots of times until the miscarriages put an end to that. Did you know that she was a Systems Analyst for General Motors when we met? She's no dummy." Lady just nodded while he rattled on. He had no idea where he was going with this. "She gave up her job to be with me and to make a family and now here we are nine years later with nothing to show. I was fifty last October—you remember the party?" She did. "I tried very hard after the miscarriages to get her to apply for adoption, but she wouldn't do it. And then the girls came along and all that sad mess. Now I'm too old. I'm not sure I even want a baby anymore. Hell, I'd look like the grandfather instead of the dad." He reached down to gently stroke his puppy who had fallen asleep on his stomach with a mouthful of slipper, his legs spread in four directions. How did he do that?

Lady rocked gently in the barrel chair, her hands folded across her huge stomach. Her entire attention was focused on listening to him, a special way she had of really hearing what he was saying. "Do you want her?" she asked, point blank, and he took his time really thinking about that.

"I want her like she was before," he said after several minutes in which Lady had just looked at him patiently. "Not sad all the time and so darned skinny." He ran his hands through his hair in frustration. "She does eat, you know, even though she doesn't cook much anymore. I don't understand it. I've suggested we see a doctor but she won't do that either."

Vernon reappeared and motioned toward his bottle and Lady nodded her okay and waved him to the back again. "You've heard of bulimia, Matt."

He looked at her blankly. Of course he had heard of it. Bulimics gorged themselves and then threw up, gagged themselves to upchuck when they over-ate. Binge eating, it was called. They were akin to anorexics. "Are you saying that's Shirley's problem? But when does she throw up? I don't hear her throwing up."

"Ah, the joys of living aboard and letting the Tennessee River swallow up your pain," Lady said sadly. "I don't know it for a fact, Matt. We had lunch at Jack's when we visited the graves in Atlanta and then, about fifteen minutes later, she said she didn't feel well and stopped at a gas station bathroom. I could hear her gagging and throwing up in there and I tried to get her to tell me, but she said it was bad hamburger or something. Mine was fine."

"Well, I'll be damned."

"I want you to call Maureen and tell her you're worried about bulimia or something like it. Let her mama try to get her to a doctor. She's close with one of her sisters too, ain't she? She talks about that one Gloria sometimes." Matt nodded. "Well, you call her and tell her that same thing. You've done all you can. A person can only do so much for someone else. After that you've just got to live your life. But I will say this…" she rolled over in her chair to put a meaty arm on his, waking Happy who reluctantly let go of her slipper and decided to snooze on his side. "I don't think being a liveaboard is the answer for Shirley. I know her well enough now to say that. I don't know what the answer is but she's not a water person. It gives her no peace."

"That leak be from the fresh water tank, Lady!" Vernon burst upon them, panic in his face. "Sweet Jesus, now we got no generator and no fresh water neither. Bad to worse. Things going bad to worse!"

"Take it easy, VJ," Matt stood up and stepped over the puppy. "Let me have a look."

Sure enough, there was very little water left in the 50-gallon aluminum tank. The tank had broken, probably split from old age, and all the water had run down into the bilge. Thank goodness VJ's aft flotation pump was working. At over eight pounds per gallon, that was 400 pounds of water, not enough to sink the boat but a lot of unnecessary weight. More important, if the marina water line broke, the Johnsons would have no drinking water at all except what they could carry aboard.

"You'll have to look in a boating catalog and order a replacement," Matt said.

"I don't rightly have no up-to-date catalog," VJ said. "I don't order too much."

"I've got them all, VJ." Matt measured the space available for a new tank. "It'll be a bitch getting the old one out but it has to be done. Let's look at the generator."

"She was working just fine," VJ explained. "I thought maybe I lost my prime but I used Lady's turkey baster and still nothing. She turns to start but she don't hold."

"Uh huh." Matt fiddled with a few things. "You have a gas tank gauge on this thing?"

"Course I do, what you think?" he bristled.

"Now don't get your dander up. I happen to know that Fred Langford has to use a stick to measure the diesel fuel level on that old Chris Craft."

"Well, this ain't that old," VJ said. "It's a 1980 and it got gas gauges."

At the helm Matt turned the keys and the port engine read full but the starboard read empty. VJ's eyebrows rose above his black-rimmed glasses. "You have a cross-over valve for the fuel?" Matt asked.

"Sure, but it always open. I never shut it. Why ever would I shut it?"

Matt went back to check and it was open, all right. He returned to the helm and rapped sharply on the port gauge three or four times. The needle dove to empty. "You don't have any gas in your tanks, VJ," he said with disgust.

VJ, however, was delighted with the news. "Well, I be dawg," he laughed. "No gas, huh? Well, that's one on me all right! I surely didn't realize we was down to it, no sir. No gas. I can fix that easy, yes sir."

He danced around the puppy, who was awake and probably very hungry by now, Matt realized. "You come on back to my boat with me and we'll look in the catalogs," he said and was glad when the foolish man agreed. He needed a buffer with Shirley and he needed to feed his new dog.

But Shirley was already gone by the time they returned to the Monticello. Her side of the medicine cabinet was cleaned out, most of her clothes gone, not even a note of goodbye. "Well, she fast," VJ waved that awful cigar but Matt was glad he didn't have to face this moment alone.

"Just let me get Happy squared away," he said as he scooped the canned Science Diet Puppy food into a shallow dish and heated it for a few seconds in the microwave before setting it out. "Don't want him to have trouble digesting this," he explained.

"Uh huh," VJ sipped from his paper cup. "You sign him up for college yet? They say to do that right soon as they born now."

"Shut up," Matt had to laugh in spite of himself. The puppy sent out his pink tongue to test his supper, found it pleasing and gulped it down, licking the plate with satisfaction before uttering a tremendous belch and curling up beside the dish for a post-meal nap.

"He fast too!" VJ observed and Matt began to laugh at the absurdity of it all and perused his liquor cabinet. Normally he wasn't much of drinker, but maybe tonight would be an exception.

Lady called VJ on his cell phone several hours later and told him to come home and VJ said he would be home "tirectly" and then stayed on for another hour or so. They had checked all the books and had found a 55-gallon polyethylene tank with close to the right dimensions in the *Defender* catalog. Matt estimated the cost to be about $220, including shipping, if they could wait for five or six-day ground delivery.

"Oh me," VJ moaned. Matt said that if he lived in a house he would have upkeep costs, so why did he think there shouldn't be any upkeep on his boat? "I ain't got no choice now, do I?" he moaned again, holding his head.

"Tell you what," Matt said. "I'll buy you that water tank and in exchange, you take care of Happy for me while I'm at work. I have one more road trip, just to Atlanta for a couple of days to wrap things up for the next guy, and then I'll be in Huntsville, like I told you about. I got a crate for him in the car and you and Lady can put him in that when you want to, but I just can't leave him alone all day." The puppy had curled into a fat ball and Matt bent to stroke him again. He just couldn't resist that softness.

VJ gave him a hard look. "I know you ain't from around here," VJ said seriously, "so I excuse you." Matt looked up in confusion. "We take the little dog for you this week till you get yourself situated, but we don't take no money for it, see? And we don't want no dog full-time or we would get us one. We had plenty dogs in our time, dogs and kids, and we done with that." VJ wasn't exactly sober but those beady eyes magnified behind thick glasses were still looking at him hard.

"I didn't mean…"

"No, now that's all right. You wouldn't know. About the money, now, Lady and me, we depression children. You know about the Great Depression?" Matt nodded. "We got a little more than we let on, see? My boy Reginald, you met Reginald? Well, that landscaping business he got in Grant, we got a part of that for setting him up in that."

"But…"

VJ waved him quiet. "I know, I know. I moan and carry on about every little nickel. Lady says it drive her crazy and sometimes. I don't know. Seems like I do it out of habit or something." He finally rose to go home, said "Oh boy!" and staggered against the arm of the chair before steadying himself. "You a good man, Matthew. I order that tank tomorrow morning and maybe you help me put it in if you around?"

Matt walked him home and handed him over to Lady, who just shook her head as her husband stumbled onto the boat and straight back to bed. "I'll have to bring Happy by at about 6:30 tomorrow," he apologized. She said he should just pound on the door to wake them up, if need be.

It was after 10 by the time he had carried all of the supplies from the car to the boat, ate supper, played with Happy and even got him to poop on the puppy pad. He tucked him into his crate, which he covered with a towel and squeezed alongside his bed. The guest stateroom had a queen bed but very little floor space and then he thought, what the hell am I doing? He dragged the crate into the master stateroom where it belonged. When he finally crawled between the sheets, he was prepared to sense his wife there, lying where she had been only last night, but he experienced nothing, not even her scent. He felt something lumpy under a pillow and pulled out a nightgown and breathed deeply into its softness, willing himself to be moved by a feeling of loss, of loneliness, of Shirley gone. But he felt only one thing, relief.

CHAPTER 11

❀

There are eleven sailboats at Sunset Marina and sail boaters tend to stay pretty much to themselves on the uncovered dock. They generally even sail the same areas of the lake together, places where they don't have to tack so often to avoid the shallows. Sailboat Dave is the only liveaboard on a sailboat, which is perhaps why he tends to socialize more with the power boaters who are around all winter.

Jimmy Lassiter has little use for sail boaters and calls them cheap S.O.B.s who would buy his fuel by the cup if he would sell it that way. Fern Hoppe from Hoppe's Marina on the Mississippi River calls them "whistle pissers" because after finding out the price of gas or diesel fuel, they whistle in disbelief and then ask to use her head.

Dave is not insulted by much of anything but certainly not by these epithets. He makes good money as a welder and says he lives very cheaply and well on his 34-foot Hunter. Several times a week, he eats the fish he loves to catch. What he can't fit in his propane-powered freezer, he gives away around the marina.

Although an avid fishermen, Dave is not at all interested in the many big fishing tournaments held at Lake Guntersville, like Bassmaster and other pro and amateur contests that offer big purses and feature big names. Even the Reader's Digest *lists Lake Guntersville as one of the four best places to catch largemouth bass and ESPN-2 tapes some of the events here. But Dave is one-quarter Cherokee, not unusual for this part of Alabama in which both Lakeside and Guntersville are on the Cherokee Trail of Tears. In fact, the man after whom Guntersville was named was married to a full-blooded Cherokee and the founder of Lakeside to a Creek. Dave likes to fish for what he can eat, not play with. Maybe that's just part of his heritage.*

—A Genuine Liveaboard

Sailboat Dave and VJ used Jimmy Lassiter's dolly to get the new water tank down the dock and onto the back of VJ's boat. It wasn't so much heavy as unwieldy in size and they knew they'd have as much trouble getting the new one down through the opening as they'd had getting the old one up and out. VJ was going to put the broken tank in the dumpster but Sailboat asked it he could have it. "Maybe I can weld it and use it for something," he said.

"You ain't thinking about a holding tank for John, is you?" VJ asked, "cause I don't know if these here tanks is all made the same way."

"A tank is a tank," Sailboat shrugged.

"But it ain't designed to be pumped out. The openings ain't right," VJ insisted.

"So we make a bigger orifice here and put in a vent here," Sailboat had demonstrated. "But I got to see if it'll take a weld first."

"If it work, John going to kiss you," VJ laughed.

"You know us 'whistle pissers' will try to fix anything," Sailboat smiled, his teeth very white against his broad dark cheeks.

"You still got that new gal friend, what's her name, Cindy?"

"I don't know. She's turning out to be more of just a friend, you know?"

"Your age, I don't think so," Vernon looked at him sideways. "What you think about Yolanda. She's a real nice girl, she don't drink so much. What you think?"

"I think Yolanda is big trouble, VJ. Ronald the Mooch been seeing her, you know." He shook his head. "I like to drink my beer and I like to get stoned, I won't deny that to you, but that one is trouble. Anyhow, I met another one now seems to be fine. I met her at that Powwow over at the flats."

"Huh." VJ pondered this information, kicking the new tank a little to hear it reverberate but the plastic just made a dull thud.

"How's it coming along?" Lady wanted to know as she slid the aft patio door open. She had all she could do to hold the squirming puppy in her arms, its tail going a mile a minute.

"Who's this?" Sailboat asked. He reached to pet Happy, making his joy complete. "You're Happy, all right," he agreed, letting the puppy chew on his fingers for a while.

"You working next week?" Lady asked him. He said he was, far as he knew. "Matt got to find someone to take care of him. One week is all I can take, cute as he is. I'm just not up to him."

"What's wrong with Shirley?" he asked and just nodded when they told him. "Something happens and I don't work, I'll take him."

They got the new water tank installed that afternoon and settled back in the sun on the front deck with Miller Lite and Jack Daniels. Sailboat said he would watch Happy for a while, and Lady gratefully delivered him into his arms and went inside for a solitaire game. "You think all them cormorants ruin the fishing eventual?" VJ wanted to know. "Seems like they got to. The count bigger than ever this year." They watched the fat little guy chew on a worn tennis shoe that Lady had given him, his ears perking up from time to time at birdcalls. When a fish jumped, he made a beeline for the water and Sailboat had to leap up to stop him. No wonder Lady was tired.

"Well, maybe they're making the fishing better, did you ever think of that? Maybe they're eating all the little ones and allowing more food for the bigger ones. The TVA electroshocked a ten-pound, three-ounce bass right near Waterfront Grocery, can you believe it. Stop that, Happy. Just stay put for a minute. Guy said there would be a picture of it in the *Lakeside News.*"

"Huh." Another idea to digest.

"What about Robert Marvel to take Happy? Maybe Gracie and Happy would hit it off just fine," Sailboat suggested. VJ didn't think that would work because Gracie would be too jealous.

"What you think bout that fisherman drowned over to Short Creek under the bridge? That be the third one to drown in this here lake already this year. You a fisherman. What you make of it?" Sailboat shrugged, put his knees together, and turned the squirming puppy over onto its back. He rubbed its belly and chest in slow circular motions and Happy sighed and went to sleep immediately. Sailboat turned him over to let him curl up in his lap. "No wonder you always got a woman!" VJ watched with admiration.

Sailboat snorted. "Women ain't ever as easy as dogs."

Vernon leaned over, lowered his voice, and took his cigar out of his mouth. "Those gals let you sleep with em? Let you do what you want to with em?" he whispered, beady eyes open wide behind black-rimmed glasses.

"How you doing with that puppy?" Lady asked through the screen and Vernon jumped in his chair and pretended to have a coughing spell and then really did have one while Sailboat laughed.

"We're doing fine, Lady." He would have thumped VJ on the back but didn't want to wake Happy.

"Yahuh." She went back to the game.

"Those fishermen weren't wearing life jackets, if I heard it right." VJ nodded when he could. That was true. "You maybe don't notice, but I always wear one when I'm fishing in my dinghy. I spent the extra money on a suspender-type preserver that self inflates because it's cooler on a hot day, but I always wear one."

"Huh."

"And I always wear a jacket in bed with my girlfriends, too," he murmured into VJ's ear as he plopped Happy in VJ's lap and left. This conversation would give VJ enough to think about for days.

Fred had found a new exhaust riser through the guy in Florida who found it in Albuquerque, New Mexico, of all places, and for a mere $500 plus shipping, had it sent to Aqua where it was waiting for them. It was unused but had been made in 1972 or 1973. Fred was elated when he actually saw the riser in the parts department at the Aqua Yacht Harbor marina. "Nice hunk of metal!" Dorie had tried to fake excitement but Fred just looked at her and she decided to keep quiet. It could be installed in-water, but since they were having *Sun Spot* pulled anyway, it was easier to do while she was in the sling. They would go ahead and make up the heat-resistant gaskets needed for the job.

"Sling, what's this about a sling?" she wanted to know, and Fred pointed to a huge machine with four wheels and posts from which draped two big cloth bands. The idea was to drive the boat into the cement bay while the bands were underneath the keel, and then the machine would slowly lift *Spot* up out of the water. Fred showed her small metal "Sling" tabs on the hull that indicated where the slings should go so that the boat had bulkhead support. She couldn't imagine any fabric strong enough to lift 33 tons.

The diesel expert said he thought the leak in the port fuel tank might be in the ballcock shutoff valve. They would have to pump out most of the fuel in the tank to find out. Fred had figured on that and had purposely run low on the trip. *Spot* had twin 250-gallon tanks, a lot of pumping if they were full.

The port transmission had worked just well enough but he could hear a grinding noise which disturbed him. They took it for a test run and sure enough, the mechanic heard it too, and when they got back to the slip, several guys pulled out the curving staircase and the floorboards beneath it to get at the Allison transmission. When they took off the transmission screen filter, they found small granules of bearing steel and they knew a bearing was disintegrating and that soon the transmission wouldn't work at all. Trouble was, with the flywheel the thing weighed 800 pounds, so getting it out was going to take a crane and then they didn't know who could rebuild it. Best house for that was up in Green Bay, Wisconsin.

Fred asked if realigning the engines might have had anything to do with the transmission trouble. They didn't know. Sometimes these old boats had operated so long with things out of whack that putting one thing right again would mess up the whole business. While they were shoving things back into place and getting grease on everything, which they apologized for but really couldn't do much about, they said how lucky that it was the port transmission. If it were the starboard, they would have to move the entire galley and didn't know how to get that sucker out short of cutting a hole in the ceiling of the salon. Oh, by the way, that blower on the port engine didn't seem to be right either.

"Let's get off the boat and go out to a nice place for dinner tonight," Fred suggested at the end of that depressing day. "Were you able to arrange for wheels?" She had, and she twirled the keys in triumph. In fact, the marina was nice enough to let them keep the keys until the morning so they could stay out as long as they liked. During busier times, they allowed the van out for only an hour or two at a time. At least that's what she thought had transpired. She really couldn't understand all of it, the accent was so thick, and she hadn't wanted to ask the dock master to keep repeating himself. "Great. So, where do we go?"

"We go to Tennessee, right over the border there," she pointed out the window. "Tishomingo County, Mississippi, where we are right now, is dry. It's so dry, liquor trucks have to drive around it."

"You're kidding."

"That's the story I was told. Hard to believe with all the booze I've already seen being carted down these docks. Anyhow, the cops always harass them if they try to go through. But there are a couple of nice places over that border. They can't serve alcohol outright, but if we take our own wine or whatever, they do set-ups, like a private club."

They found one called Willie G's, its art deco motif of stylized palm trees and neon booth dividers at odds with the country western music blaring from the speakers but nobody seemed to notice. They sat in the busy bar for a drink before dinner and Dorie was surprised when Fred asked her to dance. Too early for the band, no one else was dancing yet and their tennis shoes stuck to the floor and jerked them up short every once in a while until the cutie came from behind the bar and sprinkled dance wax around. Lots of it. Then they did the skaters' waltz until they gave up. They were tired and hungry anyway. On the way to their table they noticed several rows of locked mailboxes lined up in a hallway. "Neat idea for booze lockers," Dorie told the young man with the menus and he said something in Mississippi, which she took to be an affirmation. She just couldn't get through that accent. Apparently the problem was mutual.

"Where y'all from?" the waitress asked after they had verbally arm-wrestled through the menu, grilled fresh tuna for her and a steak for Fred.

"Alabama," Fred replied and had laughed when she looked askance. "Well, I've lived in Alabama longer than anywhere else, honey, is all I can say," and she had to be satisfied with that.

"You don't have trouble communicating with the boat guys at Aqua," Dorie pointed out.

"I think they're from all over. Besides they speak in 'Boat Repair,' a very expensive dialect but very easy to understand." He blew out his breath in disgust.

"We agreed not to talk about it tonight, honey," she patted his hand. "Tomorrow we'll hash it out."

"You know, it's occurred to me that we hardly ever talk about the kids anymore." She peered into his eyes to see if this was a complaint but he seemed mostly curious. "Do they even know we're here, for instance?"

"Of course they know! We have a system. Didn't you know that?" He shook his head no while he buttered a slice of bread. "I'm sure I told you, Fred," but he shook his head again. "We have this system where I call Mindy in Nashville, she calls Teddy in Omaha, he calls Janie in Nevada and she calls Freddie in San Diego. Freddie calls us if there's any news we should know about. They all know exactly where we are and what we're doing. Everybody but Janie thinks we're crazy, by the way, but they want to know all about what we're doing with *Spot*. I thought I told you all this."

He shrugged. "I guess you did. They're good kids, aren't they, Dorie?"

"Yes, Fred they are."

"And the tadpoles are good too, aren't they?" He was just tired enough and had had just enough gin to become maudlin, and she assured him that the grandchildren were very good too. "Teddy's back on track now, isn't he? No more drugs. I know what you went through with him, Dorie, and I'm sorry I wasn't around more to help." She assured him again but he squeezed her hand, his blue eyes misting up and thank God the entrees came before he dissolved in tears. The food, followed by coffee, revived them both. "The band sounds pretty good from here," Fred looked at her expectantly, his eyes clear again. "What do you think?"

The band was good and they danced until past midnight, delighted with each other as they rediscovered their old steps and signals. By then the floor was so crowded with youngsters there was no room to move anymore, even if they had been physically able to move anymore. The manager stopped them on the way out and handed them breath mints and said something to the effect of being careful of the "po'lice" and a "D-U-AH" and fast lumber trucks. Fred thanked him and they safely drove the short distance back to the marina exactly five miles under the speed limit.

They were awakened before 8 the next morning by pounding on the side of the boat. "Sorry to do this to you so early, Mr. Langford, but we can get you lifted out today after all. We'll bring some of the heavier tools aboard now and help you with your lines and all."

"Should I stay on the boat?" Dorie yelled up as she hustled into jeans and a clean tee shirt and Fred started up the engines. Maybe she really was losing weight, she thought. Her clothes were feeling mighty roomy. Fred thought she should get off. The main salon would be so torn up that he didn't know if she could even get to the head if she stayed. She grabbed a hooded sweatshirt and a good book and watched as *Sun Spot* left the slip, and then she ran up the pier and over to the cement bay to watch her glide in. The operator adjusted the straps over the metal tabs, revved up the powerful motor and up *Spot* came, creaking and groaning and swaying but safe enough in the sling for several workers to climb like monkeys onto the bow pulpit and disappear below.

She hadn't even brushed her teeth and she waved to Fred before she walked up the steep hill to the office building in hopes of finding a vending machine for coffee. No machine but pots were brewing in every department and she cadged a couple of paper cups full and trudged back down the hill to place one on the bow pulpit for Fred. "My lord, you're a lifesaver," he shimmied out for it and sat on the deck to sip at it gratefully while she stood on the apron below. She hadn't realized how tired he looked, his eyes bloodshot, cheeks droopy, and hair all over the place. She suspected that she didn't look much smarter. "What are we, nuts, Dorie? I can't think of a place on my body that doesn't hurt. How are you holding up?"

"Bout the same, I'm afraid," she laughed, and wished for a stool or anything to sit down on.

"I'm going to have that one guy take another look at the port transmission today as long as we have all the floor boards up. You know we're looking at twelve thousand dollars, probably more, and God knows how long to rebuild it." His head sagged between his shoulders. "I could kick myself. I thought I was so clever having the shaft logs straightened. Probably never happened if I'd just left them be."

"No use crying over spilt milk and all that, Fred," Dorie said but she was shocked at the cost and couldn't hide that entirely.

"I'm sorry, honey. I might as well have him start to take the port blower apart too. Some of the oily smell was probably coming from there too because there's a crack in the housing. They send in the whole part and get a rebuilt part in exchange. That's eleven hundred dollars minimum but at least that's not my fault. Maybe," he added ruefully. "Do you think you could get some more of this coffee? And maybe a roll or something? I need all the help I can get this morning."

"Sure," she sighed. "Should I line up somebody to come and get us?"

"Wait just a little bit longer. Maybe something good will happen."

By the end of the day the diesel expert had fixed the fuel leak, and others had installed the new manifold part. They lowered *Spot* and fired up the engines and determined that both problems were solved. "No more stinky fuel smell?" Dorie called to Fred over the racket.

"No more stink!" he yelled back. He had had them replace the ballcock spigot on the starboard engine too. But he wasn't at all happy with the work that still had to be done, and they stayed aboard that night in the work bay with a long extension cord running from *Spot* up to the building for power. "This will take weeks," he said in despair, picking at his microwaved potpie. His original budget had been blown out of the water. "And the boat will be unusable for weeks!" he ranted.

Dorie had had all day to think. "Freddy…" she began.

"Freddy? Don't you mean 'Dumbass'? You never call me Freddy!"

"Freddy Boy," she laughed at his glum expression, "y'all lighten up and listen to me now, honey chile." He almost smiled. "Fred, in a way, if this had to happen, it's good that it happened now. Suppose we had been on a trip and away from everything when the transmission or the blower went out. We would be stuck, right? And we'd still end up having the work done somehow." He grumbled but she ignored it. "Let's use this opportunity to go to the house and really get it in order to sell." His head came up on that. "We said we would be ready for the kids to come and take what they wanted by Easter week. Well, that's only eighteen days away. Let's concentrate on doing just that and not think about anything else."

"Be liveaboards?" he asked hopefully. "I figured this might sour you completely on the idea. What if *Spot* just keeps breaking down? Pretty soon we've worked our asses off and have 250K tied up in an old boat and can't afford to go anywhere in her."

"Do you honestly think that will happen?"

"No, I believe she's basically sound. And I also believe that before I do anything drastic to her again, I 'believe' I'll get an expert opinion."

"Let's plan to live aboard for a while, anyway," she smiled. "We've outgrown that big house regardless. I haven't even thought about all the stuff I knew I couldn't live without just a few weeks ago. It's always just stuff and what we're spending is always just money. If we run out, you might have to go back to work for a while. That's the worst that could happen."

"True," he nodded, beginning to cheer up. "I never thought of it like that. I don't get Social Security yet so anything I'd earn would be gravy. But that would be the 'worse case scenario,' as they used to say, because I'd much rather be boating."

"And I'd much rather be dancing with my husband than dusting Grandma Rosalind's china."

"You would, huh?" He was definitely smiling now. "Me too." He kissed her cheek. "What about the kids? You think they'll want to visit us on the boat?"

"I honestly don't think we should even worry about that, Fred. They'll come, they'll see what it is, and they'll figure it out. As you reminded me, they're not kids anymore. Let them work it out."

"You've always been able to see the bright side, Dorie."

"Okay, I'll call Margery Steel to come get us."

"Who?"

"Margery from my Master Gardener's club. You remember I took her daughter back to school in South Carolina when Margery's mother was so sick."

"Don't remember that at all."

"Well, she will. And if she can't do it, she'll find someone who will."

"You know, Dorie, something just occurred to me." He put his arms around her shoulders and kissed her. "I honestly wouldn't know who to call if I had to. I don't have friends the way you do."

"You just haven't had the time to make any, honey. Don't worry about that at all."

Margery came late morning the next day and they were "home" before dark.

CHAPTER 12

֎

In 2003, Guntersville was the only town in Alabama to be listed by a national web site called Relocate-America as one of 100 best places to live in America. It was one of only 18 places of less than 10,000 people listed. A company called HomeRoute runs the website and used the following as its top criteria: safety, activities, serenity, beauty, good schools, a healthy economy, and great neighbors. People who go to the Relocate America website learn that "The mountains in the distance complement the waters by projecting a perpetual, soothing setting found in very few cities anywhere." Well, hoorah for Guntersville, which has a very active Chamber of Commerce, but its neighbor Lakeside is even better, some people think, a well-kept secret, and they like it that way.

The boating season for most people on Lake Guntersville runs from Memorial Day to Labor Day, which is strange when many liveaboards think that late April, May, September, October, November, and even early December are good for boating, but folks are tied in with that old-time school vacation thinking. Stranger still because school vacations don't even correspond with the "season" anymore.

On good weather weekends during the season, "serene" isn't exactly the right word to describe Sunset. It's not as busy as its bigger neighbors but it hums with engines of all types, noisy wakes, children playing, dogs barking and dock parties. Some liveaboards are thankful for a short season.

—A Genuine Liveaboard

"Shirley's driving up from Florida this weekend," Matt told them at the party on Marlene and Randall's beautiful 1967 Hatteras. It was fiberglass but had lots of wood inside and out, which Randall kept in pristine condition through constant vigilance. He was forever sanding and putting on "just one more coat" and you could see your face in the transom, which Matt caressed absent-mindedly. "Be here around noon tomorrow." They were all looking for relief from the August sun and had spread their lawn chairs wherever they could find some shade. The party wouldn't really get started until sundown. "She hasn't seen Happy since he was a newborn," he said and smiled as the half-grown puppy rushed to Marlene who bent down to pick him up and talk baby talk to him. Marlene and Randall took him during the day while he was at the Huntsville office. He didn't know what he would have done without them. They were crazy about the dog and a sweeter disposition on an animal was hard to find. Happy was a joyful creature.

"How do you feel about seeing her again?" Ronald the Mooch asked, bringing him back to reality. "Sit down here, Yolanda," he peeled the miniature woman from his side and pulled a chair over for her.

"Okay, honeybun," she smiled sweetly at Ronald and sat down, crossing her matchstick legs and sipping delicately on a cold beer.

"I'm scared to death," Matt said. "We talk once in a while but she never has much to say, and it's been four months. She says she's been seeing a doctor and feels much better about everything though. She's put on some weight, she says. Oh lord," he said as he spilled his drink gesturing with it. "I shouldn't be drinking at all. It's too hot to drink." He felt miserable. The last four months had been so pleasant, so stress free. He had spent long hours starting up the new office, but he had enjoyed it more than he thought he would. He didn't miss being on the road and even if he got home late, Happy was pleased to see him. He could take the puppy out on the boat whenever he felt like it, puttering over to Short Creek or Honeycomb on hot nights like this one. Most times he came back in at first light so he could walk Happy on land, let him stretch his legs and run some before Matt got cleaned up for work. He didn't feel cooped up in that little office at all knowing he could slip those lines and be free.

Happy didn't like to swim, as the dentist had predicted, but he loved watching the water. Matt figured he thought it was alive, the way it moved, and Happy was most contented when there were small waves lapping at the hull. He had found his voice but barked very seldom, only when you played with him or when he was frightened. He was incapable of harming anyone but was a good watchdog in that way. This sweet little doggie had helped Matt stay away from Dorie Langford, and Matt had poured all of his affection out on the little guy who had welcomed it, lapped it up and asked for more. So now what? Would Shirley insist on getting rid of him? Marlene and Randall would take him in a minute. They were talking now of getting one of their own. Jesus. And he had felt sorry for Robert Marvel and Gracie.

"The new water tank fixed up real good," VJ was telling them, "but I done got another leak somewheres. Darn me can I find it. Seem to be coming right up out the bottom!" His skinny legs were dark brown now, not as dark as Sailboat Dave's, but colorful. He wore plaid shorts and a tank top because of the heat but insisted on his heavy black winter shoes with thick soles and droopy white socks. "My feet don't like them skimpy tennis things," he said. A brand new half-price haircut, the shaved bottom band looking even whiter against his tan, completed his ensemble.

"Maybe it is coming up from the bottom," Jimmy Lassiter said. "When did you have that boat pulled out last?"

"It's a aluminum hull, Jimmy. It don't have to be pulled out." VJ pointed his cigar at him. "And what you doing talking business at a party, huh?"

"I'm not talking business, VJ. I'm just saying you could have some pitting from electrolysis. You got zincs on that thing?"

"Sure I got zincs."

"Yeh? Where are they?"

VJ walked away from him in disgust to join another group. "Man think he know every damn thing there is," he grumbled. "What are zincs?" he asked Fred. Zinc deteriorates from electrolysis before aluminum will, Fred explained, so you put pieces of zinc on the hull and replace them if they disappear because the aluminum will be attacked next. Some people hang a big piece where they can check on it easily. VJ could also install a galvanic isolator but he would still want the zincs. "Where your zincs be at?" Vernon demanded. "I want to see them things." Fiberglass boats used them only on the propeller drive shafts and rudders. They didn't work on fiberglass. "This ain't my year," VJ moaned. "First the water tank and now I got to pay to have the damn thing lifted over to Alred's! And I probly got to buy me some zincs on top of that!"

"You're complaining to the wrong boater," Fred said with a grimace. They had paid a huge bill before leaving Aqua and the small ones still kept coming in the mail. Thank God they had finally gotten a good offer on the house. Interest rates had just begun to go back up and anybody even considering buying a home was in a hurry, so it looked like they would close on it soon. "Besides, you've got to have your boat pulled at least every five years for the insurance company, don't you? I do."

"S'cuse me, Freddy. You very smart an all but I got to find my Jack." VJ almost went home, he was that depressed, but he took a good swig right from the bottle, so what if Lady shook her finger at him, and then he found Georgie Lassiter standing kind of alone and she was one attractive gal even if her husband was an ass. Jimmy made him sign that he had boat insurance but never asked to see it and a good thing because he never had no boat insurance. Wouldn't have no car insurance neither if it wasn't the law and if he didn't drink regular and wasn't afraid of getting stopped without it. Especially since the accident. All them Yankee insurance companies was too rich as it was. Hell, by the time you paid the deductible, you might just as well pay the whole dang thing. "Hey, sweet thang," he smiled at Georgie who smiled back in her usual sweet way. He looked for her sourpuss husband but Jimmy was busy shooting his mouth off to another group, as usual, and he sidled up to Georgie. Opposites sure did seem to attract one another.

"This is Abigail," Sailboat introduced his new girlfriend around.

Dorie couldn't believe it—another one with unbelievable skin and a long ponytail! Abigail was so pretty that Dorie said, "Princess Summer-Fall-Winter-Spring," before thinking and startled them both. "You're too young to know, but she was supposed to be a beautiful Indian princess on 'Howdy Doody.' I don't remember that she ever did anything but show off a gorgeous buckskin dress and lots of beaded jewelry, but I loved her. And her wonderful name, of course," Dorie laughed. They made her say it over again.

"I am half Cherokee and some Creek," Abigail smiled, "and I do have a beaded ceremonial dress made of deerskin that my aunts and my mom sewed for me. But my Cherokee name means 'Good Walker.' I think I like your 'Howdy Doody' name better."

"And do you have a Cherokee name too?" Dorie asked Sailboat but he said he didn't go in for that stuff much.

"Oh, he has one," Abigail assured her, and then drew back in mock terror when he glared at her. "I won't tell if you're nice to me," she batted her eyelashes at him.

"You better not," he growled and reached under all that hair to squeeze the back of her neck.

"What's the matter?" Dorie asked. "Does it translate into 'One Defeated by a Capon with a Cape On'?" They looked at her blankly until she explained.

"Close, very close," he grinned. "I just don't always feel comfortable with that Indian stuff."

"I don't know why he feels that way," Abigail said. "The first book written about anybody from this area was about Catherine Brown, who was half Cherokee. That was in 1825. Honest," she said when he looked doubtful. "It's called

Memoir of Catherine Brown, a Christian Woman of the Cherokee Nation. I'm teaching a class on Saturday mornings about our people's history in this area," she explained. "It's really fascinating. Our heritage is everywhere when you start to look. I mean, Guntersville has an elementary school named Cherokee. John Gunter and his second wife, a full-blooded Cherokee princess, were ancestors of Will Rogers."

"I'd go to Princess Summer-Fall-Winter-Spring's class," Sailboat said, "but I can already hear the fish calling my name."

"Me too," Abigail agreed. She cocked one hand around her mouth. "One Defeated by Neutered Chicken Wearing a Cape!" she called and everybody turned in confusion and Abigail laughed and blushed, looking even prettier.

The blistering sun finally dropped behind the mountains and Marlene and Randall set out citronella candles as insects began to attack bare legs and bare anything. "Watch those dogs for the candles now," Marlene warned but the big dogs knew enough to stay away and Robert Marvel had scooped up Gracie long ago. They would keep little Happy inside the boat until Matt was ready to take him home. He was still too unpredictable to be safe on the pier.

"What you done to yourself, Marlene?" Lady grabbed her arm as she was replenishing the snacks table and Marlene looked her straight in the eyes and without sunglasses.

"What do you mean, Lady?" Marlene laughed and fluttered her eyelashes. "I got one plain, brown tinted soft contact lens. It was Matt's idea and I wish I had done it years ago. What do you think?"

Lady shook her head. "I think it's wonderful. I got to tell you, Marlene, it was hard to know which eye to look at when they were so different. I just couldn't hardly get past that, for some reason." Marlene laughed again and patted her shoulder. "Get Vernon to help you with that shrimp boil, but don't let him do the salt. He always adds too much." Marlene said she would watch that.

"Abigail is gorgeous and smart," Dorie told Sailboat when she happened to be alone with him for a few minutes. "Looks like a keeper to me," but he just shrugged.

"She's coming down off a nasty divorce. I don't plan to rush anything. Get her on the rebound, you know."

"Get who on the rebound?" Ronald asked as he and Yolanda joined them. Yolanda seemed even tinier than usual, her blond mop pulled back and clipped to the top of her head, her blue eyes enormous and bright, a pixie in size 2 short shorts and halter top. She seemed to need to touch Ronald constantly, had glued herself to his side in the sticky heat, and even though the scorching sun had set, he squirmed uncomfortably from time to time.

"Oh we were just talking," Sailboat said. "You look real good tonight, Yolanda," he said politely.

"Well, I'm standing up," she smiled and stroked Ronald's arm, long blood red nails flashing. "I'm working at Chili's in Huntsville now? You ever been there? It's pretty good and good tips too, huh Ronald?" she looked up at him for confirmation.

"From what you tell me, honey. I'm not exactly a good judge of restaurant tips, now am I?" He didn't say it in a nasty way but without much enthusiasm either.

"The tips are real good," she said with emphasis and Dorie and Sailboat murmured their appreciation before Sailboat excused himself to see to his guest.

His departure didn't seem to faze Yolanda who leaned in on Dorie. "There was one guy with a big family, five kids, would you believe, but the wife wasn't with them for some reason and he left me a twenty? I mean, they only had hamburgers and fries and cokes so the bill wasn't that much even for six people so I nearly lost it when I seen the twenty?" Her voice was too animated and too loud, her eyes jumpy, never quite focused in the dying light. When Dorie stepped back, finding it uncomfortable to be so close to the girl, Yolanda moved right with her. "I mean, you don't get that everyday, you know? I snatched it up before he maybe realized he made a mistake and asked for change? Course then you get the other end of the stick and somebody doesn't like the way their steak is cooked or something and they leave you a penny or something just to be mean? There was this party of four…" Yolanda rattled on with more anecdotes, each statement ending in a question for some reason, and Dorie could only glance at Ronald with pity. He was embarrassed but didn't seem to know what to do about it. Dorie pasted a smile on her face and escaped as soon as she could. Maybe a passed-out Yolanda wasn't so bad.

She found a group discussing the War on Terror, opinions as divided now as they had been in the 2000 presidential election. "The Homeland Security Department, or whatever they call it, should be more concerned about dams," Bobby Ray was saying. "Al-Qaeda ever go after dams, watch out. And it would be easy, too. They don't have hardly no security at all. Anybody can get close enough to Guntersville Dam to throw a bomb, for instance, whenever they feel like it. Hell, they got picnic tables and grills right next to the main lock. And nobody checks out the towboat crews, I bet. Any one of them could carry a bomb right into the lock and blow it up from the inside. Scares me to death."

"Did you get your letter of appreciation from President Bush?" Jimmy Lassiter asked.

"What you talking about?" Vernon said.

"Why, the letter thanking you for helping the Marine Police to patrol the river in front of Redstone Arsenal during the weeks after 9/11." Nobody had gotten one. "Me neither," said Jimmy.

"You really something, you are," Vernon sputtered. "President Bush don't got to send no letter for something like that. He ain't got time for that."

"No, he's too busy raising ten million dollars every month for his re-election campaign," Jimmy said and that set off a real round of arguments.

"What do you hear from your boy in Iraq, Bobby Ray?" somebody asked but Bobby Ray just shook his head and wouldn't talk about it.

"Can of worms," is all he would say. "Can of worms."

Dorie went looking for Sarah, whom she found talking with some transients and seasonal boaters. Sarah put her arm through Dorie's in what was becoming a familiar gesture and made introductions. The transients were in a 2002, 42-foot Carver and were exploring the Tennessee River before finishing the western part of the Great Circle. The couple said they planned to leave the boat at Demopolis for the hurricane season and fly home to earn money for fuel. Diesel fuel prices, and gas too, of course, had risen to from $1.60 to $2.50 a gallon with future raises predicted, and they hadn't figured for that in their budget.

"How many miles to the gallon do you get?" one of the seasonal boaters asked.

"You mean 'gallons to the mile,' don't you?" the husband said and that drew laughs. "We get .6 to .8 miles per gallon if we travel at trawler speed and don't have to fight a strong current or a strong wind. I wanted a trawler with a single screw but she," thumb in the wife's direction, "insisted on something glamorous."

"Comfortable," she protested, "and roomy!"

The seasonal boater was shocked. "I thought those newer boats would be more fuel efficient, like new cars. I get over a mile in my old 28-foot Bayliner but I sure wouldn't want to do the Great Circle in her."

Matt joined the group. He was so handsome that Dorie gently extricated herself from Sarah's companionable grasp to move a few steps away. He was tanned a golden brown, muscle shirt bulging in the right places, the gold flecks in his eyes catching the candle glow, and he acknowledged her withdrawal with an understanding nod. They had tacitly agreed that what happened before would not happen again.

But Sarah wasn't bound by any such agreement and edged closer to him. "Hey, Matt," Sarah said softly, and Dorie was struck by the longing she heard in Sarah's voice and by what a beautiful couple they made. "How's that puppy of yours?" Sarah asked. She had an inner glow, that woman, and Dorie thought her simple white sundress was stunning. Matt smiled his own golden smile and said Happy was spoiled rotten and asked if she wanted to see him. They ambled towards the steps of the Hatteras. "Bobby Ray won't let any pets on his boat, except for Gracie who never touches the carpet," Dorie heard her say.

She and Sarah had spent many days together sewing and Dorie had grown to love this child-like woman as a daughter. In fact, when Mindy and John and the two grandchildren drove down from Nashville over the 4th of July, she thought Mindy might have been a little jealous of their friendship, but Mindy was too intelligent and too busy to let that bother her for long. "You can't put love in a box and label it," is what Grandma Rosalind always said. It was far too complicated and quixotic for that. Dorie couldn't wait for Janie, her wild child, to get to know Sarah too. They would hit off beautifully, she thought.

So far only Mindy's family had spent any time aboard. The boys, aged seven and nine, had absolutely loved it although Mindy and John had hinted that they might try a motel for a longer stay. "But we'll get to sleep on the boat with you and Grandpa, won't we?" the boys had begged. They had taken the boat out in the afternoon to puddle around with others from all the marinas nearby and watch the annual 4th of July Lake Guntersville Boat Parade. Flags, banners, spangles, horns tooting, people forming tableaux on their decks of all manner of patriotic scenes as they circled the judge's boat. Maybe next year, in spite of the enervating heat, *Spot* would participate. "We'll decorate for you," the boys promised, "and not complain even if it's a hundred in the shade!"

They had gone out again at dusk to find a good spot to anchor for the night and to watch the fireworks from the boat. The night had been warm and clear, a lovely wind from the south blowing in their upturned faces as the fireworks boomed and sizzled overhead. "I wish the whole family could be here," Mindy had said and the boys wanted to know it they would all fit on *Spot* at one time and if Grandpa had enough life jackets for everybody. He said that he had jackets for twelve people and that twelve was about as many as he would feel safe about taking out at one time.

After the show, they all went up the ladder and squeezed together onto the fly bridge seats where they rocked and rolled with the wakes made by the other boats leaving for home and watched another show of dancing lights. It was well after midnight before they went to bed, the boys bunked in the forward cabin and Mindy and John on the hide abed in the main salon. The boys cried when it was time to go home. They hadn't even gotten to swim off the swim platform and had caught only a few bream with Grandpa. "Not even enough for a fish fry!" Dorie promised them a "vacation" for just the two of them before the summer was over.

None of the others had come for a real visit yet. They said they couldn't take any more time away from work since they had flown into Huntsville and taken extra time at Easter to help clean out the house and to arrange for the stuff they wanted, but Janie had promised to spend several days in the fall. Maybe with a new boyfriend, but with Janie there was always a new boyfriend.

The house was completely empty now and when she went through it, it echoed eerily and was no longer her home. Without the usual annuals she planted every spring, even the garden seemed foreign. Her best daylily bulbs had been distributed among her faithful bridge friends, as promised.

Sarah had shown a remarkable aptitude for sewing, a natural feel for what Dorie had to work at. Dorie had taught her about analyzing fabric for warp and weft, shrinkage and durability, and she had caught on instantly. Where Dorie had to measure to within a sixteenth of an inch and then didn't always get it right, Sarah could eyeball it perfectly every time. That was a gift of spatial intelligence, Dorie had told her. Finishing off was Sarah's weakness because it was tedious and repetitive, but Dorie insisted she take the time, do handwork when necessary, and Sarah had finally agreed that the results were worth it.

They had finished *Spot's* deck cushions in a colorful, mildew-resistant cotton polyester blend and filled them with high quality, dense foam. Fred had found a place in Huntsville that blasted the diesel-permeated wicker with ground walnuts and then actually submerged it in a vat of white paint and then in one of clear polyurethane. The old furniture looked fabulous. They had gone on to make new cushions for Bobby Ray's built-in dinette, although the "old" cushions were just dirty, but that's what Sarah wanted to do "to practice doing curving stuff" is how she put it. "Have you ever done Isinglass windows?" she had asked one day, looking pointedly at the scratched and brittle windows of *Spot's* deck. Now that the furniture was so spiffy, the windows looked worse than ever. Diesel fuel had permeated the blue canvas trim too and nothing Dorie tried would take it out.

"I'm sure you need a special sewing machine for that," Dorie said, "an industrial machine and a huge work space."

"Uh huh," Sarah had said.

Now she heard noise coming from the back deck of the Hatteras and looked up to see Matt laughing, his head thrown back and teeth white against his tanned face. "They're talking!" he said delightedly and she could hear growls and yips and then Sarah's head bobbed up while she yowled and disappeared again. Happy and Sarah were singing a doggy duet and Matt laughed until tears ran down.

The next day Matt and Happy were waiting for Shirley when she pulled into the parking lot. She had phoned ahead but seemed surprised to see them nevertheless, and he was certainly surprised at what he saw. She must have gained ten, fifteen pounds, he thought as he opened the car door for her. She stepped out and looked uncertainly at him, smoothing her hands down her stomach and hips. "You look great, Shirl!" he said with forced enthusiasm while Happy sniffed and then licked at a sandal and she lifted one foot in distaste before pushing the puppy away.

"Not too fat?" she asked, frowning down at the eager little guy as she smoothed her gray topknot.

"Just right," he assured her. "Happy, no" he pulled the dog back and tied him to the dock cart. "He just wants to say hello," Matt apologized, and gave her a peck on the cheek. "I'll get your things, Shirl." He opened the back of the van. "You said you had gained some weight but I didn't expect you to look this good. How are you feeling? You sure had some great weather in Florida! How's Mom doing?" He was babbling. He never called Maureen "Mom."

"She's fine," Shirley offered tentatively, "but don't take the bags, please. I'm not sure if I'm staying, Matthew."

"Oh." He was disappointed and relieved at the same time and studied the riprap along the shoreline as if he'd never seen it before. "Well, do you want to come out to the boat or should we go somewhere else to talk? I can take Happy to Marlene and Randall's."

"You do that and I'll meet you at the boat. Give me a few minutes alone there, will you?"

"Sure." He would never understand this woman. He watched her walk down the dock, her gait jerky and stiff, like someone with severe arthritis. She might not be bulimic or whatever anymore but she certainly was not comfortable with herself. He told Maureen he needed to kill some time and she gave him iced tea and they sat companionably in the shade beside the boat, Happy snoring at their feet. Randall was doing a new stanchion rail for an old Trojan at Alred's. Seems the owner had snapped canvas over his mahogany rail to save it from the sun, but he had left it on for years and mildew had ruined the rail instead. "Why is it so easy to talk to you, Maureen?" he asked, and so hard to talk to Shirley, he wanted to say but she understood anyway.

"I hope you get what you need to make you happy, Matt," she said. "Sometimes we don't see it right under," she pointed to her now perfectly matched brown eyes, "or over our own noses."

Shirley was standing in the middle of the main salon when he got there. "I've never liked this boat, did you know that? This was your dream, Matthew, but not mine. All this constant fussing with engines and water tanks and hulls. Little boys playing with toys. We had a real house in Atlanta." She gestured around the salon dismissively, waving her hand as at so much junk. "Trailer-park trash on water. That's what most of these people here are. Lowlifes afloat. Could be a movie title, don't you think? 'Lowlifes Afloat' starring Vernon Johnson, Robert and Gracie Marvel and Yolanda. Just Yolanda. Like Cher or Madonna. What do you think, Matthew?" Her teeth were clenched and her chin quivered with anger.

He thought that he didn't know this woman, maybe had never known her, but he wouldn't dignify her crazy tirade with a response, and he sat down to see what was coming next. She had to be on something, but he had no doubt that she was telling him at last what she really thought.

"Doggy got your tongue, Matthew? That's all I hear about. Happy, Happy, Happy. Sappy Happy. You don't have time for Ann or Maggie because you're always fooling with that damned dog. You said you'd go on Decoration Day but you didn't," she waggled a finger at him. "I know, see, because I flew up all by myself and rented a car to do it with you and you weren't there." She started to cry, big tears welling up, but there was no point in trying to comfort her. "I waited all day." There was no point in reasoning either. He had said he would go with her but then she had left. What did two babies care about fresh plastic flowers on their graves? What did God care? She still stood in the middle of the room, crying silently, fists clenched.

"You want a divorce, Shirley?" She nodded yes vigorously. "Do you want to initiate it or should I?"

"I already have," she choked out, sniffled and blew into a Kleenex. "The papers should be served next week. I want everything, including your pension, Matthew. You're not going to get away with this."

"Get away with what?" he said wearily. When there was no answer, he asked again.

"You're not going to have that pig Dorie, and all those women on the road, and especially not little Miss Sarah and all her money and all your money too."

"What in God's name are you talking about, Shirley? There are no women. I don't even know Sarah, for heaven's sake."

"Hah." Enough hate went into that syllable to start a small war. "I've seen the way she looks at you with those eyes. Everybody's seen it. She's gaga over you and you know it."

He wasn't going to fight with a crazy person, and he got her off the boat as soon as he could, followed her in his car to the Holiday Inn, and saw that she got checked in. She would return tomorrow for things she wanted.

He called his mother-in-law and told her what happened. "I'm sorry, Matt," Maureen said and he felt his own tears welling up at the unexpected kindness. The psychiatrist had thought her capable of traveling alone and Zoloft was helping, she thought, but they'd reevaluate Shirley when she got home. Yes, she really had flown alone to Atlanta for Decoration Day. In fact, that was what had convinced Maureen to get her professional help. That and the bulimia.

"I want you to know I have not cheated on Shirley, not on the road, not anywhere," he told her.

"I realize that now," Maureen said. "It's part of the paranoia or whatever the shrink calls it. She accused me of cheating on her father, if it's any consolation for you, and the dear man's been gone for sixteen years!" When he told about Shirley's intention to break him financially in the divorce, she told him to get a good lawyer right away but said she would do what she could at her end. She knew that the money Shirley's dad had left for her was invested nicely and she saw no reason for Matt to suffer in that way. He had suffered enough already. "I really am sorry, Matt," she said sincerely.

He was halfway through a stiff rum and coke when the tears came again, and he let Happy lap them up for the salty taste until grief overtook him and he pushed the dog away and heaved with misery. Happy sat back, cocked his head and let out an experimental wail of his own. "You tell em," Matt sniffled and they howled together until Matt's sorrow was transformed into uncontrollable laughter for the second time that weekend.

Vernon waited until August 5 just to be sure but then he took down all of the purple martin gourds, cleaned them by extracting all the mess with a long tweezers he had fashioned just for the task, and carefully laid them in the storage bin Jimmy Lassiter let him use. By the time he was finished, he was wet right through to his underwear. He didn't mind the job but it made him a little sad to know that the martins were gone, although he had noticed that the brown bats were beginning to pick up where the martins left off, bug wise, so that was good. They flew out at dusk from caves along the riverbank and looked like black butterflies in the lamplight. Still, he always missed the martins when they left.

CHAPTER 13

❋

Electric bills at many marinas are paid directly to the marina owner who usually charges a fee for reading the meters once a month and then pays the local electric company. Many disputes and bad feelings have centered on these charges, the basic problem being distrust of the marina owner. It is illegal to resell electricity but that doesn't mean it doesn't happen with the owner giving his renters such a song and dance about surcharges that it's impossible for them to determine the real price per kilowatt-hour. Boaters have been known to leave marinas over what they think are unfair electric bills.

At Sunset, Vernon complained to the Lakeside Electric Company so long and so hard that they finally decided to read the meters themselves and to bill each boater directly. Vernon is proud of this achievement and was further rewarded when the company decided that genuine liveaboards should be given residential status, which means a considerable savings on their bills. Some sail boaters and owners of small powerboats are not happy with the change because the basic commercial fee for non-liveaboards is higher than the energy they use, but they're stuck with it now, thanks to Vernon. Jimmy Lassiter is just plain pissed. Things are seldom unqualified successes.

—A Genuine Liveaboard

"Georgie said we could have that end slip on a month-to-month because nobody took it yearly yet," Vernon told Lady, "but I don't know now we got to have *Angelina* pulled out and the bottom fixed. And I see that sun going to cook us late afternoon. Still," he pondered, "we could hang us some of those sunscreens everybody's getting, those Cooleroo things they sell at Lowe's."

"You do what you think, Vernon," Lady said. She was going to the hairdressers and then to lunch with one of her sisters and was dressed up in a deep pink caftan with a low square neckline and some colored beads to match. It was big as a tent but pretty.

"Where you get that dress?" Vernon asked. "You get that from Walmarts?"

"No, Sarah made it for me. She said this was my color."

"It looks right nice," Vernon said and cocked an ear as he heard the aft bilge pump go on again. They were going to be pulled out at Alred's tomorrow, which was none too soon. He would take the van over there and Lady's sister would pick him when she brought Lady home later so they would have a car over there because who knew how long the repairs would take. He was glad that all the arrangements had been made; one bilge pump or the other was working almost continuously now. Lady no sooner got off the boat, looking for all the world like a pink barge slowly sailing up the dock, when Jimmy Lassiter came pounding on the hull.

"You the one complaining about the electric bills?" he demanded, one foot propped up on VJ's front deck.

"What if I am?" VJ matched his tone.

"You going to Alred's tomorrow, why don't you just stay there."

"You saying Lady and me ain't welcome at Sunset no more? If you ain't skimming, what different do it make about the electrical? Save you having to read the damn meters, seem to me."

"I don't like renters complaining behind my back."

"I complain to your face, Jimmy, and you brush me off. Seem to me you done forgot something. Without good renters, you don't got a good marina. You don't got a marina at all, as a matter of fact. And if you ain't skimming, how come the Lectric Company decide to do this? Cause they need the exercise?"

Jimmy narrowed his eyes at him. "It's tough to make a living with a small marina these days. I got five, six boats so far in arrears on the rent, I'm going to have to take them to Small Claims Court, and everybody goes up to Goose Pond to get the cheaper fuel that I can't buy at the prices the city of Scottsboro sells it to Goose Pond. Even if I'm successful in Small Claims Court, I can't do nothing with those dead-beat boats for a year and then I've got to fix them up first to sell them. My property taxes go up almost every damn year but I'm afraid to raise my rents or I'll lose too many folks to Signal Point or Alred's or Covenant Cove."

"C'mon in here and sit down and talk to me," VJ said with some reluctance. He didn't really want to hear Jimmy's problems, but he couldn't let the man stand out there so frustrated neither. A person had to have more kindness of spirit than that.

After pushing aside some newspapers and catalogs, Jimmy sat down on the couch. "I don't want to discuss electricity," he said edgily.

"Nothing to discuss," Vernon took his chair, folded his arms over his belly and crossed his skinny legs at the ankles. He considered this his "sympathetic listener" mode.

"I'm not losing money," Jimmy said with a sigh, "but Georgie and I are working our tails off and we're just not making much. I need to have every slip filled, with paying tenants," he added, "and that's not happening in this economy. The other marinas are hurting too, I guess, but that's little consolation."

"Which ones doing good?" He knew the answer but he wanted Jimmy to say it.

"Goose Pond has a waiting list, and so does Jackson Park. Goose Pond is talking about adding on to their docks and covering some open slips. Maybe sixty more slips. Jackson Park might expand too now."

"But they subsidized by the city?"

"Or the county. They can't make a profit. Some competition that is," Jimmy said bitterly.

"Lady and me been to Goose Pond and to Jackson Park and they nice places but we like this here spot better. Let me ask you this. Something for you to think about is all. You lower your rent ten percent, give free pump outs to your people, and fill your slips, no deadbeats...then you make any money?"

Jimmy checked VJ's eyes to see that he was serious, extracted a mechanical pencil and notepad from his shirt pocket and did the math. "I'd be satisfied," he said slowly. "I'd have to sell some fuel too and get a few transients." He looked at VJ sharply. "I can't cut the fuel because they've got so many taxes on it now I don't make much, but I could cut the transient fee. I could do that if it would bring more people." He rolled his tongue around in his mouth and looked at VJ's worn carpet. "I can't pay for a lot of fancy advertising."

"Word of mouth best advertising there is to a boater." Jimmy rose to go. "You talk it over good with Georgie. I ain't no business man, now, so whatever you decide, you decide on your own, now, but maybe I could make a few phone calls, people I ain't see for a while. We looking to do us some ribs and chicken pretty soon. I can get em here but you got to make some changes to keep em here."

"When you come back from Alred's, maybe you should take that end slip, if you still want it."

"By the month."

"Yeah, by the month is okay."

"We gone squeeze them runabouts in with her," Vernon looked at him sideways. "Maybe stick out just a little."

"You always got to push, don't you, VJ?" Jimmy shook his head but he wasn't mad and they shook hands before he left. It wasn't even near to 3 o'clock but VJ had himself a short one. He may be sitting on a leaky old boat, but by God at least he didn't have Jimmy Lassiter's troubles. He wouldn't want to own this place for nothing.

Sailboat Dave and Ronald the Mooch were installing VJ's old holding tank on John's houseboat, their headbands soaked through and sweat stinging their eyes in the sultry late afternoon heat. "We should have picked a day with some wind," Ronald grunted. He was holding the tank positioned in the lazarette while Sailboat struggled to affix the adapters from underneath. The opening was too narrow to get the tank through after the adapters were attached and Sailboat wasn't sure how he was going to get out of the lazarette when he was finished. Maybe Ronald would have to tie a rope to him and pull him past the tank. He wore a heavy t-shirt, also slick with sweat, so he wouldn't get scratched up too badly.

John was perched on the top deck watching anxiously, legs dangling, a can of Budweiser in one hand and a Camel in the other. "I can't tell you how much I appreciate this," he said every once in a while, blowing a cloud of smoke. "You sure you don't want some Bud?" Later, they told him. Keep it cold for them. "That tank welded up pretty good, huh?" he said to make conversation but they didn't respond. Too hot for small talk. Sandy barked at them curiously from inside the screen door. John told her to be quiet and lie down and she finally did.

"Okay, try it with clean water!" Sailboat yelled and they heard John flush his head and listened for the corresponding splash of water into the tank. John flushed a couple more times. "No leaks!" Sailboat announced. "Get me the hell out of here," he told Ronald who grasped him by a forearm and pulled him up until Sailboat could get a purchase on the deck and scrape himself out the rest of the way. His stomach would be black and blue, he figured, and he rolled a cold beer on it. John wanted to order some pizza but it was too hot for that, they told him, and left him smiling and thanking them halfway down the dock.

"What did you charge him for the welding?" Ronald asked.

"Nothing."

"Jimmy isn't going to like it that he can't make money off of John for his holding tank and I hear VJ has got to go to Alred's for his work. Jimmy says he's pissed. He's got that guy Jamie Raines or Rines or something to do boat work for him now but he can't make any money, he says."

Sailboat stopped to take a long swig of the cold beer. "Well, he can't do a thing about it if I'm qualified and I put in the holding tank for free. John lives pretty much on his Social Security. I'm not about to take any of that money and Jimmy gets enough of it as it as."

"I won't never forget this!" they heard John calling after them and Sailboat acknowledged him with the raised beer can. "Whatever you need, you know where to come!"

"You think if Jimmy was in trouble, John would come running?" he asked Ronald and Ronald laughed and shook his head no.

Since there was no wind, they decided to take Ronald's 32-foot Marinette over to Short Creek and throw in the hook and swim off the platform. The water was warm, almost too warm to be refreshing, but they cooled off as the sun went down and a nice breeze came up from the south. "It doesn't get much better than this," Ronald said, propping himself up on the front deck beside Sailboat with the small front seat as a backrest. Now they were hungry for the pizza, but all they had were a can of Pringles and few stale Cheetos, and the beer was going straight up.

"No offense," Sailboat said, his long black hair shiny and damp on his shoulders, "but how come you don't have a can of stew or corned beef hash or something? My stomach's grumbling, man!"

"I didn't realize I was down to it," Ronald apologized. "Want to go back and we get some burgers or something?"

"Nah, I guess I'll live. It's just funny, is all. I'm just tired."

"I could make us a catsup and mustard sandwich if we had any bread," he laughed but Sailboat just frowned at him. "I get a discount at the lunch counter and the deli, so I eat there."

"Eat where?" Sailboat propped himself up on one elbow.

"Walmart's, where I work. And all the ladies on the docks give me leftovers, you know. Dorie, and Marlene and Lady are real good, but don't tell VJ." He laughed again at Sailboat's shocked expression. "Even Sarah helps out. They don't call me 'the Mooch' for nothing, you know."

"I thought that was a joke."

"It's not a joke. I enjoy eating their leftovers; they enjoy nourishing a lonely guy who's not too handy in the galley. It's symbiosis at its best."

"Symbiosis, huh? What kind of a word is that?"

"I guess it's social worker language," he laughed. "I used to be a social worker in Birmingham."

Sailboat regarded him seriously for a long moment and Ronald's smile faded. "They got social workers at Walmart's?"

"No, no. I do whatever they need. Unload stuff, stock shelves, get the bucket for broken jars and spills. Whatever they need," he repeated and stood up. "Ready for another one?"

"One more. Then we should head back, I guess. Work tomorrow. Look at those stars." The wind was strong enough to keep insects away and the night was black with the moon not yet risen. They could hear the slap of waves against the hull and an occasional squawk and rustle as birds and other small creatures settled down. Then the cicadas set up their high-pitched buzz and the frogs their mating calls. When they heard the hoo-hoo-ta-toot of the Barred Owl, they knew that night hunting had begun. "How is Yolanda?" Sailboat asked suddenly. This was met with silence and Sailboat tried to peer through the darkness to see the face of the man beside him but he was just a dense shadow now. "She's back on the meth," Sailboat said, and it wasn't a question. "I do a little pot now and then but I can leave it alone. That meth crap scares me."

"It is real scary," Ronald said quietly. "I thought I could help her but I can't even help myself."

"You doing it too?" he demanded. The moon was rising early, a full gold-red ball climbing just above the mountains.

"No, I'm not. I've tried a lot of serious stuff but so far I've stayed away from that. Just barely," he laughed, "but I'm clean now and I need to stay that way."

"You got a thing for Yolanda?" he demanded again.

"No, not really. She's just so pathetic and I thought maybe I could help, but…" He laughed self-consciously again. "Aren't you getting awfully personal, Sailboat?" but Sailboat just grunted.

"Walmart stock boy the best you can do? No need for social workers around here?"

Ronald drew in a deep breath and let it out slowly as he contemplated the wondrous mellow yellow moon hanging just over the mountaintop. It was so big and so close you could make out some of the craters against the darker lowlands or maria. "Right there where the Man in the Moon's forehead is, that's called the Montes Apenninus, really old crater walls," he pointed out. "His nose and his mouth are made up of several craters. Ptolemaist is a big one at the base of his nose there. You see it? Way around at the end of his pointy chin is Grimaldi."

"So you want to be a social worker on the moon then?" Sailboat asked.

"Well, with my record, I'd have about as much chance getting a job up there," Ronald laughed.

"Everything a big joke to you?" Sailboat turned to look straight at him, his dark eyes piercing even in the moonlight. "You laugh at yourself all the time, Ronald."

"Beats crying."

"Maybe, maybe not. It ain't no joke if a man can't do what he's good at. You need to find a way to get back into a decent job for yourself, man bright as you are." They quietly watched the golden moon rise and fade to yellow, its rays dancing over the water in a glittering path to the boat. "Abigail has a friend. You remember Abigail?"

"Princess Summer-Fall-Winter-Spring?"

"That's the one," Sailboat finally smiled, his teeth a white flash. "Maybe we could double date sometime."

"I'd like that."

"Yeah. You don't have to be pathetic all the time, Ronald. You ever howl at the moon?" Sailboat stood up, his legs a little wobbly from all that sitting and all that beer, and gave an experimental wail that brought a genuine laugh from Ronald who joined him. Together they howled until they couldn't anymore.

Back at Sunset, Happy sat up in his bed, cocked his head, and gave a little yip but Matt reached down to shush him and soon he was snoring.

"What's that funny sound?" Bobby Ray Reynolds stumbled up to the main salon still half asleep, his hair every which way. "How come you still up, honey?" he scratched at his bare belly above his pajama pants and yawned, smacking his lips.

"Full moon, Bobby Ray. I never can sleep when there's a full moon." Sarah was curled up in an armchair on the back deck watching the moon's path, which sparkled and danced on the water. She was still in her daytime clothes but had taken off her sandals.

He sat down in the matching chair and watched it with her for a few minutes, waiting for his brain to lose that cotton candy feeling. "You been mighty quiet lately," he said, twisting to see her face but it was closed to him, had been closed to him for a long time. "Now it's stopped," he said about the sound, an eerie wail still echoing faintly in the distance. "What do you suppose that was?" but she just gave a slight shrug and pushed deeper into the cushion. He reached toward her but she did look at him then and he stopped on the edge of his chair. "Sarah, what's wrong, honey? What's troubling you? You can tell me."

"This isn't going to work, Bobby Ray," she said finally. "You're the nicest man in the world and I've tried, but…" she uncurled and reached to touch his hand, "I don't love you, Bobby Ray. Please don't hate me. It isn't you. You've been just wonderful to me; nobody's ever been nicer, but…" she pointed to the emerald ring lying on the coffee table, "I'm going to give that back to you." It caught the moon's reflection off the water and flashed green. "Please don't be mad at me. I never said I loved you."

Her lovely face was the picture of distress as she clasped two hands around his own and he almost laughed at the irony. She was the only woman he had ever wanted that he couldn't buy and now she didn't want him. All the others had raged and carried on when he dumped them, called him names and vowed to take him for every penny, but he knew enough to protect himself and they had left with little more than they brought. Except for Hannah, the mother of his boys, and he had done that for the kids. "I'm not mad, Sarah." Suddenly he felt so tired. "You're the most beautiful woman I've ever known, honey, and I hope we can be friends." He laughed and gave her hands a squeeze. "Such a corny line, but I mean it, really."

He got to his feet and she uncurled and gave him a quick hug. "I'm so sorry, Bobby Ray. You can tell everybody that you gave me the boot. That's the story I'll tell. Okay?" She looked at him so hopefully, as if that would make everything all right, that he had to laugh again.

"Whatever, sugar." He went back to bed and, to his surprise, slept until well past sunrise. When he awoke, she was gone and when he looked around, except for that ugly green flower thing and his nice new dinette cushions, it seemed as if she had never been there. He tucked the emerald into a small chamois bag and deposited it in the jewelry box on the nightstand.

"We can apply to the Lakeside Electric Company for the residential rate now," Fred said. "That should help a little." He was looking over their bill, high because they had the air conditioners on from mid-afternoon until bedtime when coolness from the water usually began to drift up to the windows and their fans would be enough. They had also bought a stand-alone air conditioner for the back deck and had vented it out the cleat hole. It was noisy like the others but it worked unless the humidity was up and the temperature above ninety-two degrees; then they buttoned down tight and stayed bellowed until after sunset.

"I miss sewing with Sarah," Dorie complained for the umpteenth time but she couldn't help it.

"'Sewing with Sarah,'" Fred teased, busy making drawings for the installation of an inverter on *Spot.* "Sounds like a TV show. Like 'Cooking with Emeril.'"

"I guess so. Listen to me for a minute, Fred. I've got something to discuss with you."

"So what was I just doing?" he protested.

"No, put the drawing aside and really listen." He did. "Sarah wants me to go into business with her sewing stuff for boats, even canvas and Isinglass. She can rent a place here in Lakeside that's big enough for two worktables and storage and she's got a used industrial machine lined up from a guy in Arab. We'd have a lot to learn but she wants me to spend some time at Ken's Upholstery and Canvas in Albertville. Ken's son is a friend of hers and Ken has agreed to teach us for a fee because he's about to retire and nobody in his family wants the business. We might be able to get the worktables and another used machine from him, depending on when he actually retires. He's been saying he would for a long time."

"Hold it, hold it!" Fred raised his arm like a traffic guard. "What in the world are you talking about? Is this the Sarah I know?" She just raised her eyebrows at him. "Well, you have to admit it's pretty ambitious for a woman who did nothing but polish her nails and go shopping when we first met her. What's the matter; does she suddenly have to make a living now that Bobby Ray dumped her? Is that what this is all about?"

Dorie had been chopping veggies for a stir-fry, but now she came around the end of the little galley. "No. It's about having fun and making money at the same time. I truly enjoy working with her."

"But when was this big business thing hatched?"

Dorie waved the big knife at him. "She talked to me…"

"Put that Goddamned thing down before you kill somebody," he interrupted.

"Think I'll just keep it handy," she joked, but she did set it down on the chopping block. "Sarah talked to me about a week ago and I didn't want to say anything then because I thought it was maybe pie-in-the-sky. But she called this morning while you were at the hardware store and has all these plans organized and so I thought we should talk about it."

"Have you two ever done sewing for money?"

"You know the answer to that, Fred. Don't patronize me."

"Honey, I don't mean to. It just sounds like a tremendous undertaking for two inexperienced people who simply like to sew together. How about y'all trying to make new Isinglass and canvas for us first? See what's actually involved?"

"If you had let me finish, that was what I was going to propose. We, you and I, buy the materials and we, Sarah and I, will rent this Ken's expertise and space while we make new curtains for *Sun Spot*. Then you, Sarah, and I will decide whether or not we want to start this business. That's not so bad now, is it?"

He looked only slightly mollified and pursed his lips at her. "But what if we decide to go cruising for a few months, like we talked about? That's what we spent all that money and effort on *Spot* to be able to do."

"Then we take on jobs accordingly and/or Sarah finds another partner. I see this as a winter thing, mainly. Just a minute…" She opened the door to the back deck and sure enough, there was the subject of their conversation in person, standing on the wooden steps and asking permission to board. "Come on down where it's cool." She kissed the pretty one's creamy cheek and so did Fred.

"Aren't you full of surprises," Fred smiled.

"I figured I better come in person. Besides, I haven't seen y'all in a coon's age. It's nice and cool down here." She was in another stunning sundress, pale peach this time, and she looked like an elegant confection, shiny brown curls pulled up off her neck with a matching peach ribbon. She wore a thick gold necklace and bracelet, heavy gold love knot earrings, and several gold rings, all simple yet beautiful in design.

"Lovely," Dorie pointed to a ring she recognized as a stylized Greek letter. "I've never seen you wear any jewelry except that huge emerald ring."

"Yeah well, I did that for Bobby Ray. So he would feel special for giving it to me. Lending it," she amended with a wry smile. "Where did VJ and Lady go? Their dock box is still there, but it's so funny to see their slip empty." They explained about the bottom work. "I've tried to get VJ to buy a better boat but he always says he's too poor. Do you think he's too poor?" They didn't know what to say to that. Sarah sat at the table and extracted a three-ring binder from her giant cloth bag. "I've got something here for y'all to decide on. I mean, I figured that whether or not we do the business, we get to do your deck curtains, right?"

"Yes, indeed, you 'get to do' the curtains, Miss Sarah," Fred said as she spread the binder on the table. "But where are you living now, Sarah? You left in such a hurry that we never had a chance to offer you our spare room, but you're still welcome to it."

"Aren't you the sweetest thing, Freddy?" She kissed him on the cheek. "Isn't he the sweetest thing, Dorie?" she gushed in her Southern Belle mode, which used to irritate Dorie until she had realized long ago that Sarah couldn't help it. That's just how she was raised. "I have a house in Guntersville, but you probably didn't know that. Bobby Ray never liked to go there. I don't know why because it's right on the water, but he always had so much business in Birmingham and he loves that boat, so we just always lived in those two places, you know. Y'all have to come visit me now." She gave them a calling card with the vital information under a sketch of the house. "I still miss the marina, though."

The binder contained samples of Isinglass and canvas, along with a price list per yard, and various zipper and screen options. After some discussion, they decided to go with the 40-gauge, double polished plastic and the fabric-backed canvas in cream. *Sun Spot's* fiberglass was really more creamy than white. Fred wanted the fine "noseeum," zip-out screens, but Sarah convinced him that the sun would eat those up in no time so he settled for something sturdier. Instead of snaps, Fred wanted turnbuckle fasteners that weren't in the book and Sarah made a note to price those.

She and Dorie would meet at Kens' Upholstery in Albertville the next morning, Dorie to bring two sections of the existing curtains to use as templates. Fred wanted to make a couple of changes in the curtains, but these first sections would be reproduced just as they were. By the time they finished, it was after six and Dorie started the air conditioner on the back deck and they went up top with drinks.

"I'm so excited to be learning how to do this, I can't tell y'all," Sarah beamed. "When we're done back here, it's going to look so nice." Dorie invited her to supper but she said no, she wasn't hungry, but she would take a gin and tonic for the road if they didn't mind.

"And what 'road' would that be?" Fred asked after she had left.

"I'm not positive, but I suspect it's the road to Matt's boat."

"Aha." He fingered the calling card. "This is quite a house."

"Isn't it," Dorie said dryly. It could easily be called a mansion.

CHAPTER 14

❀

Both Guntersville and Lakeside are wealthy little towns. Guntersville has eleven banks and branch offices and Lakeside has six; these in towns of about 7,000 and 4,000, respectively. Well, they have to keep all the money somewhere. Sarah Garrison's daddy made his money from Garrison Motors, which he started in Guntersville with money that his daddy had made when he found himself with lakeside property after the TVA flooded his neighbors' farmlands and created Lake Guntersville. Garrison Motors has expanded into the third largest Ford dealership in the South, its main offices in Huntsville now. Southerners do like Ford trucks.

But not everybody in these communities is wealthy, of course, and some try to get what they want however they can, same as anywhere. In a 2003 Boating Industry Marina Survey, 62.5% of marina owners/operators reported having been burglarized or vandalized. Things disappear from unattended boats quite frequently too; lines, power cords, fenders, hoses, flags, deck furniture, you name it. Robert Marvel once stopped a group of suspicious teenagers from "partying hearty" on his neighbor's boat. When he didn't recognize any of the kids, he called the owner and they left in a hurry after Robert called the police. John stopped two men from stealing his neighbor's dinghy. He fired a BB gun over their heads and they jumped in the water and swam to shore while John rowed out for the dinghy. Jimmy Lassiter and his customers are relatively theft-free because Sunset Marina has liveaboards year round to watch over things, and even Jimmy recognizes that.

—A Genuine Liveaboard

Out of the corner of his eye, Matt caught the swirl of the peach sundress as she was way down the dock and held his breath as she drew nearer. He and Happy were sitting on the back deck in the shade under his ceiling fan, Happy preoccupied for a few minutes wolfing down his supper. It was still hot but he had been in a dry, air-conditioned office all day and he welcomed the soggy warmth, felt he could breath better. He had just unbuttoned his work shirt and taken off his shoes and socks, glad to be home, and he wiggled his toes and sipped sweet tea as he watched her. She had to pass his boat to get to Bobby Ray's at the end but she would say hello if she saw him back here.

"Hey Sarah!" he stood up and leaned around the corner and she came smiling down his finger pier, a big cloth bag sagging from one bare arm and a paper cup in the other.

"Hey, Matt. Happy. How are y'all?" She waited for him to open the swing door and gracefully stepped over, so beautiful that Matt couldn't take his eyes off her and he caught his little toe on the edge of the door as he closed it and bit his lip at the pain. Happy left his dish briefly to sniff at her ankles, tail wagging like mad as she bent to pet him, but his dish wasn't empty and the little chowhound returned to it. "Well, I know where I stand!" she laughed and propped her heavy bag in the corner.

He gave her his chair and unfolded another for himself, setting it down in a couple of different places before he found one that seemed right, not directly facing her but where he could see all of her. He felt big and clumsy as he settled in the chair, spilling tea on his good work pants as he lifted the glass. He swiped at the wet mark a few times and then decided to ignore it. "Hot one," he said. "I just turned down the thermostat inside to cool it off, but it's still better out here. I set it up pretty high during the day when no one's around."

"Happy still going over to Marlene and Randall's then, until Shirley comes home?"

"Shirley served me with divorce papers two weeks ago." He looked at her sideways. "I thought everybody knew that by now."

"I haven't been here much. You heard that Bobby Ray and I broke up. Actually, he asked me to leave so I'm back at home."

"With your parents?"

Sarah laughed. "No, silly. At my own house. I'm thirty-eight years old. What would I be doing living with my parents?"

He shrugged. "People do that these days."

Sarah fished around and pulled a calling card from her voluminous bag. "Here's my house. You know Wyeth Drive in Guntersville? That's where it is."

Matt squinted and whistled. "Is that a swimming pool?"

"Uh huh. And there's a hot tub, but y'all can't really see it on this picture. It's here, beside the gazebo." He whistled again and tucked the card into his back pocket. "So, how do you feel about a divorce?" He caught a glimpse of thigh as she crossed her bare legs and dangled a sandal from her toes.

"Frankly, I'll just be happy to be done with it."

"Shirley with her mother?" He nodded. "Is she feeling any better?' He nodded again. "Do you miss her?"

"What is this, twenty questions?" He had tried for a bantering tone but it came out snotty and he turned toward her to apologize. "I'm sorry, Sarah," he said, feeling even more miserable when he saw the hurt look on her face.

"No, I was wrong to pry. I'm sorry," she said contritely.

"It's just that I tried so hard to make that marriage work, but maybe I'm not cut out to be married. We, Shirley and I, wanted children. Our marriage was based on that, really, although I didn't see it at the time. And then when the children didn't survive, there was nothing. I thought maybe living on a boat, doing something different like that, would shake her loose from it, but..." he took a deep breath and let it out with a whoosh. Happy had finished his supper and cocked his head at the sound, his eyes bright with mischief.

"Come here, you," Sarah hoisted him onto her lap and they kissed each other and touched noses. "Should we sing together, huh?"

"Not until you learn some new songs," Matt complained, relieved to change the subject.

"Oh, daddy doesn't like our singing, Happy." She sat the puppy up on his square little fanny and waggled his front paws, talking to him like a baby. "Our happy Happy singing," she shook him and his ears perked up with excitement.

"You do that too much too soon and you'll get his supper in your lap," Matt warned and she grimaced and set him down carefully.

"Didn't think of that. Speaking of supper, how about if I take you out for a bite?"

His mouth hung open and he looked so stunned that she thought he was going to turn her down and began to steel herself against the rejection, but he just said, "Okay," and went inside to freshen up while she played with the puppy as gently as it would let her.

"I thought maybe you and Bobby Ray were getting back together," he said as he carried the heavy bag to her car, but she said she didn't think Bobby Ray was even in Alabama. Maybe in Mexico. "This Lexus is yours too?" he asked, that stunned expression back.

"It's just been sitting in my garage. With so much stuff to haul back and forth all the time, we always used Bobby Ray's pickup." The midnight-blue beauty looked brand new, not a scratch on her, and Matt stepped back to admire it. "Daddy says I should trade it in for a newer one, but that seems foolish when it's only got 34 thousand miles on it, don't you think so?"

"So you're that Garrison?" She nodded. "Maybe you should buy dinner," he laughed.

They had agreed to drive separately to the "Chinese Palace" in Albertville. "Lead foot," she observed because he had arrived a few seconds before her and had been leaning on his car door when she pulled up.

"You get behind one of those chicken trucks, you can be late to your own funeral," he countered. They were seated in one of the booths facing each other.

"Whatever does that mean?" Sarah said after they had ordered. She had moo shu pork and he had chicken kung pao, medium hot. "How could the funeral start without you if you're the dead person?"

"I don't know." He played with the straw from his iced tea, making accordion pleats. "It's like my mother's warning to us when we were small. 'Keep that up, young man, and you'll be smiling out of the other side of your face.' Total nonsense but somehow it worked with all six of us."

"Six! All boys?"

"No, I have two sisters."

"Wow, three brothers and two sisters! Were you like 'The Waltons'?" He snorted. "Hey," she reached across and lightly slapped his hands still playing with the straw, "I used to love that show and how they all said goodnight after the lights were out. I'm an only child and I always suspected that I was cheated, but after 'The Waltons,' I knew it!" He envisioned her as a lonely little rich girl, maybe a nanny or baby sitter for company as mom and dad went to some gala fundraiser for the symphony or the museum. Lila and James Garrison were big shots in Huntsville, very big shots. However did their only child turn out to be so lovely, so unspoiled.

"No family is like 'The Waltons,' Sarah," he said. "At least no family I ever heard of and certainly not mine." The food was delivered and he watched as she filled a little crepe with shredded meat and vegetables, dabbed a little plum sauce on top, folded it neatly like a diaper, and took one delicate bite. "How is it?"

"Really good. You want to try one?"

He motioned to his own heaping plate. "Let's wait and see," he said and dug in with enthusiasm. He hadn't realized how hungry he was. "Whoa," was all he could get out after the first spices registered and his eyes began to water. "Great stuff!" he gasped and dove in again. "If this is…medium hot…I'd hate to think what...hot...might be like," and he shoveled more in, fairly writhing with pleasure. Beads of perspiration stood out on his forehead and the back of his neck.

Sarah watched with wide eyes, too mesmerized to eat her own little hand-made dumplings, until she started to giggle. Matt sniggered too but it segued into a cough when he realized he had a huge, burning mouthful and he controlled himself enough to chew and swallow. "No fair," he panted and he found himself smiling into her lovely brown eyes. "I'm having fun," he said through seared lips. "It's no good eating hot stuff unless you can suffer out loud, you know." He almost told her that Shirley would never have tolerated such a performance, even though the restaurant was practically empty. It humiliated her, she said.

"The hotter, the louder?" she asked.

"I should be screaming like a banshee," he grinned. "I'm actually behaving with decorum, considering," and he finished off the entire plate and pretended to waft smoke from his mouth and ears as she giggled some more.

"And I always thought you were the strong, silent type."

He looked into her magnificent face again. He had always thought she was drop-dead pretty, but he hadn't actually focused on her eyes, milk chocolate and compassionate, and her skin as peach-colored as her sundress, and her mouth so soft and inviting. "Just silent, maybe." He slumped down in the booth and focused on the red Formica tabletop so she wouldn't see his longing, his need. "So, what's with you and Bobby Ray? You seemed like a good pair. Are you getting back together when he gets back from Mexico or wherever?" The waitress took their plates and they hunched over their handle-less cups waiting for the teabags to steep in the little silver pots.

"I told you. He kicked me out. He got tired of me just like he gets tired of everything."

"I don't believe you," he said seriously and she reached for a fortune cookie.

She pretended to read from the strip of paper. "'You always tell the absolute truth.'"

"'Unless we are talking about Bobby Ray Reynolds,'" he read from his own cookie strip. "They're getting quite specific with these, aren't they?" He reached to pour from her pot of tea and brushed her long thin fingers with his thick clumsy ones. "Sorry," he said and poured her tea and then his own. "Nobody's ever left Sarah Garrison. She does the leaving." He smiled at her confusion. "Trust me!" he smiled, which was one of her daddy's latest TV ad phrases.

"Bobby Ray needs to be the one who broke up," she said hesitantly and he nodded his understanding.

He asked about her sewing projects and she told him about her plans and how much she hoped Dorie would go along with her because she was afraid to start a business alone and Dorie had so much common sense, was so smart and very kind too. Fred would help them, she knew, and…" She stopped at the funny look on his face. "Are you in love with Dorie?" she asked point blank and folded her hands before her to wait for the answer, a charming picture of gravity.

He sat up straighter and cleared his throat. "No, I'm not. I thought I was," he tried to match her straightforwardness, "but I realized quite a while ago that I was in love with what she and Fred have. I've given it a lot of thought. They have a strong marriage built on mutual respect and trust and generosity of spirit and love, of course, and a healthy life style that allows them to be themselves, the best of themselves. Oh boy, listen to me!" He looked down at her folded hands and wanted to clasp them in his own, just touch this golden girl. "Let's get out of here," he reached for the bill and found that his hands were shaking. He was way too old for this. "We both have to get up early for work tomorrow," he said as he escorted her to her car and took her keys to open the door of the Lexus.

"I was supposed to pay," she reminded him as he stepped back and she slid gracefully behind the wheel.

"Well, just this one time," he grinned and leaned down to wait for a hug or a peck on the cheek, a friendly Southern farewell, but none was forthcoming and he found himself nose to nose with her, gazing through the open window into those liquid eyes shining in the glow of the overhead parking lot light. "Just this once," he heard himself say again.

"Is it going to be an ugly, drawn-out divorce?" she asked, isolating the ignition key but making no move to start the engine.

"No, I don't think so. Shirley's mother seems to understand how sick she is and I've got a decent attorney. I offered to cover her medical bills for a year after the divorce because she's on my company plan, but her mother said Shirley's trust fund should handle that. I think Maureen, her mom, feels guilty for believing some of the stuff Shirley's been saying about me. At any rate, I'm grateful for any help, and I certainly do rattle on, don't I?" He stood back in embarrassment and stuffed his hands in his pockets for somewhere to put them. "Neither strong nor silent," he said dully.

"Let me ask you just one more serious question."

"Okay, shoot," he said and cleared his throat nervously, "but there might be some questions coming back at you, you know."

"Is it still so important for you to have children?"

He rattled his change for a moment before leaning down to peer into her face again but she was concentrating on the steering wheel, caressing the smooth outer rim. He reached in and caught her left wrist to make her look at him and when she did, her expression was so sad, so much like Shirley's long face, that he had to do something. "Come out here." He opened the door but she didn't move.

"I can't have children," Sarah told the steering wheel in a rush. "I had an abortion when I was fifteen and the clinic said there were complications and that it would be too dangerous for me to have children. So I couldn't even if I weren't thirty-eight and too old anyway."

"Goddammit, come out here," he commanded. He stood her up before him, holding the tops of her arms close to her sides, and he wanted to shake her. "I've done lots of things I'm not brave enough to tell anybody about. And you would be stupid to beat yourself up because of something you did when you were fifteen years old. So you can't have any kids. We…Shirley and I…obsessed on that for nine long years and look where it got us. And I don't even care about having my own children anymore. I just don't care. Not everybody in the world has to have kids, you know, Sarah. There are plenty of people in the world, too many people. I don't want to grow old alone but I wouldn't count on any kids to protect me from that anyhow. If I were you, I'd want a husband I could talk to, really talk to and love and share things with. Right now I love living on my boat but if I loved a woman who didn't enjoy that, who wanted a different kind of life, I would try to make that work because above all, what I need, what anybody needs the most, is a real partner, a soul mate."

"A soul mate," she echoed, breaking his hold and putting her arms around his neck and her cheek against his chest. She pressed herself against his length, letting him feel her body, and he held her sweetness and breathed her hair, swaying a little to comfort her. Hot as it was, they were soon stuck together there in the parking lot.

"Sarah, we have to go slow," he said into her ear. "I'm not even divorced yet. We don't know one another."

"You may not know me, Matt, but I know you." She kissed him on the mouth then, a squashy, hungry kiss that he was too stunned to return. "I know all about you," she whispered. "I've been stalking you."

He really didn't want to let her go but she had so startled him that he abruptly pulled back, his shirt and her blouse damp down the front so he could see her the shape of her lacy bra underneath, and he laughed nervously at the strength of the desire that raced through him. "Stalking?" he croaked.

She cocked her head. "You know. Not like stalking to molest you or something but like when somebody watches you and plans to be where you are as much as possible. But you never noticed me. And then when you showed an interest in Dorie, I was so mad I played up to Fred. Even got him to smoke some pot with me. It wasn't very nice of me, but I've apologized," she said breathlessly. "Honest! I just love Dorie and I'd never do anything to hurt either of them and they forgave me."

He took a moment to digest all that. "I didn't pay attention to you before because I was a married man, Sarah. I still am a married man. I have no right to pay attention to anybody yet. That thing with Dorie was wrong but it was less than what we did together right now. This isn't a soap opera, this marriage business. I don't fool around on my wife."

"I know. That's part of why I stalked you."

"But what about Bobby Ray? He wanted to marry you. Where does he fit into this?"

"I like Bobby Ray but he wants another trophy wife, something nice to hang on his arm, is all. He doesn't love me and I have never said I loved him. I don't love him. He'll have someone new before long."

"Just like you."

"What?" It was her turn to be startled.

"Think about it, Sarah. I'm no prize to most people, seems to me, but you've got me pegged for a 'trophy husband,' if there is such a thing. You've been hanging around the marina too much. Get back into whatever world it is you travel in, and you'll find someone much more desirable and much more suitable."

She said nothing, just gave him a hurt, scornful look, gunned the engine and drove off without a backward glance. Matt sighed. It would be so easy to love her and then have his heart broken again. A woman like that could have anybody, not a fifty-year-old, two-time loser. A woman like that changed men like she changed her underwear. Poor old Bobby Ray had met his match.

At Alred's, Vernon could get the tip of his little finger into some of the holes in the bottom of *Angelina,* they were that big. "Damned electrols or whatever," he said, wiped the sweat from his brow with a paper towel, and took a good bite of his cigar. They never told you about this stuff until it was too late and now what. "How you going to fix this, boy?" he asked the kid who had pulled them out on the sleigh, a kind of pulley affair that got *Angelina* to ride up out of the water on a frame with some wheels under it. But the kid didn't know, and now they had to wait for the damned welder. For a hundred dollars, the kid had pressure washed the bottom so they knew what they were looking at. If only Sailboat worked here he could get a deal on the price. Sweet Jesus but this was going to set him back.

"I'm surprised you folks are still floating," the welder said when he finally arrived and ran his fingers over the same places. "Some of these pits are over two-thirds of the way through the hull. Where abouts was the leak?" When Vernon showed him, he shook his head in amazement. "You could have been at the bottom at any time!" More head shaking. "Any time!"

"You fix em?"

"I use aluminum welding rod material to fill each of them. Going to take some time." Vernon close on his heels with his glasses steaming up, the welder inched his way along crabwise, making tsking sounds and marking red x's on the worst places. He stopped every few steps to catch sweat drops with the ends of the bandanna around his neck.

"I got a welder friend could help you out after hours," Vernon offered hopefully, wiping his smeary glasses on his damp shirt.

"Nah, I use my own guys." The welder looked at him narrowly. "I guarantee the work, I use my guys."

"I'd like an estimate, not too much trouble."

"Yessir. I'll have one for you tomorrow morning. We could get started by tomorrow afternoon, that okay with you."

Lady was sitting nearby in the car with the air conditioner on and the door open so she heard a good share.

"We don't have no choice," Vernon complained. "Already have to pay Alred three fifty just to pull us out on that contraption and then the pressure wash. We stuck."

"Yahuh," Lady agreed.

"At least we can visit some of these folks we ain't seen in a while. Tell em bout the changes over to Sunset."

"Yahuh," she said before taking off for her sister's house, the one in Gadsden this time.

Vernon waited until the car was just a cloud of dust and climbed up on the step stool to get aboard and get his Jack. It was mighty hot inside with the boat exposed to the direct sun and no air conditioning. The kid said he would run an extension cord for power but had disappeared, dammit, and Vernon would have to find him pretty soon or Lady's freezer would melt and then there would be hell to pay. He filled a paper cup and climbed down to seek the kid and a cooler place. Maybe he could convince somebody at Alred's to hang up some martin gourds next spring. Set back in the weeds the way they were, they sure could use some bug control.

Back at Sunset, Dorie and Fred were working as usual. "What's an inverter?" she asked. She had seen him doing the sketches but hadn't really tried before to understand what they were about other than that some gizmo would go under the curving staircase into which a vent would be cut and something else would go under Fred's bunk.

"An alternate, quiet power source," is how Fred described it, "to run the refrigerator and maybe a fan at night when you're anchoring out." The plan was to buy two dedicated, 8D gel-cell batteries for under his bed and mount a grid inside the control panel that would show how much inverter power was being used. When the inverter was drained of power, you turned on the generator until the grid showed that you had recharged it. Then you started all over again. "It won't run air conditioning or even the microwave, but it's great for when the dock power goes off for short periods and you don't want to turn on the generator. Or maybe you're away from the boat when the power goes off. It'll work for maybe thirty-six hours if you're not pulling much. Then when the dock power goes back on, it will recharge the inverter." Fred was getting excited just talking about it.

"That would be nice," Dorie agreed when she finally understood it. The last time they had thrown in the hook for the day, they hadn't realized how quickly the frig would defrost in the extreme heat and had come inside from soaking for hours in the river to a soaking wet carpet in the main salon and a melted ice cream mess in the drip pan. She had ended up throwing away most of the dairy products in the cooler and the meat in the freezer. They had turned on the generator then but they didn't like to swim with the exhaust drifting back at them so they sweltered on the back deck until the sun went down and they could turn off the generator again. That was when Fred had promoted his inverter plan.

"That was way down on your list, if I remember right," Dorie pointed out.

"What list?"

She shook her finger at him. "You have such a convenient memory. That was a tiny four thousand dollar entry way down at the bottom."

"I know, honey, but I saw one on E-Bay for less than half that and I think I can hook it up myself. Of course, the gel-cell batteries are expensive, maybe four fifty each, so we're back to about three K, give or take." She wanted to know why they couldn't use regular marine batteries like they had in the bilge. "Because they're going under my bunk. Regular batteries give off some hydrogen, which is highly explosive, and gel cells are enclosed so you don't have to mess with them. They can blow up too, of course, so if you smell rotten eggs, clear out. But they're safer for this purpose."

"Well, we are saving a lot on the deck curtains."

"Deck curtains weren't even on the list," he said smugly.

"Oh sure, that you can remember. They had to be done eventually and we're saving a lot."

"Even though you two wreck every other piece of 40-gauge Isinglass?" he teased.

"One piece, Fred. We've ruined one piece! And that was the first panel we did with your new doorway design so we didn't have a template," Dorie pointed out. She and Sarah still had to make two more sections and cleat covers for *Spot* and they had been amazed at the hours of work involved. At first they had gotten Ken's blessing on every step but now they could work independently, although they still debated forever before actually cutting. No matter how careful they were, there was always more waste than they figured on, a good thing to remember if they went into business. "Sarah wants us to make covers of sunscreen mesh for the glass windows so we get experience working with that material. It'll cut the UV rays and then we just snap them off in the winter. What do you think?"

"Go for it, baby. I think you're doing a terrific job. Honestly." He smiled up from the tangle of wires inside the control panel in the main salon. He had his wiring diagrams spread on the floor beside him and was trying to figure out how best to wire in the inverter.

"Sarah's been kind of pushing me to make a decision on the business. I think we should discuss it seriously."

He put down his tools and scooted over closer to the couch where she was sitting. "Should we do the pro's and con's? Make a list?" he asked facetiously, smiling too broadly up at her.

"No lists, thank you. Now be serious, Freddy Boy, or I'll have to hurt you." He nodded that he would. "Ken says if we're going to do this, we need to start soon so we get work for the winter. You can't install new canvas, plastic, and so forth if it's too cold, but you can take off the old stuff for templates now and reinstall the old stuff until you're ready to replace it during the first warm weather in spring."

"Makes sense," Fred agreed.

"The only thing is, I don't see that I'd be able to take any long trips this winter until after we fill any orders we get. That wouldn't be fair to Sarah. Assuming we get some orders, of course." She draped an arm around his shoulders and smoothed his ear lobe. "We thought we'd use *Sun Spot* as an example of what we can do. Do you have any problem with that?"

"Nope. I have so many things I want to do this winter, I don't know where to start. We're not anywhere near ready for a long trip and I'm just as contented exploring around here. I want to go to a place north of Goose Pond called Jones Creek and spend a few days there, for example, when Janie and what's-his-name are here. And maybe up to Shell Mound and Chattanooga for a week or so in late fall, whenever the leaves are turning. But that's it, so this might be the perfect time. Do you still enjoy working with her? She's seemed sort of subdued lately. She still reliable and all that?"

"She's wonderful, Fred, even though, yes, something is definitely bothering her that she doesn't talk about. In spite of that, I don't know, we just hit it off. What I don't think of, she does. Like you and Marty used to."

"Yeah." Marty had retired before him and he had missed the older man as he was wrapping up his own career. Marty had always understood what he meant the first time. "Well, it sounds good. How much seed money are we talking about?"

"None from us."

His head swiveled around on that one. "Sarah pays for everything?"

"That's what she wants."

"Will you work by the job or by the hour then?"

"Neither. We'll split the profit."

"Honey, it may take a long time before there is any profit, once you take her investment off the top."

"No, Fred, that's exactly what I said and she said she planned to write off her investment as a business loss for the IRS. She needs one, she said. She wants me to pay for half the rent for the space she has in mind, but that's only a hundred a month on my end. I think she's doing that to make me feel more like a part of it. So, whatever we make over the rent, we split. I didn't misunderstand her."

He slapped her knee. "You can buy the inverter!"

"Stick with me, toots, and you can become a kept man."

He brushed at his hair that definitely needed cutting again. "As opposed to an unkempt man." She hissed at him.

When she told Sarah the next day, Sarah was ecstatic. "I've never had a real job," the rich girl confided. "I never found anything I wanted to do before." She danced Dorie around the cutting table. "We're going to be so successful, I just know it."

"And if we aren't, we'll have fun trying," Dorie added.

"I just knew you'd say that, and I love you to death for it," the pretty one said, kissing her on the cheek. "The machines are so old, I'll try to Jew them down on the price," she said, and that was when Dorie told her how offensive racial slurs were to her personally and to lots of other people who might be potential customers. Sarah was instantly contrite. "I just never thought about it," she said. "Around here, if someone asks you what nationality you are, you tell them you were born in the South. I'll try to be more careful." Dorie told her to go ahead and make the arrangements for the machines and she would work on *Spot's* last panels alone, but Sarah wouldn't hear of it. "We've got to finish them; they're our showcase work," she insisted and they made good progress now that they were more focused.

"So what do you hear from Bobby Ray?" Dorie asked conversationally as they fitted a heavy-duty zipper to the plastic.

"Nothing," was the uncharacteristically short answer.

"Matt and Happy doing all right?" Sarah shrugged.

"I hear the divorce went through very quickly," Dorie persisted.

"Where did y'all hear that from?"

"Word on the dock. Maybe Robert Marvel. Ouch!" Dorie sucked on her finger. The edge of the plastic could slice you up nicely if you weren't careful. They kept first aid supplies nearby and she tried to peel a Band Aid open with her teeth before Sarah noticed and scolded her for not asking for help. "Haven't seen Matt around much, though. Matt takes his boat out almost every night and returns just after dawn. He disappears every weekend too." She watched Sarah clean the cut with antiseptic and struggle to feign indifference every time she heard his name. "How about if I invite you and Matt for dinner on the boat some time?" she offered and was alarmed when a big tear fell on the back of her hand. "Sarah, sweetheart, what's the matter?"

"He thinks I'm just playing with him." More tears as she wrapped the Band Aid around Dorie's finger. "He thinks I'm a spoiled little rich girl and he doesn't want to be my boy toy." Sarah vigorously blew her nose on a Kleenex. "Only he said 'trophy husband.'"

"And you haven't spoken to him since?"

"For over seven weeks. Whenever I come down to the marina, I make sure his car isn't in the lot, or if it is, I check that his boat is gone." Another round of tears. "He said to find someone more 'suitable,' but I don't want anybody else, Dorie. I really don't." Dorie handed her the tissue box and patted her on the back.

"In all of our conversations, you've never said why it is you haven't married, Sarah. It's unusual for someone your age to never have been married. Surely you've had offers, besides Bobby Ray, that is."

Sarah sniffled and half laughed, "Well, I'm not gay, if that's what you're getting at." Dorie decided to ignore that. "I don't know why exactly. I just never met anybody I wanted to be married to before Matt. And I can't have kids—don't you dare ask me why," she warned but Dorie assured her that she wouldn't. "So I wasn't in a hurry to marry anybody for that reason. And I sure don't need a man to support me financially. Well, other than daddy, of course, but he's just daddy. You know what I mean." Dorie said she did understand while Sarah hunted for more tissue and dabbed at her brimming eyes and blew her dripping nose. "I've had lots of men tell me they were in love with me, but I've never been in love before. Not really. I thought I was a long time ago but that ended in a big mess and he wasn't who I thought he was at all." Time out for more water works and nose blowing. "Matt's the real thing and I wish I wasn't in love now because I've never been so upset. He's my soul mate and he doesn't even know it!"

In Dorie's experience, crying was the one thing Sarah had done so far that wasn't pretty and, in spite of herself, Dorie felt some gratification. Sarah's eyes were red-rimmed and puffy, her flawless complexion mottled, nose swollen, snot and tears dripping everywhere and then the hiccups started and Dorie couldn't help it. "Girl, you are a mess!" She started to chuckle, and Sarah gave her a dirty look and smacked her on the shoulder before starting to giggle, punctuated by the hiccups. They ended up sitting on the workroom floor, intermittently laughing, talking, and Sarah crying until they were exhausted, but at least they had a plan.

Fred saw the two men wandering the docks, twenty somethings with baseball caps on backwards and multiple earrings. One even had a nose ring. Fred was up on the flying bridge taking measurements for a new windshield and it wasn't the caps or the rings, it was the way they were sizing up the wrong things. Most young guys looked at boat design, flashy molded consoles, techno sound systems, muscle-bound motors and imagined themselves in Speedos racing along at sixty miles an hour, the envy of their friends and every pretty girl on the lake. These two were eyeing dock boxes and power cords, walking to the ends of finger piers and looking into windows, climbing around on the back of a boat if nobody was there.

Jimmy had gone to Atlanta on business and VJ wouldn't be back from Alred's until the weekend. Mid-week after Labor Day, there just weren't many people around except for liveaboards. These days what with meth amphetamine so prevalent, you didn't want to mess with strangers all alone. A very popular chief of police in Grant had been shot to death by kids he knew well, one of them his own Godchild, kids who were crazy on meth. He saw Sailboat's pick-up in the parking lot and called him on the boat radio, and Sailboat said he and Ronald would be right there. They were both at home because they had arranged for the day off to go sailing. Fred picked up his digital camera on his way down.

"Hey, you guys doing all right?" Sailboat asked as he, Fred and Ronald approached the two. They were just climbing off the transom of a 28-foot Four Winns after rummaging in storage compartments and under seat cushions. "Pretty boat, huh?" Sailboat said with a nice smile. "You fellas finding everything you need? You friends of Jethro?"

The intruders exchanged nervous glances and finally the taller one with the nose ring said, "Yeah. Jethro said he might be selling it and this is just what me and George here…this here's George and I'm Junior…" Polite nods all around. "Anyhow, we was wondering if you might know where Jethro keeps the keys. He said they'd be under the helm seat cushion and that we could look around inside, but they ain't there, so…" he elaborately shrugged his shoulders, "we thought maybe you might know."

"Sorry I can't help you but climb on back over the transom there so Fred can get a picture of you, see how you look in that nice boat, but they both said no, that would be rushing into things. "See that boat right there?" Sailboat pointed to the Carver across the dock.

"Yeah, course I see it," Junior shifted from foot to foot, but George stood stock still, his eyes moving rapidly from man to man. He was sweating profusely, big circles of wet traveling down under the arms of his tee shirt.

"Well, that boat's private property, just like a house or a car. See that boat over there?" he pointed again. "That's private property too."

"We wasn't doing nothing wrong. You got no call to mess with us." Junior was beginning to shove out his chest, working up belligerence. "Jethro said…" Fred snapped the camera then and took a second shot, just for effect.

"Jethro who?"

"I don't rightly remember his last name, but we wasn't..." the belligerence was changing to a whine.

"You don't rightly remember his first name either." They said nothing to that but licked dry lips, apprising the odds against them. "Now I'll tell you what, George and Junior, you leave peaceful and don't come back here and today will be forgotten." Sailboat began backing off the narrow finger pier so they could leave. "We're going to post your picture on the bulletin board, and unless you're with a real friend at the marina, we see you again, we shoot first and then we call the cops. And I ain't talking about shooting pictures." Sailboat waved his arm in a wide arc. "All this here is private property, so we got rights to defend it. Now I'd like for us to shake hands like men are supposed to do." They shook hands all around, eye to eye. "I'm sure you understand," Sailboat said sincerely.

"No hard feelings. We understand right well, times being what they is," Junior assured him before they drove out of the lot in a souped up Firebird.

"You handled that like a real diplomat," Fred complimented Sailboat. "I especially liked the Jethro part. That was inspired."

"He's real good with stuff like that," Ronald agreed.

"Well, they got the message but I didn't want to completely insult them. I don't do that to anybody. Seems to me you can't take all of a man's pride away or he'll just think of a nasty way to get back at you. At night when you're asleep," Sailboat added.

"What kind of a gun do you have?" Fred asked.

"A Remington 22 shotgun. I used to hunt rabbits and squirrels with my dad," Sailboat said as they walked back to Sailboat's boat for a beer.

"I've got a flare gun," Ronald offered and they laughed. "Think about it, though. You shoot a flare gun at someone or something and you can put a good hole in it, but you can claim you were calling for help. You were just so agitated or scared or nervous, you misfired. You're covered both ways."

"I will think about that," Fred said. "I considered buying a pistol just for safety when we're anchored out, but I like your flare gun idea. I just have to put it where I can get to it easier."

"He's smarter than he looks," Sailboat teased, and Ronald blushed.

"You two going together?" It was Fred's turn to tease.

"Damn that gay marriage shit," Sailboat frowned. "It's got so a man can't spend time with a male friend unless someone looks at him sideways."

"Better watch Sarah and Dorie," Ronald shook a finger playfully and Fred said he surely would and they opened their beers and sat back. Fred admired the sailboat's clean power cord and explained his frustration over his inability to properly clean his own cords and fenders.

"That cord's more than two years old," Sailboat said. "Water soluble brush cleaner is what you need. You get it at the hardware store in the paint section. It's cheap and the rubber stays nice and supple."

"Sailboaters always know that stuff," Ronald said.

"Want to go out with us?" Sailboat asked.

Fred locked up the Chris Craft, grabbed a supply of gin and his life jacket, called Dorie, and went sailing with his friends on Lake Guntersville.

CHAPTER 15

❀

A big fight is brewing statewide over water in the entire Tennessee River, fresh water becoming scarce in places like Atlanta and Birmingham. How much water could be taken from the river, by whom, and at what price is a very complex issue, especially since this diverted water would not return to the same water system, as it now does when local communities draw it off.

Water use rights on Lake Guntersville are squabbled over in lesser ways too. Bass fishermen occasionally get into trouble with net fishermen. Professionals practicing before a recent B.A.S.S. tournament were fined after they cut a net that had entangled them. They claimed that the net had illegally held game fish, and there was some controversy over that. Recreational boaters complain that their engines become fouled by the watermilfoil and hydrilla which fishermen say are essential to have a healthy fish population. Shoreline owners claim that marinas foul the water with human waste, and liveaboards descry the inadequate treatment of waste from chicken hatcheries and pig farms, and the overuse of lawn and garden fertilizers and insecticides.

The list goes on, but probably the most constant and visible battle is between recreational boats and towboats during the season. One short-lived fight occurred between duck hunters in the Eastlake area who figured they could set up a blind wherever they wanted to. The towboat captain warned them that he was coming through and that was the end of that. During the winter, towboat operators can work for days without seeing a soul, but come summer the lake is swarming with these pesky things. Given the sheer size differential, the towboats pretty much pretend that recreational boaters don't exist, but boaters had better beware of these behemoths. If your engine fails while you're crossing in front of a line of barges, you are in big trouble. And one of the greatest fears when anchoring out is that *your anchor will drag as you sleep and your boat could end up in the shipping lane at night. The stuff of nightmares.*

—*A Genuine Liveaboard*

Dorie had been waiting for Matt in the parking lot but she tried to make it look as if they had arrived at approximately the same time. "Hey Matt," she waved him down with her notebook. "Hold on a minute." He had lost weight, his Dockers sagging around his fanny, and he plucked self consciously at the material puckering at the waist around his belt. "You're getting skinny," Dorie said. "Too hot to eat." She pulled at the loose waistband of her own shorts. "Even I've lost a little more weight, I think."

"You look fine the way you are, Dorie," he smiled. "How have you two been? I see *Spot* go out a lot. Well, I don't always see you go but your boat is gone when I come in early in the morning."

"We go over to Short Creek rather than run the air conditioners so much and we're usually the only ones there mid-week. We must come back in right after you do. I have to get to work now too, you know. Sarah and I," she was gratified when he started at her name, "are really busy. We're even thinking of hiring somebody to help out. Where do you and Happy go?"

They walked companionably toward the water. "Oh, it depends. If I'm late we just go behind that little island across from the campground. Tonight we can probably get to Honeycomb before it's real dark. One of these times we'll join you at Short Creek, if that's okay," he looked at her anxiously. "Not to raft off or anything," he assured her. He didn't want her to think he was trying to start up anything again and she nodded that she understood and assured him that he and Happy were welcome to raft off any time.

"That would be just fine, Matt." She put a friendly hand on his arm. "In fact, I wanted to catch you before you took off tonight. We're having a party Saturday night in honor of Sylvia and VJ's return and their new slip and just to have a party. Fred and I want you to come. It's our first big party."

"I don't know, Dorie. I just haven't felt too sociable since the divorce and all." They stood at the point where they had to separate to get to their own piers and he took off his sunglasses to wipe the sweat from his face. He had lost some weight in his tanned face too, the bone structure more pronounced and those gold-flecked eyes more compelling and gorgeous than ever.

"She'll be there, Matt. She said to tell you she's still crazy about you. Your divorce is final now?" He nodded yes. "Then, under Alabama law, you could remarry at any time." Those gold flecks really danced and he stepped back in alarm but she forged ahead. "Sarah wants you to know that she wants to marry you."

"Good lord!"

"She says she loves you. She's never been married, but she wants you for a husband, a soul mate." Dorie sighed and fanned herself with the notebook, relieved that she had had the nerve to say it all. "She said to be very clear about that. Am I being very clear?" She stopped fanning to look up into his eyes and he nodded. His throat was so tight he could hardly swallow, let alone speak. "You think about it for a while, Matt, and let me know if you're coming, all right?" He nodded again and headed up the pier, remembering by sheer force of habit to pick up Happy on the way to his boat.

"Well, the deed is done," she told Fred.

"Reminds me of grade school," he grumbled. "Ask Jack if he likes Jill because then Jill will like him back and they can be girlfriend and boyfriend for ten minutes. Childish."

"That's our Sarah, but I prefer 'childlike.' And that's all the further I'm going with this. I told her so. She's on her own with that man."

"Or any other man," he added.

"Agreed and bah humbug. Now, what in the world am I going to feed all these people on Saturday? And we've got to get the measurements taken on the Holman boat and their old curtains back up because they're taking the boat out of the water early for some other work. I need to talk to Sylvia."

Vernon and Lady chugged across the river from Alred's to Sunset, and four or five friends who had agreed to give Jimmy Lassiter a try would follow them in the next months. Alred's manager was none too happy but people don't leave a place when they're satisfied, Vernon told him. Next he would visit Signal Point and spend a little time with those folks. Feel out who was looking for a change.

"Let's take a little ride," Lady suggested when they had cleared the marina. It was early morning and still fresh.

"We paying two-fifty a gallon for gas, Lady, and I ain't even got the final bill from that place," he protested. He hadn't turned the generator on to save a little fuel. Lady's frig would be okay the short time they'd be on the water. They meandered downstream toward the dam at trawler speed and he had to admit that he was enjoying it. "It been too long," he said and inhaled deeply of the water smell mixed with wet pine needles and some late-blooming sweet flower. The lake was nearly empty, no fishermen around today. Must not be biting. *Angelina* was creating a delightful little breeze as she went along, and Lady sat on the front deck and smiled flat out and that was worth a lot of money, he decided. In the summer when they rolled up the Isinglass, the front deck looked much better without all the tears and rips showing. "Them Yankees throwing us a party tonight," he reminded her.

"Yahuh," she said. "It's for that new business Dorie and Sarah started up too. They call it 'Boat Works.' Dorie asked me the menu and she's making small ribeyes on the grill. We got to bring our own steak knives."

"Hope they ain't too small."

She gave him a scornful look. "You know Dorie and Fred. What you think?"

"You right," he conceded.

"You need to stop about the Yankee thing. It makes no difference they Yankees or not."

"You right," he said again. He didn't really consider them like that. Mostly he did it because it was easier than thinking of their names. "I looking forward to our new slip. You?" She was. "More money though and I don't know where it coming from, all this expense."

She turned to look at him through the screen door. "Maybe you need to help Reginald with the landscaping work."

"Well, it ain't that bad yet," Vernon protested, unwrapping a new cigar. "I let you know it gets that bad."

That was when first the port engine and then the starboard started to falter. Vernon cut down the rpms to listen better and they were definitely dying on him. "We got three-quarter tanks full," he assured Lady. "More. I filled em not six weeks ago and all we gone is over to Alred's." Now the engines quit altogether and *Angelina* began to bob uncomfortably in the current that always swirled around the steep rock cliff that formed a sharp bend near the red day marker. They were in water over sixty feet deep so their anchor wouldn't be much good. "You watch we get too close while I try to fix em," he told Lady. "Just holler out we in trouble," and he headed to the back.

"First get them life jackets out, Vernon," Lady called and he did a fast U-turn, pushed a rolling chair aside, and yanked up the floorboard so he could reach the Mae Wests.

"Oh oh," he said after he had helped her into hers, a size triple extra large, and realized that the ties wouldn't close across Lady's tremendous bosom.

"Never mind," Lady said, "I'll get me some shoestrings or something to keep it around. Go on now."

Vernon was very much aware that they were in the towboat-shipping lane, narrow at this part of the river, and he debated telling her to watch for a tow.

That might scare her good. Better to wait and see. But nothing he could see in the engine room helped him out. He pulled and jiggled wires, untwisted caps and twisted caps, peered into dark places. Nothing.

"We're drifting toward the rocks!" Lady called and he hustled back to the helm.

"Get you the pole to push us off, we need it," he told her and started calling Jimmy Lassiter on 16.

Lady had found some string for the life jacket and now she looked like a big orange balloon with twin orange torpedoes jutting in front. With difficulty, she unhooked the telescoping pole from its cradle. "It's too early for Jimmy, but maybe somebody," Lady said and sure enough, Ronald the Mooch heard them, although the signal was very weak around the mountains. Day marker 353.6, they told him, and he said someone would be there as fast as possible and for them to try to get out of the shipping lane. "Call the dam on 14 and tell any towboat coming upstream to swing wide as he can around the marker," Lady said calmly. "Anybody coming downstream can see us in plenty of time." He did that and the lockmaster assured him that no tows were expected for a couple of hours so they could breath a little easier and to let the lockmaster know when they had been rescued.

There was nothing to do but wait and drift with *Angelina* ever closer to the rocks, Lady bobbing around on the front deck hanging on to the pole and Vernon so nervous he almost wet his shorts. It was all very well for the lockmaster to warn an uphill towboat. A captain could control the load pretty good against the current, but he was scared to death of one coming downhill, warned or not. Why, a barge had gotten away from a towboat once and ended up damaging several boats docked right at Sunset. He strained his eyes hunting for towboats in the bright morning sunshine while he moaned aloud without realizing it.

"Stead of that, Vernon, let's us say a little prayer for Jesus to help us out of this mess," Lady suggested and she prayed out loud for both of them and it was just as well because he was really too upset to follow much of it.

Finally a bass boat whizzed around the corner of the cliff past the day marker and Vernon and Lady waved their arms frantically until the bass boat slowed and turned back to them. "You in trouble?" one of the fishermen hollered and Vernon waved his arms some more. "Hold on, now. We got you," they yelled again after Vernon had tied the towline they had thrown to his front cleat.

"Thank you, Jesus!" Lady hollered up to the sky but one of the fishermen misunderstood and shouted back over the engine racket that she was welcome and Lady laughed. Vernon called Ronald to tell them they were being towed back to Alred's and to hold off sending anybody from Sunset but Ronald said John was already on his way. Ronald would try to call John back. Then Vernon let the lockmaster know the situation and soon they were safe at Alred's fuel dock and the fishermen had been invited to the cookout that night.

Everybody was up and around now. "I think I might know your problem," the kid who had hauled them out said as he flipped a couple of levers that were hidden underneath where it was hard to see.

"What?" Vernon felt his ears get red. Goddamned boats.

"We shut off the fuel tanks after we pulled you out, sir, so the sparks from the welding wouldn't ignite fumes or anything. I'm really sorry, sir, but I did tell you." The kid was so sincere that Vernon didn't doubt that he had.

"Well, how did we get so far, then, fuel lines off?" he demanded.

"Maybe the current just took you?" the boy shrugged.

"Don't make no sense." Goddamned boats. "Don't tell Lady," he told the boy but he could see by the look on her face that she suspected something as they chugged out of the marina again, this time towards home. Ronald, John, Fred, Dorie, and Jimmy were waiting and helped them tuck into the end slip kitty-corner from the Langford's. "Engine trouble," is all Vernon would say, shaking hands all round and giving Dorie a big wet one. "All fixed now," he smiled, "and we so happy to be home."

"Yahuh."

CHAPTER 16

People at marinas seem to need very little excuse to party, but for folks anywhere, a genuine reason makes the event much sweeter. Not much more to be said about that.

—*A Genuine Liveaboard*

They had three propane grills ready to go; one for individual, foil-wrapped scalloped potato and onion packets, one for a big pot of calico beans, and one for the steaks. Dorie had bought several pounds of okra at the Lakeside Farmers' Market that morning and Lady would do her famous deep-fried version. Marlene would do fresh creamed corn, which they would keep warm with the beans, and others would make corn bread, salads and desserts. Sarah wanted to do the snack table by herself, she said. Something real special. As per their agreement, Sarah hadn't asked about Matt, and Dorie's heart had dropped when she saw him go out last night after work. He still hadn't returned and she was trying not to think about it, not to listen for the sound of his engines in the harbor.

"What would you think about asking the men to do a party some time?" Dorie asked as Fred and Ronald were setting up the tables, chairs, and assorted coolers, nobody working too fast. She was covering the tables with plastic liners, securing them to the undersides with U-shaped clamps. Thunderclouds rumbled in the northeast and she hoped rain was moving in soon as predicted. Maybe it would cool things off. It had reached a humid 94 degrees yesterday and it felt even worse today.

"You like peanut butter and grape jelly or peanut butter and strawberry jelly?" Ronald joked. He wore muddy gray-brown shorts and a grayish-yellow tee shirt and Dorie finally figured it out. Everything he owned was some shade of gray because he washed everything together. He too had lost weight in the intense heat and had taken on an angular shape, sharp shoulders and protruding hips and cheekbones. It made him attractive, she decided, younger and more interesting.

"I do like peanut butter and jelly," she told him. "You can make anything you want to make when it's your party."

"Then what I'd do is make is a phone call to Domino's Pizza," he laughed. "I prefer Domino's to Pizza Hut and they don't squawk about delivering on the pier."

"Are you telling me that this is a bad idea?"

"Oh gosh, no! I'm just saying it's not a very good one." He exuded boyish charm today. Dorie knew he had a date for the party and it wasn't Yolanda. Some friend of Abigail's. It would be wonderful if Ronald could find a woman as nice as he was.

She poked at Fred when he ambled past. "You have no opinion, I suppose?"

"You got that right, Dorie. Where do you want the snack table, hon?"

It poured right after they finished, came straight down in sheets. There was no lightning but low rumbles of thunder accompanied the din on the metal roof and she heard the sound of Matt's engines that, in spite of herself, she had been listening for and did a little pirouette. "My my, aren't we frisky," Fred panted and sat down heavily in a folding chair. He untied his headband and wrung it out, drops of perspiration dotting the pier. "Now if this were inspiration we'd have something," he noted. Dorie went back inside to work on the potatoes.

"I'm glad Matt's decided to come," Ronald dropped into a chair beside him. "I haven't even talked to him in maybe a month. Guess he just needed some time to himself after Shirley and all that. Divorce is always terrible. It's like a death in your immediate family."

"You ever been through it?" Fred asked him.

"Yeah. I was married for five years right out of college. It wasn't so much a marriage as a collaborative effort to experiment with every illegal drug we could get our hands on. We were quite successful," he said dryly, "but the marriage died."

"You ever see her or hear from her?"

"She's in a looney bin up in Indiana, near where her folks live. I probably should be there too," he smiled but deep sadness showed in his eyes. "You ever regret stuff, Fred? You never say much about your personal life. I don't mean to be nosy but I wonder sometimes."

"I think everybody regrets things." The downpour had ended already, rumbles growing more and more distant, and when the wind lifted again, the air was definitely fresher if not much cooler. "I don't think it's possible to get through life without some regrets."

"Give me just one of yours, one 'for instance,'" Ronald insisted.

"Okay. For instance, I wish I had spent more time with my kids, especially the two youngest, Janie and Ted. I don't know them very well. Dorie does, but I don't because I wasn't there. The thought of having to send four children through college sent me over the top, I think, and all I did was work for years and years. And they didn't all even want to go to college but I insisted, and so I missed being there when the last two grew up."

"Maybe it's not too late," Ronald said hopefully.

"Well, I think it probably is, Ronald. Some things you simply can't redo," he said kindly and shook his head. Another young one. Another grown-up child. Maybe American society no longer needed genuine young "adults." Maybe the ever-lengthening average life span affected the maturation rate biologically, genetically, so we had forty-year-olds still "finding themselves," or whatever they called it these days. "That's the only 'for instance' you're going to get right now, my friend," Fred stood up. "Got to unwrap the steaks and see what I've got to work with. Want to help?"

"Sure," Ronald followed him aboard. "Give me a chance to pick a big one for myself."

Sarah arrived a few minutes early, pulling a cart loaded with treats and a treat herself in a gauze cream-colored big shirt and cream and blue striped baggy drawstring pants. If Dorie had worn such an outfit, she would look like a house, but the slender one was cool and elegantly beautiful, as always. The main food attraction was a huge iced bowl filled with peel-and-eat prawns.

"What bank did you rob and where did you get them?" Dorie had never seen such shrimp.

"Oh, there's a place I know in Huntsville. They fly them in for you when you order ahead."

Sarah spoke as if she ordered them all the time, and maybe she did. Dorie had come to realize that Sarah could probably buy the marina if she felt like it, which made Sarah's enthusiasm for "Boat Works" all the more touching. This woman needed to make her own mark in the world and she was willing to work for it now that she had discovered something she was genuinely good at and enjoyed doing. Dorie admired that in anyone. "I'm so proud of you," she said and gave her a kiss on the cheek.

"I didn't realize you liked them so much," Sarah said with wide eyes.

"Oh, I like the shrimp, but I was talking about you, honeybunch." Dorie gave her a hug. "I'm so proud of you."

"Thanks, Dorie. I've felt better about myself ever since I've met you."

"You've got a lot going for yourself all by yourself, Sarah girl. You don't need me and you don't need any man either. Just remember that, especially tonight."

"Easy to say when you have a wonderful man like Fred."

"Nobody on earth 'has' anybody, Sarah. Fred and I are close and we love one another dearly, but there's no ownership just because we feel that way or because we're married. We live beside each other, not through each other or even for each other. Now that I understand it, I love living aboard, but if I didn't, I certainly wouldn't be here. We'd have figured out something else."

"Y'all are your own person."

"As are you. You've been as forthright with Matt as anybody could be, even though you did use a go-between." She pointed to herself. "Now the ball is in Matt's court and if he doesn't choose to play, your world will not end and you will celebrate this evening with dignity and joy, as befitting the owner of a business."

"Yes, ma'am. I believe I can do that," Sarah smiled and warm brown eyes met warm green ones. "I love you, Dorie,"

"I love you too, Sarah girl. Now, let's party," she said as people transporting dishes and baskets began coming down the pier. The shrimp were an instant hit and nobody cared when it started to rain again. At least it came straight down so they were dry under the metal roof.

An hour later Dorie welcomed Bobby Ray Reynolds, who was alone, and saw him talking quietly with Sarah for a while and then he disappeared back down the dock only to reappear a few minutes later beneath a golf umbrella with a stunning young redhead on his arm. She flashed the large emerald ring as she was introduced. "Tacky," Dorie said quietly into Bobby Ray's ear as she passed behind him and realized that he had recently dyed his hair much too dark, too obvious. She had meant the ring but he patted the back of his head and looked embarrassed for about five seconds before shrugging her off. She found Sarah and gave her arm a squeeze. "You're worth ten Bobby Rays. Remember, dignity and joy," she whispered, and Sarah straightened with determination and joined a group.

"Anybody who spends more time on their boat than in their house can call themself a liveaboard, I think," said a short woman with very thick glasses. She and her husband spent most of the time from June through early November living on their Bluewater and switched their mail over to their marina mailbox during that time.

"But Cathy, remember when one of your fuel lines broke? Two summers ago, I think it was," Maureen said.

"God yes. The stench was sickening. I still smell it every now and then, especially like today when the air is real heavy and just sits there."

"But my point is," Maureen said, "what did you do during the time it took to fix it?"

"Well, it was making us sick so we went home for a while," Cathy pushed the heavy glasses back up, "but we still spent more time on the boat than at home that year."

"But you did go 'home,' you said," John joined in. "See that houseboat over there, that's the only 'home' I got." He reached for a shrimp, flipped the pieces of shell into the lake, dipped it in the big bowl of sauce, ate half of it with gusto and went back in for more sauce. "Best shrimp I ever had," he declared. "Not for you, Sandy! Lay down over there."

Robert Marvel joined John at the table, his little dog draped over his left arm, as usual. "Gracie don't like shrimp," he said and offered the Chihuahua a prawn that was almost as big as she was but she stuck her nose in the air.

"Dogs don't got any sense," John said and dipped again.

"Gracie does. She got lots of sense, don't you, Gracie?" Robert Marvel protested. "Not everybody got to like shrimp, you know."

"But what if something happened," Cathy asked, "like our gas leak, and it was making you sick so you couldn't stay at 'home' on your boat. What would you do then? You'd go to a hotel or a motel, wouldn't you? So what's the difference?"

"Oh, I couldn't afford no motel room," John shook his head. "I'd have to stay at a neighbor's, I guess. Maybe with Sailboat or Ronald, probly. Whoever would have an old fart like me."

"Not me," Sailboat backed away, dragging Abigail with him a few steps. She smiled at his silliness with adoring eyes.

"Count me out too, John," Ronald backed off in the other direction, pulling his new date, a robust young woman with black eyes set just a little bit too close together under long brown bangs. Like almost everybody else at the party, she wore a tee shirt and shorts and when she giggled, a mouthful of braces glinted.

She looked like the captain of the volleyball team and Ronald held tightly to her free hand.

"You are turning down a man who has a holding tank and an MSD clean poop sticker," John said, nose high in the air before reaching for yet another shrimp. "And y'all better get some of these before I eat em all. They're so good, I can't hardly help myself."

"Move over now before you get hurt, boy," VJ moved in from another group. "And no double dippin, John," he elbowed him good-naturedly. "Here, you dummy." He spooned some sauce onto John's paper plate. "This is how you do it, boy. You raised in a barn or something?"

"Well, I am so sorry, Mr. VJ, sir," John countered, elbowing right back. "It ain't like I get to eat mumbo-jumbo shrimp every day, you know. The size of these here just drove my manners right out my head!"

"These'll do it," Vernon agreed, "but this here party in my honor, some of it, and Sarah said you got to leave these here shrimps for me." He grabbed a couple and began peeling. He had taken some to Lady a while ago and had gotten stuck telling *Angelina's* bottom story and then about that morning's rescue, of course. And then Fred again tried to talk to him about a galvanic something-or-other to stop the holes from coming back, but he'd have to think on it. Fred and Dorie were loaded; they could talk free about money. He would get one of them zincs, though. A small one.

"VJ, would you take me in, my gas line broke?" John wanted to know.

"Hell no. What you talkin about?"

It was then that Yolanda came up behind Vernon and threw her tiny arms around his waist, clutching at his belt loops as a lifeline. "Oh, VJ, I've missed y'all so much!" she cried.

"Where you come from, sugar?" Vernon put down his plate and reached around to pry her loose but she hung on and he sloshed his Jack as he twisted back to reach her. "Let go now, sweetie," he urged but her eyes were closed, her forehead pressed down into the small of his back and her little fanny up in the air as he lumbered around the pier trying to shake her loose without spilling any more of his drink. People backed away to accommodate the strange dance. "Someone get her off me!" he finally hollered but Ronald held on tight to the healthy girl with the braces and nobody else stepped in except to take his cup from him so he could reach back to pull her hands away. She had a surprisingly strong grip for such a little thing and he had to nearly tear his belt loops off before he could unclench her child-sized fingers. When she tried to grab at him again, this time in front, he thrust her hands high up in the air to stop her and that did it. Yolanda opened her eyes and squealed before she hit the water, the big splash getting everyone's attention. She came up sputtering and thrashing and then went down again.

"Oh sweet Jesus," Vernon moaned but nobody moved, still hypnotized by the weird spectacle.

"I'll get her," Fred said. "What is it here, fifteen feet deep?" and somebody said that was about right. He sat down on the pier, slipped off his boating shoes, checked his pockets to make sure he had left his wallet and money clip on the boat, and slid feet first into the warm water. Dorie threw him a ring buoy and he approached Yolanda cautiously, not wanting her to get hold of him and drag him under with her, but she grabbed at the ring buoy and held on, coughing and gargling while he towed her by the ring buoy line over to the wooden steps. By that time, Sailboat was in the water too, waiting at the bottom of the steps, and the two of them got the woman up the ladder, pushing her wet bottom as others pulled her up by her arms.

Yolanda sat on the pier in a daze, mascara making black rivulets down her cheeks. Dorie wrapped her in a beach towel and knelt to gently wash her face with clean water and comb her hair back. "Can you talk to me, Yolanda?"

"I'm okay," she whispered and looked around at everybody as though she had never seen them before but at least her eyes were focused. "Need a drink," she said loudly and that's when Dorie realized that her mouth was bloody.

"Get me some ice, somebody," Dorie commanded and she wrapped the ice cubes in the washcloth and got Yolanda to open her mouth. "You broke a tooth, Yolanda," Dorie said as the frightened girl lifted enormous pale blue eyes to her and began an unearthly high-pitched whine. "It's only a tooth, sweetheart," Dorie tried to console her but the keening continued as Yolanda hunched over the icy washcloth pressed to her mouth.

"It's the second one," she got out with difficulty. When the bleeding finally stopped, she quieted, handed the bloody rag back to Dorie, and felt with her tongue the empty place right in front where the tooth had been. "I need a drink," she said and they helped her to her feet. She wobbled a little but stood on her own still wrapped in the beach towel. When she began to show everybody her gap-toothed smile, they felt they could party again, clapping Fred on the back as he made his way back to the boat to change into dry clothes. He brought back some 7UP for Yolanda but that wasn't what she had in mind, she said, although she sipped at it and said her tummy felt better and the ice cubes felt good against the swelling.

"I will take her home," Vernon said. "Least I can do." Yolanda didn't want to go and began to whine but Vernon put his arm around her and talked quietly to her and she said okay. "Where your car keys?" he asked but she didn't know.

They found Yolanda's purse under a table and Lady just managed to squeeze behind the steering wheel of Yolanda's car while Vernon followed with Yolanda in the van. "She shouldn't be around the marina no more," Vernon said to Lady on the way back. "Too dangerous. I told her so and she took it pretty good. I didn't realize how sick that girl is. It's that meth crap, right? She still talking like a fool off and on."

"Yahuh. Place a real mess."

"She didn't really hurt nothin at the party," he protested.

"Her place," Lady explained.

"Oh. We got a rehab around here?" Lady thought they did in Albertville. Huntsville for sure. "How we get her into that and how much it cost?"

Lady said Ronald would know. He had tried to get her to go but she wouldn't. "This might be something we can do irregardless of the cost, Vernon. That girl needs our help. She might would listen to you."

Vernon grunted and by the time they got back to the marina, he was almost resigned to the thought of working with his son Reginald on the landscaping for a while. Not too long, though. "We were talking about liveaboards," Maureen filled them in when they got back to the party. "Why you can't have a house and be one."

"I think anywhere you think of as home is your home, no matter how many places you own," Georgie Lassiter said. "I don't see why Cathy's boat can't be her 'summer home' and her house her 'winter home.' Lots of people do that all over the world. 'Home is where the heart is,' right?"

"Georgie, you way too smart for the likes of Jimmy," VJ put his meaty arm around her. "I got a problem this here marina, I coming to you from now on, yessir. You the brains of the outfit." Normally he would have copped a little feel before turning her loose, but he was still too shook up about Yolanda.

"Going to a hotel or motel in an emergency isn't at all like going home." Dorie had to speak up, having put so much thought into it. "There's a special relationship between a person and a boat, and if you don't liveaboard, you can't have that relationship. Boats have personalities. Well, we invest them with personalities anyway, give them names and human foibles. I think people can feel that way about a home anywhere, but if they don't arrange their lives to really live in a place, regardless of how many other places they visit, it's not the same. And a boat is a special kind of home because it's so different from a house, takes so much ingenuity and expertise. People have to really love it a great deal to live aboard."

"If I'd had Dorie for a teacher," Sarah smiled at her, "maybe I might have liked school better."

"Okay, okay I'll stop," Dorie laughed.

Sarah saw Matt and Happy as they were coming over the walkway on shore and she turned away and briefly closed her eyes to steady herself. They found her away from the group at the far end of the pier, looking out as the last of the rain made dimples on the water. "Y'all are getting so big," she went down on one knee to hug the butterball, who was growing fast but still getting a puppy cut. "How much do you weigh now?" She lifted his solid little body. "Bout a hundred pounds!" she told Happy as he cheerfully gave her kisses, his fat rear end wagging all it could, sending droplets of water in all directions. "And mighty wet too!" Sarah laughed as she put him back down to shake. He started at the top and rippled on back, the violent spasms lifting him right off the pier for a split second before he regained his footing and licked delicately at her out-stretched fingers.

"He had to run through every puddle he could find on the way over." Sarah looked up to see Matt smiling down on them and she thought her heart had stopped, it was that hard to breathe, but she made herself stand up and smile back. "Y'all missed the excitement," she said calmly but stepped back a little and kept her hands in her pockets so she wouldn't be tempted to touch him as she told him about Yolanda. He smiled at her from ear to ear as if this were the most entertaining comedy in the world, his hands in his own pockets. "It's sad though, don't you think so?" she asked.

"What?" His smile dimmed only a little.

"About Yolanda, of course!"

"Oh, I guess so. I don't really care about Yolanda right now. Move, Happy," he commanded and the puppy scooted out from under Matt's big feet and resettled on his tummy a safe distance away. His hind legs were splayed any old way but his floppy ears were perked up above neatly aligned front paws, and he looked from Sarah to Matt and back again with obvious excitement.

"He's such a good little doggie," Sarah said as Matt put his big hands on her shoulders and drew her close to him and smiled into her eyes.

"I got your message and I've been doing a great deal of thinking and…" he rocked her gently and drew her hands up out of her pockets and draped them around his neck so he could put his arms around her trim waist. Her hair smelled like oranges and he closed his eyes and inhaled deeply. "And I've been thinking that maybe I've been doing too much thinking lately and that maybe I…"

"What you two up to now?" Vernon staggered toward them but Lady moved faster than anyone thought possible and twirled him around by one ear. "I didn't mean nothin," he complained but she just marched him back without saying a word.

"Maybe I should let my heart rule my head for a change. What do you say?" He blew her brown curls aside to find her lovely little ear and bent to nibble on it before thrusting his tongue deep inside and then gently blowing." Sarah shivered almost as violently as Happy had earlier and Matt laughed softly until she pushed him away from her and he saw the tears standing in her beautiful eyes. "Sarah!"

"You might be surprised how much your head would like me too, Matt," she said defiantly as one big tear and then another rolled down her cheeks. "I'm a business owner now and a damn good one." She pulled a tissue from her pocket and dabbed at her eyes while he stood rooted to the spot. Happy had edged closer, his tail down between his legs, and now tentatively licked her toes where they peeked from her sandals. She knelt to pet him and he lapped at the salty tears on her face, his chubby self so full of anxiety she'd swear he understood her. "I'm not just a pretty face," she told the puppy.

"Sarah, come on up here. Please, Sarah," Matt pulled her up and produced a tissue of his own. "Blow," he ordered and she did, sniffling into his shirtfront afterwards. "I didn't mean to insult you, sweetheart. I'm just so thickheaded, it's taken me way too long to realize that I'm crazy in love with you and I want you. With Shirley, I figured I didn't deserve any happiness at all. Then you said you wanted me and I figured it was much too soon after the divorce. Then I thought, who says it's too soon? My marriage to Shirley has been over for a long, long time. I can't even think back to when we were genuinely happy together. You see what I mean about thinking too much?" He put his arms around her. "I want all of you, Sarah, not just your body." He squeezed her hard enough to make her gasp and Happy yelped in sympathy. "Oh, sorry," he laughed and eased up enough to touch noses. "I want all of you, your sweetness and your spirit and your mind."

"Do you think I'm your soul mate?" She sniffled and looked up into his eyes so seriously that he was taken aback for a second until he felt the joy welling up in him, coursing through him like pure oxygen, and he breathed deeply, his smile as wide as the Tennessee River.

"I believe that you are my soul mate, Sarah. I love you. I want to be married to you for the rest of my life, if you'll have me."

"Can I marry your dog too?" By now Happy was circling them frantically, and Matt pulled him up and he snuggled between them immediately, a deep sigh signaling his contentment.

They decided they would have to get married twice; the first time on Matt's boat with all Sunset liveaboards and boating friends invited, and a second time in Huntsville to satisfy Sarah's wealthy parents and Matt's big family. Dorie and Fred came out with plastic flutes for everyone and went around filling them with champagne, another of the treats Sarah had provided for this very special party.

"I don't even like this here fizzy stuff but I got to drink it, under the circumstances," Vernon declared.

"Yahuh," Lady agreed and shocked everybody by taking a small sip herself. "Not too bad," she said and took another.

"And who says you can't teach a old dog new tricks!" Vernon marveled.

"Vernon, I am not a old dog," Lady glared at him and Vernon decided to keep quiet for a while.

978-0-595-36167-0
0-595-36167-6

Printed in the United States
33300LVS00006B/305

9 780595 361670